Fathom

A Novel by
Michael Gaff

First published by Dog Ear Publishing
4010 W. 86th Street, Ste H
Indianapolis, IN 46268
www.dogearpublishing.net

ISBN: 1-59858-101-5
Library of Congress Control Number: 2005937995

This book is printed on acid-free paper.
This book is a work of Fiction. Places, events, and situations in this book are purely Fictional and any resemblance to actual persons, living or dead, is coincidental.

Printed in the United States of America

For Debbie and Elizabeth

Who have always urged me to tell my
"Underwater Adventure Stories"

Chapter One

The Recruitment

The journey of a thousand miles starts with one step. The journey to the front of a Central American firing squad can start with a trip to the men's room in a Chicago convention center. I know this to be true, because that is how I set off on my circuitous route, finally ending as the center of attention of El Salvadoran national guardsmen. It was not a nonstop trek.

The year was 1969. I was 19 years old, and was attending the National Sporting Goods Association convention in Chicago. I was the picture of health, having spent hundreds of hours underwater in the four years prior to this anxiously anticipated show, featuring (for all I cared about), the latest in diving technology and gimmickry. Wet suits were becoming comfortable and tailored, dry suits were entering the mainstream, masks were sculpted and purposeful and the technology of breathing apparatus was approaching the nirvana of "think of a breath while underwater and you were breathing underwater." Gone were the days of sucking air from the scuba (self contained underwater breathing apparatus) system, to be forever replaced with the delivery of air underwater as almost an afterthought.

I knew that I was being perceived as an erudite, professional and knowledgeable sport diver as I asked probing questions, tried on gear and made suggestions to the people working the booths, not missing an opportunity to show them that I belonged. It wasn't until much later that I realized I most certainly had not impressed anybody. Virtually every product demonstrator was thinking about Chicago nightlife, drinking, and the downtown female population. No one cared who I was, where I came from or where I was going. Well... not precisely no one, just virtually no one.

As I was dutifully washing my hands after using the facilities, a ritual almost always ignored if I found myself alone, an older man next to me, gray temples and all, spoke to me. "Are you enjoying the show, son?"

"This is the best I have ever seen," I gushed.

"It's your first show isn't it?" he asked, looking me square in the eyes. I looked away just enough to answer his question.

I didn't have the faintest idea who this guy was. I sized him up, noted the narrow tie, the carefully combed hair, and stared, remembering to slam my lower teeth against the uppers, at the gorgeous Rolex chronograph covering a respectable chunk of his left wrist.

"My name is Larry Dean," he said a little too slowly for my taste while extending a decently cared-for hand, "and I wanted to talk to you because I noticed you were here alone, and keying on the scuba gear."

I was at once almost frozen in place as I realized that this was a pickup line and this guy was out trolling. I looked around, hoping it was a furtive looking around, and saw no one else in the 32-holer, with 64 porcelain places of worship. How was this possible, I thought? There must be over a hundred thousand people here and this men's room was empty.

"I'm not a faggot," widening his grin as he added, "and you don't strike me as much of a catch if I were."

"Oh I didn't think that," I lied, "I was just looking for my buddy."

"You don't have a buddy here, Tommy Conklin. Like I said, you are here alone. You live in Fort Wayne, Indiana, in a 12 foot by 55 foot house trailer that you bought when you were 16 years old. You work as an apprentice electrical/mechanical designer in an anti-submarine warfare lab in the Magnavox Company. You are a good diver, hold a secret security clearance and have more time underwater than I have in the shower. And I love a good hot shower."

"Uh oh," I retorted.

"Exactly, son. Uh oh"

My antennae were extended to the limit. I was a nothing trainee, but I did work on gear, like the sonobuoys that were used to help the US Navy find and track Soviet submarines. I had even made a few trips to the US Virgin Islands, in Navy P3C Orion submarine hunter aircraft and helped tweak a few moored buoy underwater surveillance systems. I am naturally given to paranoia, and I really hoped that this guy wasn't a spy, or Russian representative of some kind. I am not given to bravery either, but I wasn't going to help the Russians and I really didn't want to find out what happens to their recruiting failures.

"What is it you want, Larry Dean?" I wanted to be a little cocky and work up to appearing confidant. I achieved cocky, but slipped on the way to confident.

"I want to give you a chance to get rich, have some adventure and help your country," Larry said, sounding vaguely like a Mutual of Omaha commercial. "I represent a little government agency. We are interested in furthering relationships in Central and South America. Toward those ends, my company, as we are given to say, has helped some other companies establish some resorts in a few out of the way places. We are hoping to build tourist interest in some often overlooked countries in our very own hemisphere."

"And you want me to visit these resorts?" I asked, my confusion obviously amusing the guy.

"Not exactly, Tommy," Larry grinned again. "We, meaning the little government agency I represent, want you to sell and give away all your possessions, down to whatever fits in a duffel bag, and move to Honduras. You will be given the chance to share in the proceeds from whatever treasures you may find and recover. We want you to join a treasure hunting expedition. You will be a shareholder of record, join in the hunt for pirate treasure and live on a beautiful tropical island. So, Tommy what do you say-are you on board?"

"You're putting me on, right?" I was not a quick study sometimes.

"No, Tommy, I am not putting you on. My immediate job is to find people we can trust, and who have the right temperament and skills to fit in our little expedition. Did I mention that it is called Fathom Expeditions and that you will be buying a five percent stake in the company? You will live on the island of Utila in the Bay of Honduras, and you will be helping to build an underwater park and a museum."

I can also be marginally perceptive at times, and this was one of those times. Even through the fog of words, I could see that this was no chance encounter. I knew I had been selected for something and this guy was massaging my ego. I quickly did an inventory of my life, concluded that I could certainly leave my trailer, pickup truck, boat and few other possessions. I was an average engineering talent and vaguely worried at the prospect of the career stretching out ahead of me being just another small cog in the giant military /government/industrial complex that was all the talk of the Vietnam era. I had even enlisted, been part of the warrant officers program, and been given the chance to get out after being hurt in a physical training exercise. I was a little concerned that I was a coward. An expedition, pirate treasure and diving in tropical waters every day for the foreseeable future held the promise of another chance to validate my life.

I established eye contact, took the proffered hand and shook it firmly. "I'll do it."

This bathroom encounter was my first step toward a waiting Central American firing squad. It's a complicated story, so I will start with a little background information..

Chapter Two

My Teen Years

The idea of scuba diving didn't just pop into my head. It was thrust upon me while I was devouring the recent issue (October 1965) of Skin Diver magazine. I read the first person accounts of sport divers checking out local quarries, diving among the reefs of the Bahamas and spearfishing for carp in Midwest lakes and rivers. I didn't kid myself about ever diving in exotic locales, but where I lived in northeastern Indiana, lakes, rivers and quarries were everywhere.

I ached to put on the diving gear that was always in the front window of Sappenfield's Sporting Goods Store in downtown Fort Wayne. The big double hose regulators just like those used by Mike Nelson, who was played by Lloyd Bridges in the Sea Hunt television series, called to me. I had fantasies about my diving life.

I could foil the bad guys' plans to hide stolen loot underwater, recover who knows how many sunken cars and boats and even.... most likely, save an entire family trapped underwater in the family sedan. Everybody knows that bridges ice over first and it would be just a matter of time before a car skidded out of control and crashed through the railings of a bridge, sinking into the river below. I would always have my scuba gear in the trunk of my car, ready for any underwater emergency, just like Mike Nelson.

The fact that I was only fifteen years old and didn't even have a learner's permit didn't dim my vision of glory. The lack of a license didn't keep me from driving my beautiful Honda Super 90 motorcycle. I had bought it from Mike Saunders's dad. He was a stern minister who ran a nursing home. He had grounded Mike for irresponsible acts involving the motorcycle. I had paid $360 for the bike and learned about the clutch, shifter and throttle in a crowded storage room deep in the bowels of the old institution. Because it was a quiet bike and was already running, I decided I would carefully idle it down the long corridor, make the right turn at the nexus of the building and out the big french doors just another hundred feet after the turn. I didn't realize just how easily it would pick up speed and I am certain that if I hadn't slightly grazed that old guy's wheelchair hidden around the corner (he wasn't exactly creeping along either), Mike and I would be friends to this day.

But first, I needed to learn how to dive using scuba, and the library was the place to learn. I have never been one to take advice, including instruction, if I could possibly learn on my own. I jumped on my Super 90 (I never thought of it as a motorcycle; it was always the Super 90) and took off for downtown. I checked out a book entitled <u>Introduction to Scuba Diving</u> and went home to learn. It really isn't a dig deal, you know? A few laws about the reaction of gases to varying pressures and temperatures and remember to never rise faster than your bubbles and to breathe regularly pretty much covered the basics. The fancy stuff about nitrogen narcosis, decompression sickness (the bends), oxygen toxicity, etc., just didn't apply to me at this time. After a thorough study, taking nearly an hour, I was ready to go scuba diving.

I had no scuba gear, but I did have a job. I pumped gas at

a Gulf service station and talked people into buying air filters. I had sold so many Purolator air filters the previous summer (more than a thousand), that my boss won a national contest and got a free trip to the Bahamas. It was easy really. I had a round metal platform in a box at one of the islands. Sticking out of the center of the platform was an always-lit 25/watt light bulb. On top of the platform, surrounding the light bulb, was a brand new round paper filter element. All air filters were round in those days, and paper filters had been around for only a few years. These replaced the old foam-in-an-oil-bath filters of yesteryear.

When I checked the oil, and I always checked the oil, I would spin off the wing nut holding the air filter assembly to the carburetor. Before the driver could stop me, I whipped out the air filter and plopped it on top of the new air filter in my box. I would cover the now double-decker air filter with the special lid, sealing in the light. When the driver saw the blazing light shining through the new air filter and the blackout caused by the dirt in the old filter… I had him. Another three or four dollars and all the savings in gas mileage made us both winners. I knew I had a shot at winning the national contest, which I did. It never occurred to me that my boss and his wife would take the grand prize on behalf of the winning service station. But I did get to keep my eighty-five cents an hour job.

And this brings me to the scuba gear. It was a given that I would be buying used gear. I knew every piece of equipment that would be needed. After all, I had read the whole book. In a few weeks, I acquired everything I would need for my first dive. I had most of a wet suit, lacking only gloves and booties, a satisfactory single-stage double hose regulator (so primitive a regulator that you would have to go to a museum to see one today), an ugly galvanized steel tank, a mask, fins and snorkel. I purchased a lead weight mold and melted down old wheel weights from the service station to make several three pound weights.

My best friend was Greg Fox. We had grown up together and had been partners in several acts of petty vandalism over the years. Living in a new addition, as sub-divisions are called in Indiana, we had great opportunities for mischief that mostly eluded less fortunate kids, the ones having to suffer with adult supervision. I was lucky enough to come from a poor family that needed two incomes to accommodate five kids, meaning little adult supervision.

An example of what passed for fun would be starting up construction machinery and putting dirt back in the basement and foundation trenches. It was always great to see the looks on the faces of the workmen the next day. One legendary feat of daring involved starting and operating one of those big tracked sewer-line digging machines. It was the kind with the wheel of toothed buckets that ate into the earth and emptied the dirt into a chute off the right side as the buckets got to the top of the wheel. We got it running, but it was a diesel and we didn't know how to stop it. Like rats scurrying off a sinking ship, we left it to its own devices and went home as the sun went down.

By morning it had chewed its way through several new foundations and one newly erected set of two-by-four walls before butting up against the new four lane highway. This exploit made it into a mini-documentary about senseless vandalism. I stayed terrified and paranoid for weeks, but that didn't stop Greg and me from taking credit for it after the heat subsided. Among my gang of reprobates, this was the stuff of heroes.

It was natural that Greg would be with me for my first scuba dive. The sky was entirely overcast and there was no wind. We had the little problem of getting to a lake with the gear. We decided that Pokagon State Park on Lake James would be perfect. It had a beach and we knew we would be alone. It was December. A skin of ice was just appearing on the surface of the lakes. I squeezed my skinny frame into the wet suit, donned the wet suit hood and secured the weight belt. Greg strapped on the tank and backpack assembly. The rest went into a cloth bag. I straddled the Super 90 and Greg climbed on behind me. This was why he had to wear the tank. He was on the back of the bike. We knew we looked cool as we blew north to Lake James, bent low for streamlining.

Arriving at the beach, I spent a little time with my hands stuck in my armpits to warm them. The temperature was in the neighborhood of twenty degrees. I figured the water couldn't be any worse because it couldn't get much below thirty two degrees. It was much worse. As I waded in, the skin of ice broke apart. I laid face down in about three feet of water and slithered under the surface. I was so excited that I was able to ignore my freezing hands and feet. The water was exceptionally clear and I gaped at each thread of sea grass and pebbles. Finding a Coke bottle made me gasp. It was all so exciting! Descending to a shelf paralleling the beach, I found myself down to about twenty feet. I crawled under the shelf and let my eyes adjust to the gloom. As a huge mouth with an attached handlebar mustache materialized, I was shocked to realize I was mask to muzzle with the largest catfish in the world. I backed up so quickly that I dislodged my mask, took in a lot of water, and began snorting myself sick. I slowed my movements and cleared the mask by holding the top and looking up while breathing out my nostrils.

I was breathing so hard that I was actually tiring of sucking in air. With a double hose regulator, a head down position put the demand portion of the system in a lower pressure environment, meaning greater effort in breathing. I had done enough. I followed my bubbles to the surface, kicked my way to the shore and emerged as a champion. My hands and feet were frozen to a point beyond pain, and I had almost lost the use of those appendages. My feet were like boards. I could only walk on my heels.

Greg helped me shrug off the gear and asked, "How was it?"

"Cold, but I saw a Coke bottle and a fish," I answered. Real men didn't gush, I knew, so I remained calm. But inside I was ecstatic. I was now a scuba diver. We huddled back onto the Super 90 and blasted down the interstate to my house. It took hours to get my hands and feet working, but I didn't care.

The following spring found me heading to the lakes and quarries every available weekend and afternoon. I was in school only in the mornings all through high school because our building was not yet built. I attended one of two schools using the same building. Luckily the high school half of this arrangement started at seven and was out by noon. Even after the high school was finished, my class was allowed to keep the schedule of the previous two years, due to jobs and college classes that had been started by many.

I attended school, pumped gas and went scuba diving as much as was possible. I taught myself the art of spearfishing for carp, which made me welcome at every lake in Indiana. I would go spearfishing until well after midnight quite regularly. I would keep the carp and take them to a few favorite chicken farms, but only the egg producers. They would dry the fish and grind them up into the poultry feed. I was obsessed with night diving, which coincided nicely with my predilection for very little sleep. Even today, decades later, that hasn't changed. I require only three to five hours of sleep a night. Really.

I continued to study the physics and physiology of diving, lied my way into an assistant instructor position at the YMCA, and became something of a professional diver. I made myself available for every salvage or repair operation that came up, sometimes making very big money, at least by my standards. I once was paid exactly one hundred dollars an hour standby pay and two hundred dollars an hour for underwater time over a four day period, working to recover a six-hundred-pair telephone trunk cable that had been damaged underneath a flooded plain that had iced over. I dove underneath the ice every winter, traveled to the Great Lakes with friends, while students paid my way, and dove on scores of sunken freighters, ore carriers, and a few passenger ships. I was a regular visitor to the Georgian Bay, a Canadian inlet off Lake Huron, about the size of Rhode Island. This bay is littered with wrecks, including hundred year old schooners like the Aruba.

I left home when I was sixteen, found a house trailer that was affordable, considering my jobs at the service station and the very early morning janitor work that I did for a McDonald's restaurant. I was a loner to the extreme. I could never stand to be taught anything and generally learned new skills by trial and error, usually after getting the chance at the trial by exaggerating my experience level. If we truly learn only from our mistakes, then I became a gifted diver. It would be fair to say that by the time I was nineteen years old, I was relatively well known among the diving circles of northern Indiana, Ohio and Michigan. It was this notoriety that would lead to the encounter with Larry Dean in Chicago.

And this is what happened…

Chapter Three

Honduras

The whine of flaps coming back and down, the distinctive clunks of the main gear locking down, and the concomitant change in power to compensate for the increased drag, jolted me out of a sound sleep. We were on final approach. Looking out and down, I got my bearings, noticing that the sun was immediately off our right wing and relatively high. We were landing to the north, passing over a shabby collection of lean-tos, rusty tin- roofed sheds and a teeming mass of people. I could clearly see the people. They were milling about in muddy streets, pockmarked with hundreds of large puddles of water. I didn't like the sight and felt a sense of foreboding descending upon my psyche. This would be San Pedro Sula, second largest city of exotic and tropical Honduras.

The aircraft touched down and decelerated with little braking. I looked out upon a ridge about one hundred feet above and running parallel to the runway. Parked in a long line along this ridge, wingtip to wingtip, were about twenty World War II-era fighters. This buoyed my spirits. I knew airplanes and these were F4U Corsairs, even sporting the gleaming blue paint that matched my mind's eye when I thought about this aircraft type. These were the distinctive bent wing aircraft flown by Navy and Marine pilots from islands and aircraft carriers in the South Pacific. Pappy Boyington and his famed Black Sheep squadron had flown this type. An aviation buff beyond the pale, I couldn't take my eyes from the sight.

I dutifully pulled my duffel from the overhead bin and shuffled down the aisle with my fellow passengers. Nothing in my experience could have prepared me for the blast of hot, moist air that enveloped my body and invaded my nostrils at the cabin door. I would have likened the experience to that of standing in front of a large furnace, except that this air was definitely wet. My snappy looking paisley shirt, hinting of those ubiquitous burgundy pears and baubles, and my equally attractive bell bottom pants with vertical black and silver stripes, fell into a wet slump that clung to my body like Saran Wrap. The customs fellow stamped my passport, almost sneering at me from the vantage point of a crisp green uniform covered with enough ribbons, medals and pretty little ropes to shame a Chicago Ritz-Carlton doorman. The hat was festooned with enough scrambled eggs (gold embroidery) to feed a family of four. He looked comfortable and menacing. I was feeling a little ashamed from my lowly status as a sweating tourist.

Finding my way through the concrete and tiled terminal building, I stared almost open-mouthed at the level of decay and neglect that permeated the building. This place was the pits, and it was my newly adopted home; for how long, only the fates knew. At curbside, I spied a guy holding up a decrepit mini pickup of obvious Asian design. He wasn't really holding the little truck up, but it was certainly leaning in his direction. I knew that this was Richard Dinerman, president of the incorporated Fathom Expeditions. He watched me as I neared him, and didn't even straighten his pose, which was reminiscent of those leaning cowboy silhouettes one still sees along the lesser highways of America. You know the ones. The cowboy's back languidly leaning against a post with arms crossed and the hat brim stretching out in simulated shade over a dangling cigarette. Except that this hat was straw and silly looking. Richard slowly raised his head a few degrees, attempted an eye contact, which appeared to make him uneasy, then inquired, "You got the money?"

Now I am still a rather easily duped person, tending to trust people until taken to the cleaners, but this was absolutely naked capitalism. It's not that I ever had anything against capitalism, but it was unseemly. Without so much as a "how do you do?" or even an appreciable shift in position to acknowledge my presence, he had just asked for three thousand dollars. I saw my hands counting out the requisite thirty Ben Franklins. When the last bill crossed his surprisingly well manicured fingers, the clouds parted and a sunny disposition beamed forth.

"Alright, Tom," he gushed, "welcome to sunny Honduras. Hot isn't it? You know it's not really the heat that gets you here; it's the humidity. After a few weeks you won't even notice it. Where did you get that outfit? I hope I didn't take your last dollar. Actually, I don't care if I did. Ha, just kidding there, you know. Hell, you'll hardly notice the heat after a few weeks. And it really is a lot better out on the islands. Tradewinds and all that, you know? So what do you think so far? Course you haven't been here long, but you'll get used to it. Or you won't. Some don't you know. They come here, they pays their money, they get a feel for the ambience of the islands, and they leave. Just like that. It doesn't matter to me, long as they get the 'pays their money first' part right. And they all do. Know what I'm saying here?" The word "saying" was so perfectly nasal, that I winced at the word.

I nodded my head dumbly. I reeled from the extreme New York accent and the staccato speech that left me some sentences behind in listening. He went on to apologize for the mode of transportation, the heat (as if he were somehow complicit in the extremes it had reached) and the general state of everything in Honduras. I felt the thought flit through my consciousness that this was a con man of spectacular proportions, and that I had just been led to the slaughterhouse with a smile. I understated to myself the enormity of the con and the man, as I was going to learn soon enough.

As Richard prattled, I shifted my brain into automatic and simply uttered monosyllabic replies and grunts, which are not worthy of recounting. I understood that we were waiting for another man, and then driving in the little pickup to the coastal town of Puerto Cortes. When the other man arrived within the hour, my very recently suppressed sense of foreboding returned full force.

Sergei Kotova arrived, the whitest white man I had yet seen in my young life. And he was tall. He was at least six and a half feet tall, with forearms that would have shamed Popeye. Hell, he was Popeye. His skin was of such fair complexion that a vision of eighteenth century women jumped into my mind, when the most worthy of the genteel looked a ghostly pale. But this was no ghost. He was too real. He was a Russian who had defected from the Soviet Union by literally jumping ship and taking his chances with the ocean and a rudimentary life preserver. After a debriefing of some sort, he was foisted upon Fathom Expeditions. As I later learned, he simply took over operations. His imposing presence accompanied with the deepest bass voice known to mankind, joined to help him force his way into the position of head of operations within weeks. He had been running the expedition for more than three years now. He looked weary and wary.

Richard waved in my general direction by way of introduction and it was understood immediately that I was to ride in the back as there was no chance that the little truck cabin could accommodate the three of us. I threw the duffel against the front bed wall and clambered over the side after the bag.

Astride the duffel and facing aft for the ride was going to give me a good view of the country on this sunny afternoon. The driving was aggressive and the view was fascinating.

San Pedro Sula was what is generally referred to as a "bustling city." It did not enjoy the scale of bustle attained by a Hong Kong or Tokyo, but it was definitely bustling. Much of the activity had to do with trying to make money. "Generally worn" would describe most of the people. It was quite a shock for me to realize that the women squatting by the rocks pounding out tortillas were usually only aged in the twenties and thirties, as was evidenced by the toddlers and children clinging to them. They looked every bit as old as my grandmother, who was in her late sixties by then. I saw much social intercourse and mostly brown-toothed grins. It was obvious that the desperation of their situations was wearing these people down. Less than an hour in the country, and I wanted to go home.

Shacks made from cardboard, odds and ends of wood, plastic and any old sheet of metal were everywhere. People were sweeping the streets and open-door hovels with brooms made from branches tied to sticks. Pride of ownership had no level of worth too low. They were trying to keep their areas neat. At the traffic lights, children and adolescents put on juggling displays, gymnastic acts and even trained animal acts. As the light was nearing a change to green, the performers walked among the stopped cars and held out tin cans and hats to accept any coins offered by the motorists.

And what the motorists were driving was a real surprise to me also. This place was a study of fifties' vintage cars. I had never liked the 1958 Chevrolet. I had decided, years before, that it was one of the ugliest cars ever built in America. It was evident that this city was the eventual home for thousands of examples of the 1958 Chevy. Many cars had started existence as sedans and coupes back in the world, only to spend their final years in this moving graveyard as homemade pickups and roughly hewn flat bed trucks. *Cutting torches must abound in this city*. The charred edges of metal cut by flame were evident on many vehicles.

The creatures populating this city were tearing the heart out of my chest. I was no bleeding-heart liberal, but the conditions these people were living in made me want to buy food and clothing and hand them out to almost every urchin and wretch I saw. And I saw them everywhere. The dogs were so ubiquitous that I mulled over the thought that at least the animals weren't being eaten. While I was taking in the distended stomachs and the rib bones pressing almost out the sides of the animals, I wondered if being eaten wouldn't be a good thing.

We passed out of the city and plunged into the jungle, and this was truly jungle. Shades of green were everywhere. I had visited many Caribbean islands and was not a complete stranger to tropical vegetation, but these plants were somehow denser, greener, and more invasive than I remembered. Canopies of branches took our little truck into near darkness, which eventually gave way, and we were awash in brilliant sunlight. I thought of strobe lights and occasionally closed my eyes because the effect was often dizzying.

How Richard could be driving so fast in these conditions was beyond my understanding. And I haven't even mentioned the roads. To call them paved would be stretching the term. I decided that hard surfaces were achieved by decades of splashes of anything that hardened. The principle road upon which we traveled was generally black asphalt. The road crowned at the middle, and fell off too steeply toward almost nonexistent shoulders; which ended abruptly in steep embankments. Richard achieved parity with the right side of the too narrow road by applying constant corrections to the left. It was fun to watch. The inhabitants were not fun to watch.

The people didn't walk along the road as much as they watched one foot step ahead of the other in a perpetual head-down slouch that I would later learn to associate with all of Central America. These were not happy people. This was not the tropical paradise of the travel brochures, and this was not a happy place. As we tore down the road, the average person ahead of us would make a shift of the head allowing a view of approaching disaster. Without gracing the driver with eye contact or even a real acknowledgement of our presence, a sad resignation would evidence itself in body language, and a begrudging shift would be made in the direction of the even more sloped shoulder of the road. The resulting clearing of that area of the road was what allowed us to pass. With our passing, the void would be filled with a slight shift of the pedestrian. Repeat the action thousands of times, and you have an image of our progress.

The animals were entirely different in their reactions to our little truck making its way through their world. The dirty pathetic dog must be the national symbol of Honduras, I thought. While one dog would run from the road in a panic, tail tucked firmly against its belly, the next would barely clear the asphalt and strike a pose as we passed. This type seemed to not care if it were hit. Then it would climb back up immediately upon our departure from his patch of the road.

A few hours of this, and we entered the town of Puerto Cortes. I felt as if we had gone back in time at least fifty years. Many of the streets were dirt and the sidewalks were actually wooden and very old. Chickens, dogs and glimpses of cats completed my survey of the animal population. The men and boys wore dirty-to-filthy trousers and loose shirts. The female population was entirely clothed in plain dresses, bringing to mind scenes from any old B-grade western.

Richard was still intent on trying to at least put another dent in the sad little truck, swinging mildly back and forth to give the appearance of concern for the locals. I got the strong impression that he wanted to brush a few out of our way, being an important American and all that. Making more turns than must have been necessary, up and down paved and unpaved streets, we seemed to stumble onto the wharf. My spirits went down the tubes yet again this day. Before me was a third world seaport of lowest order. *Some of the ugliest sea going craft in the world must be represented here.* Tramp freighters with large swaths of rust streaming down from the scuppers, truly ancient and rotting wooden trawlers, and hundreds of lesser craft lined the various docks and piers. The concrete seawall itself served as tie down of choice for the largest freighters. I was not suffused with a feeling of having happened upon an exotic port of call.

I looked at the rat guards on the hawsers leading up to the ships and did a quick survey of the area around the truck as I jumped down from the tailgate, which looked incapable of being swung into the closed position. Honduras was wearing thin on me, this after an investment of some three hours in country. Richard jumped out, ran over to the sea wall and did what he could to raise the sea level. Sergei unwound himself from the cab of the little truck.

He made a brief eye contact with me and walked off to disappear around the corner of a black wood building that just had to be a warehouse. *Where do these tropical places get all this black wood anyway?* This brooding giant with the forearms of a gorilla was essentially my boss, and he barely recognized my existence. I was feeling bile rise to my throat. I wondered if this could be the beginning of a panic attack. I had heard of such things, but had no understanding of the concept until first experiencing Honduras.

Richard returned from his mission. "Alright, Tom," he said in the high pitched voice that I was beginning to resent. "Here we are, home of the Island Queen. She is the transportation between the mainland and Utila, your new home. You're gonna love it here."

"It's Tommy," was all I could think to say. I was a little behind in the conversation department.

"Right, Tom… I got it. Now the boat won't leave until sometime tonight, but you and Sergei will run into a couple of our guys around here somewhere. It will take all night, but you'll be at the government dock on the island in the morning. Don't want to make the harbor entrance in the dark, you know. The light doesn't always work, and it can be dicey if the captain tries to make the cut in any weather. You know what they say, 'if you don't like the weather, just wait a couple hours and it'll change.' I gotta go. Any questions? No? Good. I will probably be seeing you in a coupla months. Later."

He scampered back into the little truck, twisted the key and held it seconds too long after it started, producing that expensive sounding clash of metal parts that always made me wince. He then ground the gears as he tried to shift it into first before the clutch pedal was fully depressed, then let the clutch out abruptly, nearly stalling the engine as it leapt forward. The little truck, and Richard Dinerman, president of Fathom Expeditions, Incorporated, and most of my money, were gone, leaving only a trail of dust and a whiff of too rich a carburetor setting.

What had I just done? I was now officially in the middle of nowhere with less than two hundred dollars left. I felt the bitter regret of having fallen for a scam, and I couldn't have felt more alone.

"He's a piece of work, isn't he?"

I must have visibly jumped at the sound of an unfamiliar English speaking person just a few feet behind me.

"I can't stand to listen to the son-of-a-bitch rattle on in that fast talking New York City accent," the stranger continued. *What's this, trouble in paradise?*

I turned to size up the person talking. He looked to be in his upper twenties, had short black curly hair, and a similarly short black curly beard. He was wearing the faded denim bell-bottom Navy work jeans with which I had become so familiar in my Virgin Islands trips. He looked as if he were onboard a Navy ship. He returned the appraisal and sized me up in a slow bottom to top scan. He pursed his lips slightly and made the slightest shrug of his shoulders. Apparently paisley shirts and polyester striped pants had not yet reached haute couture status in Central America. In spite of his appraisal of me, he offered his hand in greeting. I slowly took the hand and he squeezed the blood from mine until my wrist expanded. I felt my knees weaken.

"Welcome aboard, kid. I'm Nick, Nick Hatchet. More new meat for the grinder, eh?" he started, "So what are you in for; the two… or the three thousand dollar package?" I was somewhat taken aback by this opening, but quickly realized that he was referring to the shareholder packages, two and a half percent for two thousand dollars, and five percent for three thousand dollars. I had shrewdly jumped in for the five percent. Nick easily read my thoughts and laughed.

"Well, you were going to find out soon or sooner anyway. You and I are five percent shareholders of a company with at least 30 other five percent shareholders and a few two and a half percent owners. Do the math. And that doesn't get to the fact that Richard holds the majority of shares in the company. And you will find out soon enough that Sergei owns a ten percent share of the Company."

I was doing the math. I turned and looked down the grimy street, trying to get even a glimpse of my retreating money. I couldn't see beyond the mass of peasants, boxes, cars, trucks, or the laundry. "Oh, man," I whined.

"Forget it," he grinned as he talked. "You won't need money out here, until you really need money, and then you'll have it. You have a name, or am I just going to call you the new guy?"

"Uh, it's Tommy," I managed to say.

"Okay Tom, let's go get a beer."

"It's just Tommy, okay?"

Nick stopped, looked me full in the eyes, considered the request, waited a moment and said, "Right, never assume. Let's go have a few, Tommy. The boat won't sail for hours, and there's nothing else to do in this… place."

He walked past me with an interesting gait. His feet were thrown out to the sides just a little more than was the norm. *Sea legs.* I caught up with Nick just as he mounted the rickety steps of the boardwalk. No question that this was meant to keep the people out of the mud. It reminded me of a western movie set. We pulled up short of a beat up and less than ordinary wooden door. Nick studied the door with his hands on his hips. The door had no window, but it did have what appeared to be nothing more than graffiti scrawled on it; the Poke and Eat, it read in green paint.

Apparently satisfied, Nick reached out with his left hand at eye level and pushed the door aside. We entered a gloom enhanced with cigarette smoke and without the benefit of a window. Our intrusion bathed the wooden floor, wooden tables, wooden chairs and wooden people with bright sunlight. The whole place was only about twenty feet by sixty feet. Just before that wall was a bar made out of rough wooden planks and topped with, what else, rough-hewn planks of wood. If I had any illusions that my being an American would impress most of these third world types, those illusions were being dispelled. Not one denizen of this dreary establishment even looked up as we passed the tables of quiet people. I saw no hint of so much as a peripheral glance in our direction.

We climbed up on bar stools, and Nick asked the woman for two Salva Vidas. When she returned minutes later with two bottles of beer, I really felt I was back in the tropics. Nothing happens fast in Central America, excepting temper. But now I had a real problem. I didn't drink. I had nothing against alcohol, per se, but I simply had never been around people who drank. The few times I had tried to drink beer were unsuccessful. I just didn't like the stuff. I sure as hell wasn't going to tell Nick I didn't drink beer.

So I tried not to grimace noticeably as I sipped at the bitter liquid. I slouched over the bar and looked around. The most prominent artifact of note was a large retouched photograph featuring the Kennedy brothers, Jack, Bobby and Teddy, as was pointed out in script along the bottom of the piece. It was set in a heavenly haze surround, making it appear that they were emerging from clouds. *Very tasteful.* I looked for some black velvet paintings that would have complemented it perfectly.

"So what is with the Kennedy photograph, Nick?" I asked in my first full sentence to him, getting my bearings and starting to get a feeling of belonging. I felt so dependent that I would have begged him not to leave me alone in this town. I was pathetic.

"Shhh, Tommy, lower your voice. The Kennedy's are like gods all over Central America. I mean, if you want to be beaten to death by a mob down here, just start bad-mouthing the Kennedy family. It has something to do with their giving away so much of other people's money to buy votes from Mexicans and negroes, that and being Catholic. These people all live for the next world. This one is crap." I looked at him incredulously enough that he followed with, "No, really."

"Sorry, I didn't have any idea. So, what's it like on Utila?" I asked.

"Different from anything I've ever been around. We are spread out all over the town. Two to four guys in a hooch or house. No organization, no goals, other than looking for the wrecks; no structure of any kind, but it works, in a zen kind of way. If you want to work a site, you are working a site. If you want to look for sites, then you are looking for sites. If you don't want to do anything, don't do anything. Food and stuff will be there and you can just be." He stopped and looked at me rather more carefully after his preamble.

"It's hard to explain, man, but we are just window dressing." He stopped and looked at me carefully yet again. "You do get that, don't you?" he asked. "I mean, you were only graced with the presence of Richard because he wanted to get your money before you found out that the shares don't mean a thing. You could just show up on the island, say you want to be part of the expedition, and you're in, unless of course you are a complete asshole. In that case, it wouldn't matter if you 'owned shares' or not. We **will** run off the assholes. Except that we can't run off Sergei or Richard. And they are both assholes, but in completely different ways. Richard wants your money, which I know he has or you wouldn't have gotten the limo ride, and Sergei needs divers and worker bees. But it's a life, and if you needed to disappear from the world, for whatever reason, you have just disappeared."

"So, how did you get here, or shouldn't I ask?" I asked.

"Oh, no sweat man. I just mustered out of the navy, about a year ago now." He paused to reflect on that as if it were a revelation of some kind. He took on that faraway look that people in deep thought get, visibly shook off the reverie, and continued. "I was a submariner, I went to sea for months at a time, had a few duties back in port, and then was off duty for months at a time. I was based in Charleston and would just take off for the Bahamas and not go home until I ran out of money or had to get back to work. I was just thinking that maybe I should have stayed in the life."

I was really getting attached to this guy. I don't mean that the way it might sound, but Nick had a relaxed way of letting me in on his thoughts and he exuded confidence. He had a swagger with none of the pretensions and an easygoing manner without being too easygoing, if you get my meaning here. I had been having second and third thoughts all day. I felt like an idiot for handing over three thousand dollars, then finding out that it wasn't even necessary. The expedition was apparently some kind of scam that I definitely didn't understand. I found myself almost desperate to get a sense of being part of something. When you are deep into nowhere-and I am telling you here, Honduras is way deep into nowhere-a feeling of not being on your own can be the only thing that keeps your scared little inner child from taking control of your mind.

The feelings of loneliness and despair that can be felt when you are on your own in a foreign country can be debilitating. A perfect example of the desperation that can be felt was to be illustrated some months after my arrival in Honduras. It is absolutely true that a hijacker, starting in the states with a gun and an imperfect plan, commandeered an airliner, demanded and received several hundred thousand dollars and a trip to Honduras. He wandered around the country for a while, spent some money, and generally attempted to make a life for himself in a country with no extradition agreement with the United States. The word from some of the Fathom public relations people in Tegucigalpa was that the hijacker became so despondent over conditions that he simply wanted out. Within a few months he walked into the American embassy and turned himself into the authorities and went to prison in the states. A federal pen was more attractive to the guy than being rich and stuck in Honduras. There are only two kinds of stories in the world, "once upon a times," and "this is no bullshit" This story belongs in the latter category. Look it up.

When I heard the story some months later, I couldn't help but think back to my first afternoon in Honduras and how I was feeling in that bar. I generally knew that I had torn apart my safe little world for a life that was open-ended and would have no routine. I suppose it was a kind of buyer's regret. You work methodically toward the goal of acquiring something, to the exclusion of everything else. When you get it, you are disappointed.

The back wall of the establishment, directly in front of us as we sat at the bar, had a doorway that was obscured by strings of those multi-colored glass beads that always made me think of hippies. I caught glimpses of a kitchen whenever the woman would duck into the back room to get a plate of some obscure food or beers. Occasionally I would see a very pretty little girl staring out at me. By little, I mean little in stature. She could not have been more than four and a half feet tall. She looked to be in her teens easily, but she was gorgeous, like a dark skinned porcelain doll. When I was into my third or fourth beer (it wasn't as bad as I remembered beer tasting by now) this little doll rather noiselessly, save for the tinkling sound of the glass beads as she parted the strands, padded her way out of the back room. She made her way around the side of the bar to my right. Without saying a word she softly glided up to me and ran her left hand down the right side of my face. She traced the outline of my neck and shoulder, then slowly continued down my right side, which was somewhat exposed as I had my right arm extended to the bar. I was squeezing the beer so tightly that I considered the possibility of the bottle breaking.

Her left hand stopped at the waistband of my polyester, vertically striped, silver and black, bell-bottomed pants, which she grasped with a firm squeeze of her delicate left hand. I looked around the room, which was dimly lit by several bare light bulbs. Not one person, male or female, looked our way. This pretty girl then pulled the zipper down with her right hand, having secured the top so perfectly. I wasn't at all certain as to the correct response to such an overture, but I had the fleeting thought that this probably wasn't the first time that she had done this kind of thing, and she would let me know what I was supposed to do next. What I didn't expect was Nick grabbing one of her arms and roughly pushing her away from my lap.

"Tell her we don't have time for this tonight, Tommy," Nick said in the most offhand way imaginable.As embarrassed as I was a few seconds ago, I was now startled. The other people in the bar had ceased to exist and I thought I definitely had time for this. "Push her away, man," he said again. "We have to be dockside in a few minutes."

I stared at Nick and he stared at me. He was serious, very serious. My embarrassment was replaced with a complete sense of disappointment. I looked to my right, established eye contact with the girl, and shook my head back and forth while I readjusted myself. I zipped my pants back up as discreetly as possible under the circumstances. I also noticed that no one had even looked our way.

What happened next started me down the road of a life of cynicism. The beautiful little senorita leaned over my lap, her weight almost entirely given to my right thigh, her elbows brushing against me in fleeting fashion. She proceeded to start her routine all over again, but with Nick as the recipient of her ministrations. Nick just kept on talking. I haven't the faintest idea what he was saying at that point. The sensation wasn't entirely bad for me, but I will likely never again experience the simultaneous explosion of emotions of such differing characteristics.

I felt pleasure, resentment, amazement, embarrassment and an exhibitionistic pride, all at the same time. We didn't have time when I was the target of opportunity, but now we had time. I never asked Nick about the episode, and I was to know Nick for almost two years after this night. It was as if it never happened. When this thing that never happened was over, Nick readjusted himself, the young lady straightened herself back to full height, which wasn't much, and disappeared into the back room, the swinging strands of glass beads tinkling softly as the only proof that she had ever existed. I never went back to that bar again, and I never saw her again. One of life's mysteries, I guess. Nick placed a twenty lempira note on the bar.

"Better drink the rest of your beer, Tommy." We walked out of the bar into the gathering darkness. It was time to board the Island Queen.

Chapter Four

The Island

I wasn't disappointed when I first saw the Island Queen. I was too shocked to be disappointed. *Were we actually heading out to sea, at night, in this*? She was way up on the ugly scale. I estimated her to be at least eighty feet long with a beam (width) of about 20 feet. Her prow was absolutely vertical. From its condition I had to assume that the captain took a particular delight in ramming every piling, jetty or piece of flotsam that had the audacity to get in his way. Patches were everywhere, and these were not polite patches. It was apparent that when a hole appeared, a board or sheet of indiscriminate pedigree would be found, then cut, broken or hammered to the rough dimensions needed and nailed over the offense. *Nails? What were these people thinking*? Any seas more than a chop, and pieces would fly off this boat like shrapnel. This was a work boat, intended to haul supplies and goods between the Bahia Islands and the mainland. My attitude began to head south yet again.

"She ain't much to look at, is she, Tommy?" Nick asked, standing with his arms crossed in front of him.

"That is the second ugliest boat I've ever seen," I replied.

"Really, it's only the second ugliest?" He retorted, grinning at my obvious discomfort.

"I'm trying to be charitable here," I replied.

"Yeah, well, she floats, and the captain is a nice guy. That's him in the pilothouse."

I looked up to the pilothouse and saw a typically dark skinned Honduran. He had the look of just about every other middle-aged peasant I had seen so far. But he had a pipe, and was puffing away on it. It gave him an air of shabby sophistication. He caught sight of Nick and waved, grinning around the stem of his pipe and I knew I was going to like him. Just like that.

He motioned us on board and Nick strode up to the old man. He was at least fifty years old. They shook hands and slapped each other on the shoulders and talked. I was relieved to hear English. I cannot explain it to this day, but I hate the sound of people speaking Spanish. They talk far too fast. How people can hear words in that stream of sounds is a complete mystery to me. It was something I hadn't even considered when I decided to move to Central America. A few locals boarded immediately after our arrival and we soon cast off. It was after sunset, but I knew that there would be a nearly full moon, and I was at least mildly looking forward to the view over the ocean. Utila, of the Islas de la Bahia, was about one hundred nautical miles east and north, and it would be an all night voyage. I watched the moon for the first hour or so, and decided to find a berth to get some sleep. One look at the filthy cabin, lined on both sides with tiers of tiny bunks of sagging hammock style mattresses, made me reconsider. The stench from the cabin convinced me to find sleep elsewhere. I made my way topside and stared at the huge pile of bananas covering the top deck. They were obviously very green, so I looked around to be certain that no one would see me burrow into them and make a bed. It was not uncomfortable, and I soon dozed off. It was in the morning that I found out that they weren't bananas at all, but plantains. To me, plantains look just like bananas, but really, they are bigger, firmer and I guess people slice them up and fry them or something. I never had much interest in them.

Plantains are about as comfortable to sleep on as they are good to eat. They take some getting used to. I woke up several times, kept repositioning myself until I was splayed out across the top of the pile, getting a good breeze and less vibration and noise from the engine than anywhere on the boat. I was congratulating myself on my resourcefulness and wondered why no one else had chosen to sleep on this huge and relatively soft stack. It was during these ruminations that I felt something moving around my stomach. Then it was full on my stomach and making its way up my body. I raised my head, tucked my chin into my upper chest to get a look and clearly saw the several hairy legs of the world's biggest spider. I didn't want to get it excited. I lay still, tingling with excitement as it continued up my torso. It stopped to probe my chin with its forelegs, it then moved onto and over my face. When it cleared my scalp, I sat up and stared at the plantains all around me. Movement seemed to be everywhere. I was not alone. Climbing down as if the plantains were sticks of dynamite, I eventually exited the pile and tiptoed across the deck. I had solved the mystery as to why I was alone with the cargo.

I found my way to the galley, poured coffee into a cup that was clean enough by my standards and went to the bow to await the dawn. There would be no sleep tonight. At first light, we made the island and rounded the jetty into the harbor. I made the usual pest of myself and helped get the lines out and moor the boat against a wide and long dock.

If I were expecting some fanfare, or even a welcome, upon my arrival, I was soon to be disappointed. I walked with Nick down what he called Fathom Dock. There were two small sheds attached to the dock and cantilevered out over the water. Their purpose was a mystery to me. They were too small to be used for any kind of storage and they looked for all the world like outhouses. I looked at Nick, who was watching me and reading my thoughts.

"Those are the crappers," he offered helpfully. I was beyond being shocked by much at this point, but I was at least startled. I didn't want to process that kind of information to start my day. I stopped, looked at the sheds, bending down slightly to see who knows what. I looked down at the perfectly clear water. I estimated it to be about ten feet deep. It was so clear that I could easily see details such as the texture of the moss-like coatings of the rocks on the sandy bottom. I looked at the angled supports reaching out from the pilings of the dock and saw mottled black and brown streaks.

Crabs were poised all over every board beneath the sheds. "When you gotta go, and you want a little privacy, this is where you go. Everything is filtered through three feet of air before it hits the ocean. They are just one-holers, but your output will be graded, and the comments will take some getting used to." Now I was shocked.

"What about all those crabs?" was about all I could think to say.

"Oh yeah, those are a special breed of shit-eating crabs. If you are going to sit down in there, you might want to kick at the boards pretty hard and try to knock them off. But that is actually a kind of signal to the rest of them and they come running when they hear somebody pounding the dock anywhere around the crappers. I guess Pavlov had it right with that conditioned response stuff. They hang upside down all over the bottom around the seat and if any of your equipment is hanging down, those claws hurt like hell." I knew that there was no way that I would ever use these "facilities." I was to be wrong about that, too.

"If you're taking a leak," Nick continued, "you can aim for the little bastards and knock them off. You can go for number knocked into the water or go for size. I go for number myself." He said this all very matter-of-factly and walked off toward the shore, leaving me standing there stupidly, my specialty, watching his sea legs propel him down the dock.

I caught up with him as we stepped off the dock onto a soft sandy path that was outlined by that thick bladed grass that grows in sandy areas.

"Let's hit the cookhouse," Nick said. "Rosie makes breakfast at first light and keeps at it until about nine."

We crossed a sandy dirt street that paralleled the shoreline, offset from it by about two hundred feet. Utila is an oval shaped island, similar to the shape of a speedway, laid out with the straight-a-ways on the north and south shores about seven miles long, curving around to three mile long back stretches on each end. The town is ranged around a perfect harbor, looking as if it were carved into the southeast section of the speedway. This southeastern end of the harbor, and the island, terminated in a two thousand foot runway, surfaced with hard packed, crushed sea shells and coral. The town stretches around the harbor for about a mile. The cookhouse, like most of the wooden structures, rested on concrete and wood pylons and was about a quarter of a mile from the western end of the town.

We climbed the worn, wooden steps to the cookhouse. It had a narrow walled off section on one end that looked to be about eight feet deep, with a doorway that opened into a twenty foot by fifty foot room. The center of the room held the massive kind of picnic tables with attached benches that one sees in every state or national park back in the states. The room had three exits to the outside and none of the tall wide windows had glass in them. The sills of the windows were about three feet above floor level and several of these were the seats of choice for a really rough looking group of guys. Of the twelve to fifteen people, a few looked to be about my age, with the rest ranging from about 25 to 50 years of age. Not one was wearing shoes, a few were wearing shirts, and every one of them was wearing shorts of various descriptions, though most of these were cutoff blue jeans.

They almost greeted us when Nick and I entered, but caught sight of my polyester ensemble and, as one, looked back down to their plates of food with a shake of their heads. I felt like a college boy at a redneck barbecue. I wondered if they were going to beat me up to start the day off right. I would later realize that I wasn't considered to be important enough for the honor. I was going to have to lose the pants, shirt and shoes. Now that I think about them, they went to the bottom of my duffel and remained there for almost two years.

And these guys were tanned. I mean really tanned, the dark rich shades of brown leather. This being March, and my being from Indiana, I probably reflected sunlight.

Along the wall of the kitchen was a sturdy table laden with covered dishes and pots. As we went down the table, grasping heavy plates that made me think of coal miners in a company cafeteria, I found scrambled green eggs, sausages, tortillas and chunks of bread. What brought me up short was the last pot, one of those big five gallon stainless steel rigs that took me back to my youth in the Salvation Army soup kitchens. When I lifted the lid, a fog of steam and odor assailed my face. Peering into the hot liquid, the head of a large fish, complete with bulging black eyes, peered back at me. I jumped back, losing both my composure and my grip on the hot lid, which clattered off the pot and onto the floor. The room erupted in laughter. Ribald suggestions and rough language were the order of the moment, and I wanted to be in Indiana more than I wanted to breathe. For the first time in my life, I was homesick.

"I should have warned you about the fish stew," Nick said

through tears of laughter. It's always there. Rosie doesn't waste food of any kind. Every piece of anything carved up in the kitchen or out on the docks goes into that pot. And it's always hot. You'll acquire a taste for it, eventually."

I doubted that I would ever be able to even look in that pot without getting nauseous, but again I was to be proved wrong. Months later I would be ladling out what I considered to be the better parts of the gruel, as we called it, and even enjoying the hot liquid on a rainy windy night. Go figure. As for everything going into the pot, Nick was exactly right. Within days, I was to shoot a large snapper and filet it out on the dock. I carefully cut away the white meat leaving only a well-trimmed carcass, complete with entrails, fins and head.

I threw the carcass into the water and watched as hundreds of fish, including some small barracuda, attacked the remains. With a yell that made me jump, Danny, a local boy who had become the virtual mascot of Fathom, rushed past me and jumped off the dock, right into the middle of the feeding frenzy. He dragged the carcass to a ladder and climbed, fish snapping at the carcass and him. This very little boy, maybe weighing sixty pounds, made a point of unsheathing his knife and laying the fish out beside me on the dock. He lectured me about rich Americans throwing out perfectly good food as he trimmed off the fins, cut away the entrails, and strode off down the dock with an indignant aura emanating from him like a cloak, heading for the kitchen. I had no doubt that I would see the face of my snapper again.

But for breakfast this first morning, I selected green scrambled eggs and sausage. Latin Americans in general enjoy some kind of green sauce that is poured over just about any food. A few chunks of heavy bread and really good coffee did much to restore some calm to my troubled soul.

I didn't know what the protocol was for mustering into the

outfit. I supposed that I should be checking in with somebody, maybe given some orientation or gear, that kind of thing. As it happened, nobody cared that I was here, and nobody cared what I did. I struck up a conversation with a slightly built kid who looked to be no more than 15 years old.

"My name is Tommy Conklin," I started hesitantly; "I just got in this morning."

"Yeah, I know," he replied softly. "They don't exactly roll out the welcome mat down here. But everybody notices a new face. Especially if you're American, and only an American dresses like that." He looked me up and down and added, "No offense."

"Boy, have I felt like a clown the last couple of days."

"Tell you what; I live in a hooch almost in the jungle. There's an extra bunk and I could use some company. So how about it, Tommy?"

We were a couple of lost souls. I sure didn't have any other offers. *So much for the registration and orientation procedures.* "And my name is Henry Porter."

We were to become good friends. I suppose I became an older brother with whom he could actually relate. Henry wasn't even a diver, so I fixed that. He stayed only another few months after my arrival on the island, but he went back to the States a practiced diver and a wiser young man. He was running away from a situation of some kind. He once said that if I hadn't befriended him and shown him that he had real ability and was a decent person; his life would have been ruined. I think he was a little melodramatic, but I found that in investing some time in him, I had earned some of the same benefits. It was one of those things you learn about life only after you know it all.

Henry and I walked westward down the sandy street, which was barely distinguishable from the surrounding sandy soil of the island, except that it was outlined on both sides by foot high concrete curbing. We talked a little about the sites that had been found so far. Utila had been the home of the infamous pirate, Henry Morgan. It was believed that between his activities and the sometimes sudden and extremely violent tropical storms and hurricanes, the reefs in the surrounding area held the remains of many Spanish ships. Some of these ships had been noted in records archived in Spain and were known to have been carrying gold, silver and jewels taken from the ancient Aztecs and Mayans.

The little houses we were encountering as we walked became shabbier, sometimes unpainted, and more scattered. Henry turned seaward, to our left, walked down a short path littered with palm fronds and coconut husks and I found myself looking warily at a small tin-roofed hut, about half the size of my recently departed house trailer back in Indiana. We went in and Henry pointed at a handmade bunk that looked more like a slab on sawhorses than anything else. But it did have a thin mattress topped by what was obviously a government issued sleeping bag of surprising quality. Shelving along every wall served as storage space and for furniture, there was a rattan chair.

It would be easy, and wrong, to think that I was entirely unused to primitive conditions. My childhood, until the age of ten, was spent in a very rural area of northeastern Indiana. My family, with six kids, all worked the landlord's farm to earn the rent. The house that I had spent more than half my life in was built in the mid-nineteenth century. It had been wired for basic electrical service in the thirties, thanks to the Rural Electricity Act of Congress. "Basic" was defined by a few overhead wires and one electrical outlet in exactly two rooms of the old two story brick farm house. We had no running water in the house save for what I think was called a dry sink. To this day I do not understand the term, for this dry sink had a hand pump at one end connected to our well just outside the wall. When you wanted water, you poured a cup of water into the priming chamber of the old pump, and pumped away.

Outside, in the warm months, we had another hand pump directly above the well. We all drank from a handy community tin cup which conveniently hung from a hook on the apparatus. Drinking from that cup, and eating peat moss, probably gave me immunities that the less fortunate among us just never seem to acquire. I cannot remember ever being sick for more than about a day in my life. In the twelve years of schooling that I had received to this point in my life, I missed exactly three days of school. Really.

About twenty feet from the well was a two-hole outhouse, and as Jack Paar used to say, "I kid you not," it was replete with a very old Sears catalog, the kind with the newsprint pages, for comfort. The glossy pages of the newer catalogues were generally eschewed by outdoor plumbing aficionados. This is true actual fact, to paraphrase my Uncle Jim. Indeed, because I now was in the tropics, I felt that my home on the island had at least one big advantage over the old homestead. The old house of my youth was not insulated and the old coal furnace in the hand-dug basement barely gave off enough heat for the first floor to be habitable. Many was the morning, far up on the second floor, that my body sweat from the layers of quilts and blankets froze into a patina of ice so stiff that I could feel the crunch when I rolled around in my bed. *This was not going to be a bad place to live.*

I unpacked my duffel, and laid out all my worldly goods on the shelves nearest my bunk. The pragmatic aspects of suddenly moving to the tropics included preparing for an almost unrelenting sun. Knowing what was in store for me to some extent, I had brought four pairs of white jeans and several white -sleeved cotton shirts. Two pairs of tennis shoes and a stack of t-shirts just about completed my wardrobe.

I changed into white, from head to toe. For a while, my

signature white was the topic of some discussion. Comments would soon trail in my wake about the new white guy and his long-sleeved shirts and full length pants, topped with an oversized straw hat. I was immune to the ribbing from the beginning. I had seen people burned by the tropical sun and I was determined to not let the sun touch me. I dove, worked, roamed the town, and slept in my white outfit. What happens when you stay protected from the sun in the tropics is that you are never protected from the sun in the tropics. The sun will find its way to your skin. But you can slow its progress. I never got sunburned, slowly tanned, and in a few months, when on the island or the ocean, was down to nothing but cutoff jeans, excepting my thick layer of leathery brown skin.

I spent the first day walking the length and breadth of the town; the breadth being just a few irregular side roads removed from Main Street, as the principal street was known. I was most surprised when I reached the end of the island, which was the airport. Baking in the afternoon sun was a tiny, tandem, two-seat taildragger of an airplane of the type known to every living being, a Piper Cub. The little engine produced sixty horsepower and provided for the most basic flying, slow and fun. Next to it was a truly good looking twin engine Piper Aztec, a six seat airplane that was renowned for its load carrying ability and docile characteristics. It turned out that our expedition had an air force. I was definitely starting to recover from some of the culture shock. I was formulating some plans. I walked back to the west, the full length of Main Street and took refuge in my hooch.

I occupied myself with evicting most of the tenants, hundreds of insects, along with many of their predators, the lizards. I knew they would be back, but I wanted to mark my territory. In the late afternoon, I walked east to the cookhouse and did my best to socialize. I do not mix well with strangers, and everyone was a stranger. I must have looked pathetic as I sat at one of the tables, drinking warm water and watching the comings and goings. But at least my first night in country was spent eating some truly great french fries and fried fish of various species. I would learn soon enough that if any food could possibly be edible when fried, Rosie would fry it in coconut oil. Rosie's food probably took a few years off all our lives, but none of us would ever begrudge the damage done.

I even felt pathetic as I attached myself to the one person I knew, Nick. But he cheerfully took me in and became my mentor. My first lesson was to be in the fine art and subtleties of playing cribbage. It is an almost ancient card game in which the players keep score by moving "pegs" along a track of sixty holes drilled into wood, or any suitable surface. In the previous century, seamen of every description played cribbage, as the scoreboard was temporary and not subject to being disturbed by the pitch and roll of a ship. Whalers made cribbage boards out of whale bone that are, to this day, highly collectable. The cookhouse even had electricity provided until about 11:00PM, when the town manager shut down the diesel generator out near the airport. Anybody could tap into the bare lines that ran down all the streets and use what they needed. Fathom paid for almost all the diesel fuel that was brought to the island and it did much to make us tolerable to the islanders. It may sound trite to most, but some of the best evenings of my life were spent playing cribbage in the cookhouse, with the cribbage board illuminated by a bare light bulb hanging overhead. Another valuable skill acquired during these sessions was learning how to truly cuss like a sailor. It is a talent which I have put to good use over the years.

Chapter Five

The Expedition

I didn't know what was expected of me, or what I expected of Fathom. Having low-to-no expectations about things in general has always served me well. Some would argue that mine was a defeatist attitude that guaranteed failure or below average results. I would counter that my low expectations shielded me from disappointment, while making little successes major achievements. I decided to take it slow and learn about my surroundings.

Needing little sleep, first light of the second day on Utila found me already awake and heading for the government dock, which was virtually the property of Fathom. I headed east, noting that the cookhouse was not yet stirring. There were usually at least six of our guys living in the cookhouse. They had staked off small areas for their cots with the ubiquitous mosquito netting and associated framework. These personal spaces lined the three walls left to them. The fourth wall was the divider for the kitchen. It featured a permanent buffet table running the entire length. This was also the only building in Fathom control that had running water, gravity fed into a basic plumbing system that started at the rain barrel.

The rain barrel was a story in itself. It was worth some studying and it was ingenious in both its design and execution. The need for rain barrels on the island was obvious. There was no fresh water on Utila or any of the several keys that we controlled. A gutter system that linked all of the roofs of the cookhouse and the houses on either side emptied the collected rainwater through the mostly covered top of the rain barrel, which sat upon sturdy concrete pylons directly in front of the cookhouse and surrounded by a decking. We could walk on the deck, either getting there from a door of the cookhouse or by just stepping through one of the four windows on that side (remember, no glass).

I climbed to the deck, and taking the community cup, filled it with clear fresh water with a twist of the wooden handle of the tap. It had been inserted about three feet above the bottom of the ten-foot-high barrel that looked to have a diameter of about eight feet. This was a big barrel. I later asked about the position of the tap. It seemed to me that it did not allow access to at least a quarter of the water. I was told that the depth below the tap was to allow the settling of blown debris and the bodies of rodents that occasionally drowned after falling in. But mostly, that lower area was packed with the remains of millions of insects. The system worked great right up to the point when one would get a cup of wet insects instead of water from the tap. To forestall that unpleasant moment, just before rainy season every year, some few of our group would crawl down into the barrel and stand in feet high mush of rotting debris and pass buckets of the stuff up to be thrown on one of the gardens. I was to eventually acquire a taste for the beer.

I walked the few hundred feet to the dock, taking in the long narrow two-story building to my right. It was across the main drag from the cookhouse and reached to the water's edge, just offset from the dock. This was the Bahia Lodge. It was owned by a married couple, Brian and Theresa Hopkins. Brian had left an industrial supply sales job, having lived in Bloomington, Illinois, and bought the small hotel about a year before. There was virtually no tourist business on Utila, but Brian, a red-headed, fair skinned, former American entrepreneur, now hotel magnate, was convinced that it would become a popular tourist destination. Time would prove him right, but not soon enough for his success in the business. He should have waited at least two decades. If it weren't for the drinking budget of Fathom people, the place would have folded years before it did.

Brian was about the age of thirty, *still spry*, and happy to the point of being goofy all the time. His life was ruled by Theresa, who was a Honduran native he had married almost upon arrival to Utila, and also by his mother, June. June was a great old broad of at least fifty years of age. I thought it was really odd that she had moved down from the States with him. Everybody was made aware of the fact that she was a widow. Nobody was surprised. She had an appetite for young men that seemed insatiable.

June was making her way through the ranks of the thirty to forty men of Fathom, and its roster was constantly changing. She was handling the challenge well. I would later hear that conventional wisdom held that she had simply worn out her husband. She especially liked to do something special for birthdays, but not hers. June did not have birthdays. There were few in the expedition who hadn't awakened the day after a birthday to find a pair of pantyhose hung over their mosquito netting and vague memories of the previous night.

I pressed on and sauntered down the length of the dock. Most of Fathom's boats were berthed here. There were four matching center console boats. This design is popular with fishermen and divers because they have lots of deck space. Each of these had a dive platform at the starboard stern and each was equipped with a gorgeous one hundred twenty horsepower Mercury outboard engine called the Black Max. There were also a number of fourteen to twenty foot run-of-the-mill row-boats, some with outboard engines.

There were three ugly, wooden, rafts that were reminiscent of childhood tree houses in their quality of construction. Each was laden with at least two engines, a compressor and sported a manifold assembly that facilitates what is called hookah diving. These rigs could supply breathing air to six divers at a time. Next to the hookah rigs were chutes and piping, that were fashioned into air lifts. An airlift looks like a central vacuum system. Instead of air suction like a vacuum cleaner, an air line is plugged into the lead pipe inlet that is held by a diver and swept back and forth over the sandy bottom. As the compressed air escapes from the fitting, it flows up the six or eight inch pipe in a rush of effervescent-like cascading bubbles. The ascending air displaces water and drags water and whatever is caught by the resulting current up the piping. It was essentially an underwater vacuum cleaner. It was a simple and effective machine for the removal of the overburden found on a sunken wreck. Before the vacuumed water is allowed to flow back into the ocean, it runs down a chute and through screens of varying grades. This last action sifts through the sand and mud and reveals lots of pebbles, pieces of coral, chunks of wood, and sometimes, artifacts and even real treasure.

But what most got my attention was a strikingly purposeful-looking wooden trawler. It was about forty-six feet long and had a beam of about twelve feet. The pilot house was amidships and the wheel about eight feet above the waterline, empty as the boat was now. The stern was complete with a rugged dive platform, and there were three distinct deck levels. Now this was, to my primitive tastes, a fixer upper with some potential for traveling on the ocean.

Turning back toward the cookhouse, I looked at the out buildings hanging over the water on each side of the dock. Being a modest person, I looked the length of the dock, saw that I was still alone and entered the western side establishment. The scurrying of the crabs, clicking along and underneath the facilities, was eerie. I knocked three into the water before running out of ammo (it's a guy thing). The shit-eating crabs were out of luck.

Entering the cookhouse, I was aware that I was under some scrutiny from several pairs of eyes. It made for just a bit of tension. I knew that I was an interloper, breaking the casual routine just a bit. I was approached by a man whom I estimated to be about thirty years of age. He sported a trim blonde beard and mustache and was no more than five feet eight inches tall. I watched warily as he wound his way around a few of the tables and strode into my space, which generally extended out some three feet at all times.

"I saw you here last night playing cribbage. My name is Jack Crabill. I wanted to extend my sympathy for whatever sins you have committed that eventuated in your arrival to one of the armpits of the world." He had a lot of intelligence in his eyes. I introduced myself and we exchanged brief resumes. Jack was a geologist and researcher for the expedition. He had spent time in Spain looking for evidence of the final resting places of sixteenth and seventeenth century ships. He was the man who pointed the grunts in a general direction to start looking for a site. Over the next several months, I was to listen to him hold forth on all things geological, such as the structure of the Honduran basin, the kinds of rocks and sediment to be encountered, or the prevailing theory for the Cambrian explosion, for example. Much of it was lost on this gang of misfits, but some took away solid information from his lectures.

We ate breakfast and he gave me an ad hoc briefing of the different tasks that went on in the expedition, the disposition of the searches and what sites were being investigated. *Here was the intellectual of the enterprise.* He suggested that I find Duane I were interested in jumping into the thick of expedition activities. Duane would be the guy to steer me to a group of the less volatile people.

"What with you being a cherry and all, it would be best to get with Duane soonest," he advised. "Besides, he knows about your arrival on the island and is expecting to hear from you."

My defensive paranoia system kicked in upon hearing this. I had a thought of being called to the principal's office. It was not a feeling with which I was entirely unfamiliar. My colorful past had included more than a few episodes of officialdom taking an interest in my activities.

"Uh… okay," I uttered, and where would I find this Duane?

"He has a desk in the Fathom House. He usually spends a little time there in the mornings," Jack replied. He studied me for a few seconds before adding, "You look like a kid caught with his hand in the cookie jar. Relax. Duane is just the guy to make you feel at home here in our little tropical paradise."

"Yeah, sorry," I said quickly. "I'll get over it. I just kind of go up and down on the nervous scale lately."

"You'll be fine, Tommy. I can tell already that you have more on the ball than half these reprobates." He said this in a stage whisper as he looked around the room. It earned him a few catcalls and several chunks of hard bread were tossed in our general direction. This helped. I left for the headquarters building, called Fathom House.

It was on the opposite side of Main Street, and to the east of the dock, while the Bahia Lodge was on the other side and to the west of the dock. Between these buildings was a square reaching from Main Street to the water of the harbor. The square was about two hundred feet a side and was simply the park. Near the water, yet in the park, was a two-room jail; each cell an eight foot by eight foot, cinder-block lined room, with a dirt floor, a heavy iron door and one high, small, barred window in the back wall facing the park. Near the road was the two-story, unpainted, leaning, very decrepit cabana, or schoolhouse. Some park.

Fathom House was the home and office of Sergei Kotova, the big Russian with whom I had shared a ride just two days ago. That thought alone gave me pause as it seemed at least a week ago. This building was also the center of operations. Decisions about equipment, people, tasks and food all emanated from this unpretentious, two-story bungalow. It was the only building belonging to Fathom that featured an actual staircase, leading to a real front porch. The photography dark room was in this building. Photographs used to ensnare the unsuspecting into Richard Dinerman's web were generated there.

Upon entering the front room, I was surprised to see scores of really beautiful examples of sea life taxidermy. From small tropical fish to sharks, the room was a gallery. Sitting behind a gray steel desk, the kind seen in a stereotypical social security office back in the real world was, Duane, the de facto head of operations. He was pondering a few coral encrusted artifacts. I had been watching Duane the few times that we were in the cookhouse together. He had very dark hair, black even, and was just shy of six feet tall. I had already picked up on some deference being given him by my peers. He spoke sparsely, smiled just enough to seem cordial, but seemed to have his mind otherwise occupied when he spoke. Not that he seemed rude. Not at all; he just looked as if something were weighing on his thoughts. Nick had opined that Duane took this whole thing too seriously.

"Good morning, Tom," he started, "I saw you playing cribbage in the cookhouse and asked about you."

"Actually, I'm more comfortable with being called Tommy," I explained once again. "For some reason, I just don't feel old enough to be a Tom. I hope I'm never a Thomas."

This got an actual laugh from Duane. "Now that is funny.

Don't worry kid, you'll feel old soon enough. I'm aging in dog years down here. So what do you think so far?" he asked.

I looked at him for more than a few seconds and decided there was no time like the present. "Is this for real?" I said in just the wrong tone, and intimated more than I had intended.

Duane considered the gravity of my countenance I think, because he fixed his gaze upon me and replied, "Kid, this is as real as it gets. You would have to be a moron if you didn't soon realize that there is much at stake here. Not so much here on the island, but here in Honduras. Richard pulls people in, takes their money, talks about the riches at the end of the rainbow and generally feeds the same crap to both governments, Honduran and American.

"But at least our government knows it's a line of crap. But that is not what matters. He looks like, talks like and acts like he has a legitimate interest in building an underwater park and tourist trap. So he gets money from the worker bees as well as the queen bee. It gives the people in Washington something to hang their hats on and a reason to be down here where they can have some influence on the Honduran government; like influencing their wallets." He stopped and looked hard at me. "If that isn't real enough, don't doubt that when you are out on, and under, that ocean out there, everything is real. You can get your ass killed. And Richard will look even more serious if you do.

"Will you get rich down here? Not a chance. Will you do something important down here? Definitely. You already have. You are a beachhead on the soil of Honduras. You will be paid about one hundred dollars a week, more or less, depending on our situation. American dollars spend as well as the local money on the island, but lempira is the lucre on the mainland. You stay with the group, you get paid." This was much more than I had expected to hear. So that was it, no beating around the bush. We were a store front. Pretty cool. I decided right then that I would get my money's worth.

"Okay then, where do I start?" I asked.

"Why don't you go find that crazy Frenchman, Jan Merasak? He is the only real photographer here, so that makes him the official Fathom photographer. He is going out to what we hope is the Santiago. It sank in a verified hurricane right here in 1660. Its cargo, including some of the last of the Spanish plunder of the Aztecs would be worth several million dollars today. You can dive the site, work the site, or sleep over the site. Whatever you want, it's up to you what you get out of this.

I finally found my voice. "I guess I'm a little out of step here. As soon as I quit feeling like an outsider, I'll do better. I'll go look up Jan right now." I turned and started for the door.

"Hey, kid," Duane called after me, "sorry about jumping on you like that. Sometimes I just don't feel like beating around the bush."

"I appreciate it," I replied, wondering for about the hundredth time in two days just what I had gotten into. I would never have guessed what I was about to "get into."

Chapter Six

Shark Pups

It was not hard to find Jan. He had cameras. He also had (*what else?*), a black beret. I took my time walking up the dock to his boat, one of the center console sport fishermen types. I listened and watched him as I approached. He looked to be at least forty (*quite a few old guys here*), and he looked like a European, at least to my limited experience. He was a little overweight, not particularly tanned, and punctuated his guttural speech with large hand and arm gesticulations. I took in all this from a distance. Gregarious is the one word description of Jan Merasak.

When I was standing on the dock, looking down into the *Calypso*, Jan took notice of me. "You have a name, mon ami?"

"I'm Tommy," I said, startled at the directness of these people yet again.

"That is not a name for a full-grown man. I will call you Grouper. Now that is a name." And he laughed, not just the sound of a laugh, but the kind that originates in the stomach and makes the sound secondary to the theatre of the thing.

"Okay, whatever. Duane said you were going out today and I would like permission to join you. If it's okay that is," I added, sounding more like a little, lost kid the longer I talked.

"Of course, of course, it will be the three of us then. My Nazi friend Gunter Spitzer will be here soon. Are you diving today, Grouper?" he asked with a wide grin that ran up to the corners of his eyes, displaying his self-satisfaction for having tagged me with a moniker. I knew instantly that he was the type to make certain that the name got around to everyone, reflecting back on him as a great wit. I was going to protest, but just as quickly reconsidered. It could be worse, and I knew it would be if he suspected whining.

Many years later, I would think back to this episode when I saw the movie, Animal House, specifically, the scene where John Belushi chooses the frat names for the pledges and bestows Flounder on the hapless fat boy. Jan was just that kind of person, cutting a wide swath through life. I had met a few like him in my young life. His swath through my life was going to widen rather dramatically this afternoon, but I am getting ahead of myself.

"Great," I said, suddenly realizing that I was going to be making my first dive in Honduran waters, "I'll be right back. I need to get my gear." I ran down the dock and through the park. I turned left on Main Street and ran all the way down to my hooch. I retrieved my regulator, mask, fins and snorkel then ran all the way back to the *Calypso*. I sweated profusely, soaking my long sleeved shirt and white jeans, not to mention my wide brimmed hat. I had just bought it the day before from a delightful and chatty Negro woman named Sadie Berry.

She and others on the island had made it clear to me that they were not blacks; no sir, they were Negroes."Look at my hand, *mon*," she had said while I was buying the hat for five lempira (two and a half dollars). "Where do *mons* get off calling us black. I am brown, and not much brown." I was to get the same speech one day from Rosie, our cook. And I was surprised to find that everybody on the island spoke English; and

I mean everybody. I would learn that when a person used Spanish on this island he was ignored. If someone took to living on the island, it was expected that he would learn their Creole-like English.

Jan had watched my sprint and could not contain himself. "Mon ami, you will have to do something with all that speed and energy. If you are to become an example of industry and efficiency, you will have to be killed," he pronounced, looking at me somewhat disgustedly and shaking his head the entire time. "Put your gear in a locker and we will wait for our Nazi friend."

Our "Nazi friend" appeared at the slip of the *Calypso* in the form of a lean and very hairy man who appeared to be at least thirty years old. He was carrying a big load of gear. He brought two weight belts, two five foot long spearguns and a net bag filled with basic dive gear. He also had two Scubapro, adjustable-demand regulators slung over a shoulder and was wearing a single, 72 cubic foot, galvanized steel scuba cylinder in its backpack. I looked up at him from my lowered vantage point of the sport fisherman. Without a word, he held out the gear bag and let go. I caught it, as well as the rest of the loose gear as he shed it in my general direction. One loquacious, almost formal sounding Frenchman, and a no-talk German. I thought once again that I sure wasn't in Kansas anymore.

Two more men made their way toward us up the long dock. One was referred to as Captain Mike, a tall muscular man who immediately made me think of the Saturday afternoon wrestling performers in far off Fort Wayne. The other was Craig Morton, a slightly overweight, quiet man of about forty whom I had seen several times already, generally in the periphery of activity at the cookhouse. I had overheard him telling stories at a table, relating to groups he had been with in the past. I had not yet seen him talking with any one person, if that makes any sense. I had pegged him as one who talked *to* people, not *with* people. With the five of us on board, and me still feeling more the observer than a member of a team, we cast off. Gunter was at the wheel and he drove the boat aggressively from the start. The Mercury engine had some guts. One hundred twenty horsepower outboards were cutting-edge technology.

We headed straight at the western tip of the harbor which was only about a mile out. It was at the end of a peninsula which formed one half of the harbor. If you held your arms out in front of you, like a body builder striking a pose for the camera, complete with your fists clenched and wide apart, you would have a scaled shape of the harbor. It was a perfect natural harbor on the southeastern side of the island. It was in the best possible location because it was leeward of the prevailing winds. I was mildly surprised when we slowed as we got within a few hundred yards of the tip of the peninsula. We were on a line with a utilitarian, not picturesque, lighthouse, and the end of the government dock. Gunter sighted down a handheld compass toward the airstrip on the other side of the harbor, triangulating to confirm our position, and spoke for the first time.

"This is good. Drop anchor," he said, looking and sounding exactly like that Von Trapp fellow in the movie The Sound of Music. *Wasn't that Christopher Plummer?* A perfect goatee and mustache with the same accent complemented the analogy. He turned his attention to me. "You are the new man. You and I will go spear fish."

Having made his pronouncement, he turned and began suiting up. There is really only one order in which one dons dive gear. We moved in unison as I attached the regulator to my tank, assigned to me with a nod from Gunter. I turned on the air and tested the airflow with a tap of the purge valve. We stood behind the tanks in their backpacks, lifting them up and over our heads while slipping our arms into the webbing as the assemblies descended. The weight belt was next. I looked at the four weights, weighing about twenty pounds total. It was my general belief that it is best to start a dive with negative buoyancy. As you breathe air out of the tank, you become more buoyant. I cinched it very tightly over the backpack harness already in place. I sat on the starboard gunwale, back to the water. I spat into my mask, rubbing the mucous around with an index finger, then reached down to the water with mask in hand to rinse it clear. This keeps the mask from fogging, at least for a while. My large dive knife was in its usual place, strapped to my right calf. My small dive knife was secured to my backpack webbing. All that remained was to don the very large and heavy black rubber fins and to place the mask over my eyes and nose. I pulled the strap up over my head while carefully seating the split in the strap above and below the crown.

I looked across the deck at Gunter. We still had not had the least bit of conversation. I never doubted that I was being evaluated. He took the business end of one of the very long spear guns, much longer than I was used to, and handed it across the deck, butt end first at eye level. It was almost a salute and definitely was a signal to leave the boat. I tucked the spear gun against the right side of my chest, being careful to have the spear point well above my head (more than one person has run a shaft into his neck or head making a back entry with a speargun). I then let myself fall in a graceful back flip into the ocean.

I let myself sink while I got my bearings. It may seem silly, but knowing up from down is the first association a diver makes with his surroundings. It is a nearly weightless environment after all. Just think of the videos you have seen of astronauts training for space missions, fully clothed in space suits. I quickly located Gunter, signaled that I was going to arm my speargun, and did so, pulling the three long hollow rubber slings with the integral steel bands back and into the three notches on the spear shaft. The shaft is held in place by a simple tab and notch arrangement. Pull the trigger, the tab ducks down out of the notch and the shaft leaves, very quickly, propelled by three one foot loops of rubber extended to about three and a half feet.

The water was, of course, incredibly clear, with the hint of blue-green as I looked to the limits of vision, some one hundred fifty feet away. I have been asked scores of times over the years to describe the sensation of being underwater for long periods of time. I have always truthfully remarked that it looks exactly as it does on television. To say more seems pointless. The eyes do not contact the water, so the diver is viewing all through a window. I can't tell the difference. That's it. Hundreds of hours of wreck diving, spear fishing, instructing, quarry diving and reef exploration, and all I can really convey to the non-diver is that diving is just like watching television, only wetter.

Gunter and I met on the descent and hovered above a reef which appeared first as large brain coral, becoming more complex with mixtures of elk horn coral, sea fans, anemones and sponges covering a rocky geologic formation. The reef seemed planted in a sand-covered sea floor at about seventy feet. The usual suspects of tropical fish were present in abundance. The small species, sergeant majors, butterfly fish, clown fish, grunts and the like moved effortlessly around us, seemingly unconcerned by our presence. The next larger species, represented here by angel fish and coral eating parrot fish were also entirely unmoved by our transit through their neighborhood. The fish we were after were not so accommodating. We didn't expect, nor wish them to be.

The psyche of hunting requires a quarry that is wary. This was not the Florida Keys, where fish are so accustomed to humans that they will stop and stare down the shaft of a speargun. We were going to eat more of our kill than I wanted to acknowledge at the moment, but we were here for food. Still, I desired the challenge of the hunt. I knew that we wanted mature snapper, grouper and several species of jack. They are the sport fish. If a big ol' ugly hogfish showed up, he was going down, or up as it were. Hogfish have the finest textured, best tasting white meat known to seafood eating man.

We cruised over formations of coral, getting a feel for the layout. I expected to find the snapper and grouper hiding under ledges and darting through tunnels and caverns of the formations. I made my movements as fluid as the environment and dropped down to the sand, aware that Gunter was watching. I drifted under an overhang and caught a glimpse of fast movement. I let my eyes adjust to the dim light of the cavern and saw the tunnel into which the fish had disappeared. I unsheathed my small dive knife with my left hand and broke off a piece of coral, making an underwater popping sound. This startled a yellow-tail snapper and it shot out of the dead end, heading up and out for open water. I dropped the knife and grasped the barrel of the long speargun. I had been holding it loosely arrayed to my right and away from the ledge. The yellow-tail was moving fast, but from my left to right, naturally slowing as he cleared my position. I led him with an easy arc to the right and fired ahead of him. He swam into the shaft as it was about ten feet from the end of the speargun. This was a very powerful speargun by my freshwater standards. The snapper was impaled just behind the gills and two feet of shaft protruded on each side.

Gunter swam down to the fish and shaft, closed and locked the barbs and pulled the shaft out after securing the fish to his catch line. He handed the shaft to me butt end first and nodded his head. We took turns watching each other checking out holes and covering exits.

In less than an hour, we killed eight snappers and groupers. We had taken our time and spread the hunt over a line extending more than two hundred yards from the boat. It was understood that we were not going to clean a reef area. In fact, it would be almost six months before I even looked at this area again. We surfaced and snorkeled along the surface to the

Calypso. We had split the kill between us, and we were cautiously trolling for sharks, using us as bait. Not really, but if you believe all the tripe about sharks that has been written, we were just asking to be eaten. It wasn't even remotely true. Sharks are curious. They can follow a blood trail from miles away, but they do not attack everything in the ocean. In fact, they are scavengers. When confronted with a full grown human, they generally assuage their curious natures with a "flyby" or two and disappear, almost always.

By the time we arrived back at the boat, it had been joined by one of the rafts. A couple of guys were in the water and setting out lines to anchor it securely to the position. Just north of the raft, toward the island and the town, were regular formations of coral that suggested man made geometry. Most of the area was sand. We were going to remove the sand and take a look. This was the beginning of a six month excavation. In time, I would work on this site, as well as many others.

Gunter and I shrugged out of our gear and handed each piece up to helping hands in the boat. We climbed the boarding ladder only when we were down to our weight belts, knives and clothing. We were a study in contrasts. I had a mostly pale body encased in the white armor of long-sleeved shirt and long, white trousers. Gunter was wearing only cutoff blue jeans, completely dark in a rich tan and very black hair sprouting seemingly everywhere on his body excepting the soles of his feet and the palms of his hands.

He sat next to me on the gunwale. We watched the site activities and began our first conversation. "So, Grouper, you are not used to such a long gun." *Grouper? Jan had already gotten to him.*

"It showed, huh? Yeah, I'm used to a 42 inch gun. It is just easier and faster to handle." I offered this as an excuse for my slightly clumsy performance.

"You are a good diver. You will find your 42 inch gun and

we will work together from now on," he rejoined. "I get food for the people, and now you will too." And that, as they say, was that. Social nuances must have been left in the States, I thought.

"Where are you from, Gunter? That sure isn't a New York accent." I was being rather blunt for my tastes. And I had noted that his name was pronounced like "goon ta," accent on the "goon."

"I am Austrian. And I am certainly not a Nazi as that silly Frenchman tells everybody. Many here think that my father was a friend of Adolph Hitler because of his talk."

"I see your problem," I replied. "How about we lose the name Grouper for the same reason?" I asked with a grin. "The name is Tommy, okay?"

Gunter just reached out his right hand, we shook and the name was gone, at least for him, and the conversation was over. Gunter and I would go on to form a real bond. We would dive together scores of times, even risking our lives together on one occasion, but our conversations were never much more than that which had just transpired. Apparently it really does take all kinds "to make the world go around."

While some were actually making preparations for what was to become a working site, others were lazing about. A few were stretched out, taking in the rays, or trying to escape them, and taking advantage of the breeze. Captain Mike, the muscular captain of the trawler, and Craig were hauling on a line. They were wearing thick gloves that were coated with a rough canvas. I had already used a thinner pair as reef gloves on my dive. The line was of rough hemp and looked to be at least three-eighths of an inch in diameter.

They weren't talking much, just pulling in line that was moving back and forth across our horizon. Occasionally, something would pull back hard on the line, causing them to lose their grips, and the line would pay out again very quickly. Captain Mike would stomp a foot on the coil of hemp and arrest the escape of line. Getting some purchase again, the hauling in of the line would then resume.

I watched with mounting interest. I was being careful not to appear as a "whafo." A whafo is loosely defined as a goober who hangs around a dive site, noses around the equipment and is constantly pointing at things of interest and asking, "What is that for?" There was no way I was going to ask what they were doing. It took every bit of thirty minutes to get the fish near enough to the boat to identify it.

"Aw, man," Captain Mike moaned, "it's a damn black-tip shark. I ain't eatin' no more damn shark."

"You do not know that of which you are speaking, *mon ami.*" Jan had been watching with about the same level of interest as myself, but was now up against the gunwale (by the way, this is pronounced "gunnel" by every salt in the free world) and leaning down with a handled, four foot gaff hook. He snagged the shark perfectly in a gill set and manhandled it up and over the side. It was poised for just the briefest moment at the apex of its climb into the boat. A powerful twist of its muscular body sent it crashing to the deck in a spray of blood and water. It landed belly side up, exposing white skin its entire length, up to and past a two foot arc of grinning mouth punctuated by scores of sharp and jagged teeth. But it was an orifice very close to the base of the tail that had our collective attention.

Sticking out and wriggling free of the opening was a little shark. A newborn shark is called a pup, I knew, but I had never seen one entering its existence before. I was in new territory here. I sat transfixed by the scene, juggling the feeling of some pity for the plight of the shark with the emotion of raw amazement. Captain Mike was seemingly not conflicted by either of these notions. While I did nothing, he pounced on the tail of the mother and yelled at me.

"Get some line across the head of this thing. I don't need

it biting my ass off here."

I jumped at his voice, grabbing at the line running from the shark's mouth. I ran the line back and forth between low cleats, obviously meant to be used for securing gear. Instead, I was securing the sharp end of a black tip shark just as it was beginning to give birth. "Gone With the Wind popped into my head *I don't know nothing about birthing no sharks.*

But apparently Captain Mike did know something about birthing sharks. He was still wearing the abrasive-coated gloves and was able to snatch the wriggling pup from the slimy deck. Grasping the pup with both hands, he tossed it up and over the side of the boat. I will always remember that the little shark stiffened as it went airborne and had an expression of surprise on its face. It is funny the way our minds record events, thinking of the scene now.

Captain Mike got a grip on each side of the lower abdomen of the shark and started milking it. I mean, he massaged the old girl, obviously plumbing its insides with his thumbs and forefingers. When he felt a lump moving around inside her (I was starting to think of the shark as her), he worked the lump toward the orifice. When a head emerged covered in milky slime and some blood, Captain Mike, methodically and tenderly, I thought, took hold of the emerging pup and gave it the same flight path. It occurred to me that the slap of the water was analogous to the smacking of a baby's bottom immediately after birth. To this day I have no idea as to whether or not this is actually done.

After witnessing the hand-milking of eight brand new sharks, I figured that I had seen just about everything the world had to offer. I look back on my time in Honduras now and easily recognize that it was nothing more than a side bar in life. I was to experience much more than Honduras had to offer.

Craig and Jan, like me, had been mute observers to what was gelling in my mind as an absolutely cool event. I was used to the violence of hunting underwater. Fish are not warm and fuzzy, as say, deer and bunny rabbits are. I killed fish of all description, hardly giving a thought to the lives of the hunted. I certainly have never felt any particular affection for fish, but I was thinking about this shark differently. She was a new mother. I wondered if there were something I could say or do to get her back in the water.

Jan had witnessed the same event, but he certainly wasn't having the same reaction. The shark was obviously spent, having almost no movement left in her. Jan looked at the shark, and then he looked at me and said, "It is time to put her out of her misery, yes?"

Jan pulled his knife from the sheath attached to his belt. It took seconds for me to realize that he was going to stab the shark. I couldn't let this happen. I jumped to my feet, and for the first time since arriving on the island, found my true voice.

"Leave her alone, dammit," I yelled.

I grabbed at Jan's arm. I suppose I was trying to break his focus and train of thought. Unlike the movies, in real life people do not drop weapons with a slap to their arms. In fact, I realized that Jan had tightened his grip on the knife. He was going to kill her. In a move unexpected by us both, I pushed at Jan's chest with both fists, following through with the weight of my body. The top of the gunwale reached only to about mid thigh on us both, but I had the surer footing. With as much amazement as I have ever seen on a person's face, and arms flailing as he tried to regain his balance, Jan hit the gunwale at the back of his thighs. His inertia did the rest as he did an ugly back flip, arms and legs extended. He disappeared over the starboard side.

I scooted over to the nearest cleat that I had used to secure the shark and quickly unwound my trap. I tried to pick up the shark, but she weighed too much and I only managed to get her turned over. Without a word from me, Captain Mike moved in alongside and we lifted and slid the shark up the freeboard and over the port side. She did a couple of slow three sixties in her descent to the water. We stood as one, staring down at the shark. She drifted a few feet down into the very clear water, twisted her muscular body back and forth and few times, seemingly catching her breath, and majestically glided back in the direction from which she had been pulled.

The entire episode had not taken fifteen minutes. As I watched her swim barely below the surface, the feeling of relief and sense of accomplishment that had washed over me was suddenly and heavily replaced by a feeling of impending doom. I had just slammed a senior member of Fathom in the chest, and let more than 100 pounds of perfectly good seafood escape. Captain Mike and I looked at each other. We rushed to the stern ladder. Jan was swimming toward it. I backed away, not at all certain what he would do in retaliation.

I really did not have time to formulate a response, prepare for battle or initiate an escape before I heard Jan's loud yell rise from the water. As I stared, I was trying to remember which foot should be forward to afford me the best position to take the attack. Jan struggled to pull his body over the stern rail. He was scrambling, grabbing for any part of the boat that would advance his progress and coming directly for me.

When he attained a foothold with reasonable stability, he pushed off, throwing his weight entirely on me. I was slammed backward onto the deck with such force that I felt my head bounce off the textured fiberglass. I have never been a fighter. The best I ever mustered in any fight in my life was to take a good shot at the head of an assailant, and watch hopefully for the resultant collapse. I considered diving overboard, and then heard his laughter.

"I just wanted to show you that we French always return a favor," he gasped out while spitting up sea water. He picked himself up, and then pulled at the arm that was not twisted behind me, in an attempt to get me back on my feet. He seemed to have been having some little trouble catching his breath in the last few seconds, but now he was sucking in air with a rasping sound and releasing it in a staccato laugh that made me think he was having a serious respiratory problem. He was just having some fun. Duane's description of him as the crazy Frenchman seemed most appropriate. I was convinced he was crazy.

"So, *mon ami*, I have come between you and your woman, have I? We Frenchmen respect such passion. You are not the little grouper after all. You are to be congratulated, *oui*?" He looked at the empty deck, then up to me with a quizzical expression. I pointed to the south and his gaze followed my movement. I turned and looked at the same time. The gray fin with the two inches of black tip was still in sight. I looked back at Jan, he looked me full in the eyes, grabbed me by the shoulders and pulled me into him, whereupon he gave me huge, big-lipped kisses on each cheek. Still laughing, he released me and started looking around the deck.

"My knife, what have I done with my knife?" Without a word, I grabbed my mask, fins and snorkel. I quickly suited up and climbed onto the rail while adjusting the mask. With three or four deep breaths, holding the last, I made an efficient vertical foot-first entry, making certain to point my fins up as well, while holding my mask in place. With a graceful jackknife maneuver as I passed through about six feet, I kicked my fins with long sure strokes, pointed straight at the bottom. Well before reaching the forty foot bottom, I saw the knife, laying in bold relief against the light gray background. I grabbed it and made a slow ascent, looking around for some of the pups.

As I climbed back into the boat, Jan offered me a hand to clear the aft well and steadied me on the deck. I handed him the knife, hilt first. He took it rather slowly I thought, shook his head knowingly and said, "*Merci*, Tommy." *So much for Grouper.*

Chapter Seven

The Salva Vida

Within a few days, I had settled into something of a routine, at least a morning routine. My ability not to sleep (I preferred that to the term "my inability to sleep"), allowed me to prowl in the quiet hours of the day. Nobody does anything in the very early mornings on a tropical island. I was an anomaly, and not just because I was up very early. Henry and I were living on the extreme western edge of the town of Utila, almost outcasts. It was generally understood by us that this was so because we were different, in different ways.

I was new and an unknown entity, as well as pretty young. There are few nineteen-year-old people who have actually moved to Central America on a whim. Henry was different because he was amazingly young, an almost unbelievable fifteen years old. We all had the freedom to do anything we wanted as long as we were part of the expedition population, an American enterprise. But I am convinced that no one expected anything out of Henry or me, ever. Henry met their expectations spectacularly well. He never, not once, worked on anything.

I wasn't cut out for doing nothing. It is axiomatic that only those who do things are in the position of making mistakes. I made mistakes. I broke things while trying to fix them or got blamed for forgetting to do something, because I was willing to assume the responsibility in the first place. It has always been this way in my life. If I have a motto in life that is constantly and consistently reinforced by reality, it is this: "No good deed should go unpunished." My part in the expedition was no different.

It was this penchant for doing good deeds that made me first mate of the *Salva Vida* in my second week on the island. On my very early sojourns from the hinterlands, almost the jungle, of Utila, I would very quietly sneak into the cookhouse and make some coffee. The cookhouse had water and the only stove, which used propane gas fed from a manifold system connecting several standard, thirty pound propane tanks. Somebody had to lift the cylinders and judge whether or not they were empty, disconnect the ones that were and through a simple but confusing system of shutoff valves, disconnect and reconnect as necessary. And that is what I started doing on my third morning on the island, while the coffee percolated in the old aluminum pot.

With coffee in hand, I would leave the cookhouse and walk through the park to the Fathom Dock. I would then check every mooring line on every boat, use the facilities if needed, being very mindful of the shit-eating crabs, then climb aboard the *Salva Vida*.

This was a boat with a colorful history. The story was that she had been built in Cuba at least twenty years ago. She made her living as a ferry, mostly moving people across the very wide Havana harbor, then on to a few coastal towns and back again. When Fidel Castro took possession of her as a result of the "People's Paradise of Socialism," she continued to be used as a ferry, but with less care being lavished upon her. No pride of ownership will lead to entropy. Check out the old Soviet Union, East Germany, et al. The last time her engine needed an overhaul and parts, it wasn't possible, because the United States was not happy about Fidel's being in charge and trade had stopped. Not really a problem though, because Nikita was apparently in a giving mood then and a big overbuilt, Soviet diesel tractor engine was fitted to her engine room. Soon afterwards, she left on a decidedly unscheduled trip.

She was commandeered by an extended family as a tropical depression arrived over the island of Cuba. She was then taken to the western tip of Cuba where some more potential vacationers from the socialist utopia were loaded onto the boat. They then intended to tun north; her new owners anxious to visit the Florida Keys. Only she didn't turn north, or at least she didn't stay turned north. I can only imagine the surprise of the crew and passengers when they disembarked in British Honduras, now Belize.

One might reasonably ask how they had managed a southwesterly course when the compass, secure in its brass binnacle to protect it from the elements, had clearly pointed to about 360 degrees the entire trip. Without benefit of the sun during the day, because of the weather, that would have likely prompted an earlier investigation into the heading, the helmsman trusted the compass blindly. The problem was in the binnacle with the compass. It is said that several passengers blessed the compass upon embarking on the boat.

A few of the rabbits' feet and religious icons that were placed in and on the binnacle were magnetic. North on the compass swung to point toward the trinkets and icons. North became south of west and the Florida Keys were missed by a few hundred miles. Some of the miss was caused by a lack of fuel and prevailing winds carrying the boat wherever they were going. Eventually, Fathom bought the boat, or stole it for all we knew, and she had a home on the island. She was renamed the *Salva Vida*, after one of the two Honduran beers. What with the other Honduran beer being the Imperial, sounding way too pretentious for the name of a trawler, the decision was made.

And this brings me back to why I was visiting the *Salva Vida* in the early morning hours. She was sinking. She wasn't sinking quickly, but she was taking on water, many gallons everyday. In the typical tropical manner of solving problems, no attempt was made to stop the leaks. However, a hand pump was thrown into the bilge, along with a couple of hoses for the ingress and egress of the bilge water. I had heard about the leaks when Captain Mike had held forth in a general harangue in the cookhouse. It was a classic bitch session in which several of the veterans of Fathom were trying to out whine each other.

Without asking permission, a habit I have carefully nurtured all my life, I began boarding the *Salva Vida* in my early morning sojourns around Fathom facilities. I started by holding the wobble pump in my hand, feeding the inlet hose into the pool in the bilge, then paying out the other hose until it reached overboard. It was uncomfortable working the lever back and forth while holding the pump still enough to keep the hoses in place. By the second day of this, I had mounted the pump on a bulkhead and secured the inlet line to the lowest point of the bilge. I quickly located an existing outlet through the freeboard and attached the output line of the pump. My stealth visits to the bilge of the *Salva Vida* continued for more than a week, until I was confronted by Captain Mike at breakfast.

He sat down beside me while I was enjoying my eggs in green sauce, sausage and slabs of heavy bread. His sudden appearance startled me. I always ate alone, having not yet attained the familial feelings that were shared by many. He broached the subject of the *Salva Vida* in his usual delicate manner. "What the hell is wrong with you, Grouper?" he growled. "You trying to ruin the work ethic in this dump? Every day I go out to the *Vida*, check the damn bilge and it's almost empty." He paused, looking at me while shaking his head side to side.

"Sorry… Captain," I stammered, "I just like to keep busy and I thought it might help you out a little. Sorry," I said again.

"Sorry my white ass," he roared, slapping me way too hard on my middle back, "You may be the only swinging dick in this outfit that doesn't have to be told to jump in and get something done."

"I see you out there every day. You help load gear, you clean the gear and you and Gunter are bringing in the best catches I have seen in my year on this landfill." I worked to keep my mouth closed as he talked. It's rude to stare at a person with one's mouth hanging open like a lout. I was too stunned to say anything. He pressed on.

"So, you are going to be my first mate. Congratulations." He punctuated this with another massive slap to the middle of my back. I looked back at him and tried not to sound as stupid as I felt.

"That would be great, but I am really into the spearfishing, you know," I reasoned.

"Yeah, yeah, I knew you were going to say that," he quickly rejoined, "But the *Vida* only goes out a few times a week and an occasional trip to La Ceiba, so the guys can get laid, you know. When you ain't divin,' yer the first mate. Keep up the good work." With his proclamation ended, he stood up, sloshing some lukewarm coffee on the both of us. He made no comment about the spill and left the table to trade insults with one of the older guys who had just started talking to Rosie, near the doorway to the kitchen.

This was not the kind of man with whom I was willing to argue. Besides, I was rather honored by the offer, ignorance being what it is. Watching Captain Mike and the guy I only knew to be called Seaweed, my attention fell to a little, dark-skinned kid, probably no more than two years old.

He was naked, which was more common on tropical islands than most Americans would likely believe, and swinging around and in between Seaweed's legs, regularly looking back at Rosie. Much more surprising than his nakedness was that he had a string tied around the end of his penis. Attached to the other end of the string was a set of steel washers. As the little boy moved around, the washers were thrown back and forth, banging against his fat little thighs. This was a new one on me. It would be a few days before I was to learn something about this little mystery.

Jack, the geologist, was on the Fathom dock and talking with a couple of guys who had just come in from one of the many little keys southwest of the island. They had been working on some outbuildings intended to house a new scuba compressor and a desalinization unit that were on their way to Honduras. As they were offloading some scuba gear from one of the almost nondescript launches that simply appeared from time to time, the toddler was lurching around the dock, getting into everything of interest, and that was everything. No one showed any particular concern for the kid's safety, so I just took his presence on the dock in stride too. One of the guys called out to him, calling him Little Sergei.

"Has Sergei taken credit for the little guy yet?" One of the newcomers asked Jack. Jack seemed to be the repository of all knowledge concerning people on the island. He was a great guy, but definitely given to gossip.

"Hell no, and he never will," Jack responded. "And unless you are tired of having a little peace in your life, you better not let Sergei hear you calling the kid 'Little Sergei' either. He'll make our lives miserable for weeks."

"Do I look crazy to you?" he asked. He looked a little crazy to me, but I was working on some marlinspike seamanship and forming an eye loop in the end of a mooring line. I was learning to keep my opinions to myself.

"And what the hell is that hanging down between his legs anyway? Did he get himself caught on something?" he asked, while bending down to get a look at the weights and string.

Jack barely looked up from his inspection of a scuba regulator as he replied, "Isn't that something? Rosie did that to the poor little guy. She adds a washer to the string every now and then. She thinks it will enhance his manhood some day by stretching it out. Some of the guys are already calling him Tripod."

"Good God, this place is really beginning to wear me down. I think it's about time I went back to the real world," the other man said, walking down the dock, shaking his head and mumbling to himself.

As it happened, the only affect that Rosie's brilliant treatment had on the little guy was pretty predictable. The string was tied just tightly enough to shut off some of the blood circulation. The foreskin died south of the loop of string. The dead skin simply rotted away. But he did develop an infection. Shawn, our medic, was able to treat the infection, but not without resisting the temptation to march over to the cookhouse and chew off a piece of Rosie's ample derriere. The temporary bad blood between the two spilled over into her ability to cook for the rest of us meddling Americans. For about a week, the meals were even less inspired than usual. We eventually sweet-talked her into not holding a grudge and things returned to normalcy, the word being loosely interpreted when used to describe life in the expedition. And that was just pretty much the way things were on the island. The odd became the norm, and the norm just chipped away at you, bit by bit.

Chapter Eight

Spearfishing

I tore myself away from the fascinating discussion concerning Little Sergei. I felt the need to get away by myself, something I did as often as possible. I entered the *Salva Vida* and retrieved my mask, fins, snorkel, and buckled up a weight belt with about twelve pounds fitted to it. I picked up what had become my spear gun, a 42 inch long, three-sling Scubapro rig that suited me perfectly. I climbed through the companionway, disembarked, and walked down the dock, saying nothing to the few who looked my way. I knew I was being tagged as somewhat of a loner, but I was comfortable with that. I was little more than a curiosity to the others in Fathom. I will say that we were the least judgmental group with which I have ever been associated.

I made a right onto sandy Main Street and headed for the airport, about a mile away. It was a route that would take me entirely past the town of Utila. I was barefoot, but otherwise attired in my usual white jeans and long-sleeved shirt. Some of the island kids picked up on my presence and fell in with me, jabbering about what kind of fish I was going for and how far out I was going to go. They also knew that I would stop at one of the small stands that sold fish sandwiches, conch fritters and candy. I didn't need much money for myself and I enjoyed being able to help the kids a little. I didn't disappoint them. Everybody got a sandwich and I pressed on toward the airport, leaving them without being missed.

Arriving at the airport, I made my usual check of the Cub and the twin-engine Aztec. I had not yet flown, and I made a mental note to beg Jack or Duane at the next opportunity. Surrounding the peninsula that jutted out from the southeastern tip of Utila were some of the most regularly arranged, beautiful reefs in the world. Not that I had yet been around the world, but I had made it my business to know a lot about the world's reefs. Nothing could much excel the average of 150 feet of visibility, every species of sea life offered by the tropics of the Western Hemisphere and hundreds of coral buildups extending out from the shore in a spoke-like array alternating with sandy surge channels.

Diving without a partner is considered the height of stupidity by even the least experienced of divers. But that is just what I was going to do and would do many, many times over the years. The other side of the simplistic rule of never diving alone had occurred to me in my few years of teaching scuba diving. Most new divers were of little help to me. I had already been put in harm's way by the actions of several of my student dive partners. If I were only responsible for my actions, my reasoning went, wasn't I safer?

I sat down at the water's edge on the far side of the airport, seated on a perfectly placed, half submerged boulder. I pulled the reef gloves out of the foot pockets of my slotted, heavy black rubber fins, checked to see that the securing rubber loop of my sheath secured the dive knife on my right calf and spat into my dive mask. I swirled the mucous around thoroughly and rinsed it in the ocean water. I slid into the water, stood on a sandy patch of seafloor and adjusted the face mask while taking the mouthpiece of my snorkel between my teeth. Lying down on the surface, I quietly kicked my finned feet with extended legs making certain to keep the fins under the surface. I held my hands at my sides and barely grasped the speargun with my right hand, keeping the point down and away.

I swam head down, completely relaxed and breathing easily through the snorkel. The wave action was just slightly choppy. I compensated for the little swells that swept me gently from left to right by crabbing a little to the left. I swam this way the couple of hundred feet out and to the end of the natural channel. I took my time and watched as thousands of reef fish, comprised of hundreds of species, swam under and around me. The antennae of lobster were sticking out from the ledges some twenty feet below me the entire distance. Clown fish darted in and out of their homes, the sea anemones. Grunts, numbered in the hundreds per school, moved as one large body. Parrot fish grazed on the reef, mostly in steeply head down maneuvers that allowed them to eat at the coral. The large blunt front teeth were prominent and effective at chipping away the crusty material. The sound of the coral being destroyed carried through the water and was easily heard. They regularly expelled clouds of crushed material from a ventral orifice. Almost no one would bother to eat parrot fish, the taste being below average, but few mourned the parrot fish being shot and used as bait in lobster traps, in spite of their beauty. They destroyed hundreds of pounds of reef material every day around just this little island.

I cruised up and down the surge channels for a couple of hours and watched as several sand sharks and an occasional black tip shark made investigative passes at me. I wondered if I knew at least one of them. When I tired of the restive beauty somewhat, I finally armed my speargun and went to work. I tracked a red snapper with a gentle sweep of the speargun. He looked to weigh about ten pounds. With a little remorse, I fired just slightly ahead of him when he was about five feet from the end of the shaft. The click of the shaft always startles the prey. They quickly accelerate at the sound. But just as the quarry of a fighter pilot flies into the stream of bullets from a fighter's machine guns, so the fish always swim directly into the path of a well aimed spear.

Over the next hour, I shot three snappers, a hogfish and two black groupers. I had most attached to the line from my weight belt. I swam up the surge channel to the shore, followed closely by a school of interested barracuda. As menacing as they looked, I expected no trouble from them, and got none. I can tell you that barracuda are virtually never a threat to a diver, not even hundreds of barracuda, no matter their size. I had barracuda take a quick bite from a speared fish, but I was never threatened by one. They are a threat to shiny pieces of metal. If you are wearing the shiny piece of metal, you can become collateral damage. I crawled out of the water, shedding gear and struggling with more than eighty pounds of fish. We would eat well tonight.

I tied the loose equipment up with the fish, slung the whole thing over a shoulder and trudged back into town, stopping at the little store I had visited earlier, leaving one of the groupers to the grateful proprietor. I had decided to become a one man state department. I made a real effort to establish a relationship with the islanders. I had early on noticed a certain resentment of Fathom Expedition people. We had thrust ourselves into the midst of their almost ancient town. The Fathom people tended toward the arrogant. We had a seemingly endless supply of money. It is not enough to say that it was spent around the island in the main, benefiting the local populace.

Utila was virtually a shanty town, its inhabitants scratching out an existence from the ocean's resources. We were taking the same resources, making it look as an afterthought. We were doing this sporting a fleet of boats, taking over and developing several of the keys with impunity, and openly displaying our freedom to come and go as we wished. The islanders were well aware that all of us made regular and, by their standards, lavish trips to the big cities of Honduras and other Central American countries. We also traveled back and forth from *Los Estados Unidos*, where the streets were paved with gold.

For all these reasons, I had started a campaign to befriend the islanders. When I did these little things for them, I was careful to let them do little things for me. I got extra large helpings from the proprietors with whom I shared my catch, and I grew accustomed to getting help from the boys with whom I would share lunch regularly.

This day was an example of their help. Several of my little friends appeared the moment I entered the town. They divided my gear and the fish among them and I was not allowed to carry a single thing back through the town and out to Fathom Dock. The older boys fought over the filet knives and cleaned the catch expertly. I must have looked like the Pied Piper on my triumphant return. The smallest boy in the group, probably five years old, proudly carried my speargun at shoulder arms, looking for all the world like a soldier on parade. A few helped clean the fish and I made sure that each got a share of the meat.

It was a good day on the island. Serious trouble awaited me, but days of spearfishing and playing are the ones I most often associate with Utila, these many years later.

Chapter Nine

Setting up a Work Site

By the third week, I was beginning to think that I was not destined to work an actual site. I had no one to blame but myself. Since my arrival, I had immersed myself, so to speak, in spearfishing and the pursuit of all things nautical. Captain Mike had taken a shine to my enthusiasm for working on the *Salva Vida*. Our personalities meshed perfectly. He was looking to avoid work, and I was working just as hard to avoid having nothing to do. I had found a Chapman's, the Bible of seamanship, in the Fathom House library. I was determined to learn some marlinespike seamanship, the science of knot tying and braiding multi-strand rope to form splices and eyes. I made an eye splice in almost every line used for mooring the many boats. These projects lead to my finally taking an interest in actually doing some work for the expedition.

I talked to Duane about my desire to get on a site. He suggested I get with Nick and just take on any dive job that would help the most. I found Nick on the Fathom Dock.

"Well, look who's here," Nick greeted me before I could get a word out. "Who would have thought that the skinny little boy from Illinois would turn out to be the Great White Hunter?"

"Yeah, well actually I'm from Indiana," I corrected him, "and it was either spearfishing or sucking sand off the bottom with the working class." Nick let the allusion pass without so much as a flicker of an eyelid and stood up, all five feet eight inches of him. He looked me over, taking in the signature long sleeve shirt and white jeans.

"It's good to see you bleached all the color out of that hippie crap you were wearing when you showed up on the dock in Puerto Cortes, looking like a lost puppy. You been weaned yet, or you still learning how to drink like a man?"

I decided that I wasn't going to get the last word in, but I didn't want to quit trying. "I thought I might take a break today, and lie around on the bottom with you vacuum sweepers. Maybe I could run the floor polisher." At this Nick finally grinned, took me by the shoulders and turned me around.

"Why don't you make yourself useful as well as incredibly boring?" He gave me a generous shove toward a pile of hoses, dive gear and boxes. "We need to get this stuff out to the air lift at the *Santiago* site and you have been selected to stow it in any place that makes you the most comfortable." With that, he turned away and walked off toward the park.

I really only wanted a project. I jumped to it and loaded the wooden launch that was moored just below the equipment.

Ten minutes later, Nick sauntered back up the dock with the sea leg gait that was uniquely his. "Man, it's about time," he stated, picking up the previous line of good natured insults. "Do you think you can get us out to the site without sinking or stopping to rape a reef? We don't have all day to wait around while you try to take out a species."

I knew I was in the presence of greatness. I didn't try to respond in kind. I shook my head wonderingly, jumped down into the launch and looked at the few switches and levers that constituted the instrument panel on the old boat. I looked up at Nick and said, "Permission to board the vessel granted. Cast off, hold on and especially shut up."

With that, I started the engine, took it easy in idle and watched as the tachometer smoothed and the oil pressure gauge steadied at some unreadable level. I motored away from the dock with gentle movements and we headed south-southwest, straight for the lighthouse.

After mooring against the raft with a few bumpers strategically placed between the two vessels, Nick and I worked without talking for a few minutes, transferring the gear and hardware to the raft. Two men were already working on the raft's engine and compressor system and Nick introduced me in his diplomatic way. "The tall ugly guy is Brian. He hails from Long Beach and is out on parole. The uglier guy is Rodney. He's Brian's probation officer." They just shook their heads, barely looking up from the tasks at hand. Nick was just one of those guys who could say anything without most people taking offense. It is people like Nick who can break the tension caused by the close proximity of diverse people.

"Guys, this is Tommy. He's taking a break from giving Gunter spearfishing lessons. He wants to show us what we have been doing wrong out here, lo these many months."

"Tommy," Brian said, "you've been making a reputation for yourself on our little island, especially since you haven't even been here a month. Good hunting out there. If you brought your speargun with you, I'm sure we could find a target for you today that ought to keep Rosie cooking for the rest of the week," he finished, looking right at Nick.

Nick was nonplussed by Brian's suggestion and launched right into a short briefing of what he expected of me. "Tommy, you and I are going to use hookah and lay out the floats along the airlift line and adjust the buoyancy at each attach point to keep a not-too-steep angle so we get good lift from the air. If we set the angle too steep, stuff tends to roll right back down the tube. Mostly we will do set up work today with some test runs.

These clowns will erect the chutes and screens up here and hopefully get this scow down current from the site so the debris doesn't fall right back down on top of us. But don't count on it. Got it?"

I just nodded and grinned at Brian and Rodney. They simply exuded confidence and looked competent. I knew we were a crew. A guy doesn't get insulted in this outfit if he is incompetent, he gets ignored.

Nick and I strapped on our weight belts. Besides wearing a knife, a diver wears a weight belt every time he enters the water. By today's diving standards, we were purposely risking our lives. What I mean is that we wore weight belts with anywhere from six to twenty pounds on them, but we never had buoyancy compensating devices of any kind. And we almost always put the weight belt on first. A modern diver, paying attention to the order in which I donned my gear would be most critical of my technique. My excuse for these egregious acts are simple. Buoyancy compensation devices were virtually non-existent in the late sixties diving community. Secondly, we were constantly taking our gear off while underwater and removing the weight belt every time was just too bothersome. We all seemed to be infected with a mood of fatalism and invulnerability.

We both selected and unwound an air line that was connected to an expansion tank. This tank was routed to a very special compressor used to provide oil-free, breathable air. At the end of these lines were fittings that allowed us to connect an otherwise standard single-hose, double-stage scuba regulator. Rodney started the engine that drove the compressor. We watched as the pressure quickly built to around 120 psi and stabilized. At his signal, Nick and I adjusted the mouthpieces and took test breaths. Satisfied with the taste of the air, we both slid into the water from our seated positions on the raft.

Brian fed the six inch plastic tube into the water. It was

put together from eight foot long sections that were held together by inserting sleeves that matched the slightly smaller inside diameter, then secured with large radiator clamps. The site started at only forty feet, but the angle up needed more length than the depth and the raft had to be away and down current from the site. Attached to the tube, every ten feet or so, were bleach bottles. The bottles were tied so that a little air in the bottles resulted in a neck down vertical attachment. All that we had to do was extend the hard plastic end of the large vacuum cleaner-like hose to the site, where I attached it with a line to a waiting anchor. Then Nick and I adjusted the angle of the weighted hose by releasing small amounts of air into the plastic bleach bottles until we liked the overall angle of the hose. At the other end, Brian and Rodney secured the open end of the hose so that water and sand would empty into a sluice system that looked just like the old nineteenth-century sluice boxes that we have all seen illustrating the work of gold prospectors of the Old West.

The principle is simplicity itself. We attached a line from yet another compressor; this one not needing to provide breathable air. When the simple valve at the pickup end of the air supply line was opened to any level of flow desired, the air rushed up the hose, displaced water and pulled at the surroundings with suction.

From my vantage point on the sea floor, it was not at all obvious why anyone would consider this to be the site of a sunken ship. Some pattern only observable from the surface or even from the slow moving Piper Cub must have presented itself to the searcher. *I am going to have to ask about that.* Something other than natural sea floor was here. Duane and Jack had combed the area with a sensitive magnetometer and had ascertained a higher than background level of ferrous material. Metal was here, but it was covered.

It would be a mistake to think a ship that went down some

three hundred years ago would simply be resting on its keel, otherwise presenting itself as a ship, possibly with a hole in its side to indicate the reason for its sinking. The ancient ships usually went down in some violence. Hitting a reef at any speed would guarantee a ship's eventual destruction from wave action and the taking on of tons of water, unless the ship were beached in relatively safe shallows. Of course a ship dashed on the rocks and reefs by high winds meant destruction within minutes, or no more than a few hours. Fire was another common reason for the loss of a ship. Those ships were dried out piles of lumber that once burning, were almost never saved.

But the destruction of the ship itself would still have left some, or a great deal of wreckage. The single most common reason for the almost complete destruction of the wooden ships was...worms. In these instances, a specific and tiny mollusk called *teredo navalis*. These worms attacked a ship's hull by burrowing its way into every ancient sailing ship that ever plied tropical waters. But these worms could only live in the salt water itself or in wood that was well soaked in salt water, such as the surface layers of a ship. Once a few worms established their homes by eating tiny tunnels into the surface of a ship's exterior, the demise of the ship was inevitable. It was only a matter of time before the worms multiplied and burrowed deeper. They carried the salt water deeper into the wood, and provided more suitable habitat for more worms. This continued until the ship was riddled with tunnels and weakened beyond use. The only protection for the ships, against the mollusk, was a mixture of tar and pitch; slapped and smeared all over the bottom of the ship. The forests of England and much of Europe were depleted of all kinds of timber used in the building of tens of thousands of ships, and even more for the production of the tar and pitch.

The best kind of wood for making tar and pitch was pine. The pine was cooked slowly in pits, not burned, until the tarry substance oozed out of the charring wood. This goo was collected and distilled, then shipped in barrels, which were made out of (what else?) wood. By the eighteenth century, the most important export of the new American colonies was pitch and tar. If today's environmentalist wackos think that our forests are threatened by the logging industry, which plants more trees than it harvests, they are mired in an ignorance of history. From the seventeenth century and through the nineteenth, loggers wiped out hundreds of thousands of acres of trees in Europe and the American colonies with no thought of replenishment, mostly to produce tar and pitch.

When a wooden ship sank in the tropics, the teredo worms always claimed the majority of the ship. The only thing that stopped them from getting all of the wood was sand. As sand shifted on the sea floor and covered some sections of the wreck, the mollusk was sometimes stopped. If we were to find sections of a sunken ancient ship, we had to remove the sand. That is why Nick and I were setting up the air lift.

With the system set up, we surfaced to discuss our next course of action. We both flipped our masks up to our foreheads and treaded water. "Nice job, Tommy," Nick said, spinning around just enough to look back at the raft. "We've done more this morning than the rest of these clowns accomplish in a week. Your days of reef raping have come to an end. From now on, you work with me. We'll both be rich and famous."

"No way, Nick, this is too much like work. I was watching for targets the whole time we were down there." He looked a little disappointed, but mostly he just grinned.

"I figured as much," he responded. "I saw you looking over your shoulder every coupla minutes. Damn, you are one paranoid son-of-a-bitch. It wouldn't be long before you put a shaft in me just to keep in practice."

While we were talking and treading water, which is very easy to do when wearing fins, I could hear a persistent humming sound. I saw that Nick had heard it too. We both began looking around. It is very easy to be run down by a boat when bobbing around in the middle of the ocean. We both did thorough scans of the horizon as we pirouetted slowly in place. A slight movement just above the horizon and in the direction of the mainland, which was some twenty-five miles away, caught my attention. Not having to say a word, I got Nick's attention with my obvious fixation. He swiveled his head, followed by a subtle shift of his body to align it with our direction of sight.

The movement was now two distinct black shapes, one slightly overlapping the other. The silhouettes were growing, and made me think of the simple sea bird line art drawings that are so common on greeting cards depicting a beach scene, accompanied with some drivel like "Wish you were here." But these silhouettes were growing, and growing fast. The hum deepened and became a growl. The silhouettes reflected a round center section, sprouting wings that started out from the center at a down angle, turning slightly up and out, similar to flattened check marks. *Of course, they were F4U Corsairs.* And that was all that I was able to say; "Corsairs."

I was captivated. I was an airplane nut. This was too cool for words. The shapes became aircraft, the two aircraft became one as the wingman went line abreast and they aimed directly at us. I wanted a closer look and I had a front row seat. I was treading hard and wanted my head clear of the water for a better view. I was late in seeing the danger. The Corsair has a huge three bladed air screw, as it was called in World War II, which was about fourteen feet in diameter and literally cutting a trough out of the ocean.

I stopped kicking and brought my hands up from my waist with palms extended and parallel to the horizon, which forced my body in the opposite direction, down. As soon as my head was immersed, going down like a submarine in emergency dive, the first Corsair's air screw blew through my position, tearing at the water as if it were a horizontal tornado. My body arched painfully and my feet were pulled toward the horizon at the same time that I was hit with a twisting motion that spun me out and away from the center of some violence that I couldn't comprehend. Before I was able to get stable, the second tornado exploded into my consciousness, such as it was. This one hit directly over my body and slammed it into the water with such force that as I involuntarily descended, my eardrums registered an explosion of epic proportions. I was still holding my breath, and squeezed neck and jaw muscles, reflexively trying to equalize the pressure.

As quickly as the violence arrived, it receded. I kicked toward the surface and gulped in air and salt water in equal amounts. I coughed and spit water until I felt some semblance of normalcy. I looked for Nick as soon as I completed a damage survey of myself. I was surprised to see only empty water.

I reached for my mask. I figured that he had made a dive like mine, but had simply stayed underwater. My mask was no longer in its raised position over my forehead. It was just gone. I took several quick breaths and jackknifed my body while I thrust my heavy fins into the air, letting the weight of my legs push me into a vertical descent. The view underwater without a mask is not spectacular, but it is usable. I was able to discern the general shape of a body, and it was descending. I kicked hard toward Nick and reached around my waist, getting a hold on the hookah line and the attached breathing regulator. As a test, I pushed the purge button and a gush of air burst from the mouthpiece. I stuffed it in my mouth, took a careful breath and continued kicking hard and down.

When I reached Nick, my worst anticipation was confirmed. He was unconscious and drifting down, pulled by the sixteen pound weight belt. I took the regulator from my mouth and shoved it into his, simultaneously pushing the purge valve to force air into him. Bubbles frothed around us, but Nick was as limp as a rag doll. I groped for the weight belt buckle. Finding it quickly, I pulled it out and away, forcing the webbing out and allowing the belt to fall away.

I ran through the options available to me. I could not help him while underwater, but there was real danger in taking him to the surface if he had taken a breath from his regulator before losing consciousness. If you breathe from a scuba regulator at even ten feet, hold your breath and ascend, the resulting expansion of the air will rupture your lungs, damaging you very badly, even enough to kill you. The condition is known as an embolism. It is a fascinatingly simple way to kill oneself.

While these thoughts ran through my mind I started an ascent, kicking in a vertical position from behind Nick with my hands stuffed up under his armpits. As we approached about fifteen feet of depth, I slid down from behind him and gave him a squeeze, much the same thing as a Heimlich maneuver, but I don't think the term actually existed in 1970. Almost no bubbles exited Nick's mouth and I knew I could continue to the surface without killing him.

Upon reaching the surface, I ditched my weight belt with one hand as I turned my body sideways and forced Nick up over my right hip. In a classic lifesaver's carry, with my right arm around Nick's right side neck and grasping his left armpit, I headed for the raft, about two hundred feet away and up current. Brian saw us first and dove in a reaching stretch, followed with hard swimming. We divided the load of Nick's body between us and made the raft as quickly as possible. Rodney dragged him up and away from us and laid him on his back while shoving a wet suit jacket under the back of his neck.

I kicked and pushed myself out of the water and onto the raft. Rodney was already blowing pretty aggressively into Nick's mouth, alternating with several chest compressions. When I scrambled to Nick, I realized that I was going to have to breathe for him and allow Rodney to perform the compressions. It wasn't working and I didn't have much left in the way of ideas. Then Brian rolled Nick up on his side. Spittle flew from his nose and mouth, and he was breathing.

Nick sat up in a crouch and continued a raspy breathing regime. We could hear the gurgle of water being expunged from his respiratory tract. His breathing improved until it sounded almost normal. He looked around.

I made eye contact with Brian and said, "If you tell anybody that I had my mouth locked on that bearded orifice of his," I said, "I'll deny that I was even here." Not very witty, but it seemed appropriate to make some small joke out of it, for whatever reason.

Brian stood up, stretched and looked down at Nick, then slowly raised his head till his eyes locked on mine. "Nick, there aren't a handful of people in this outfit who would have done what Tommy just did for you. You would be fish food right now if he hadn't gone down after you." An emotion welled up inside me that I had not yet experienced. I was relieved and a little proud, but very embarrassed.

Nick reached over and pulled me toward him, embarrassing me even more with what can only be described as an embrace. That just did it for me. I felt tears run down my cheeks and I couldn't even wipe them off. Nick then pushed me back, holding on to my shoulders and said, "Tommy, I'm not sure exactly what just happened, but you are now on my A-list. I may even have to let your sorry ass win at cribbage every once in a while."

I just grinned stupidly at him.

"Well, guys," Brian said, "unless those fighters are going to come around for a strafing run, let's batten down the hatches on this thing and head in for some serious drinking."

With that, we secured the raft, covering the machinery with tarpaulins and checking the anchorage. We boarded the launch and I carefully took us back to the dock, where it was business as usual. As we tied up at the dock, I just had to ask, nobody in particular, "Would somebody mind telling me why we were just run over by the Honduran Air Force?"

"It's an interesting story, Tommy," Brian replied. "After what I have just seen, you are shaking out to be more than just another pretty face in the crowd here. I think maybe we need to make some introductions and you deserve a little background information. Let's head up to the cookhouse, get some sand-wiches and a few beers. Okay?"

"Sure," I said, not sure of anything.

I fell in behind Brian, Rodney and Nick. As usual, I was tagging along, bringing up the rear. But in our little group, something had changed. I had a sense that there was some drama that I was missing, but for the first time since arriving in country, I had some feeling of being one of the guys. When you are a world away from home, that feeling can save you from a despair that knows no limit.

Chapter Ten

Soccer War

It was now mid-afternoon and the cookhouse was empty. The four of us each got a *Salva Vida* from the chest-high Coca Cola cooler that I figured must have been stolen from the mainland. Brian suggested that we take the far corner table and bench, away from the kitchen. He sat in the corner. I got the distinct impression that he wanted a view of anyone entering. He started the briefing, for that is what it was, with an almost ominous preamble. "Tommy," he said, stopping me in mid descent to the bench, "what you are going to hear in the next few minutes does not need to be repeated."

"Yes, sir," I answered, surprising myself with the formality of my reply. I didn't even know who Brian was, but I had an inkling as to what was about to be said. There are secrets and there are open secrets.

"I know you have been wondering when you were going to be told just what it is we are really doing here. First of all, you have noticed a certain 'them and us' quality to the relationships in the expedition. You are now being brought into the fold as an 'us,' at least from my perspective. You, like Nick here, were carefully vetted before you were approached in Chicago.

Fathom Expeditions is a legitimate enterprise, owned and operated by its shareholders." Saying this, Brian stopped himself and shook his head.

"The word *legitimate* is to give this thing a patina of respect that Fathom probably doesn't deserve," he continued. "The whole thing is a scam, really, and its purpose is to benefit Richard and Sergei, along with a few others. Money is brought in, equipment is donated, and the outward respectability of Fathom is cultivated. You have been tested and observed. We-meaning myself, Craig, Rodney, Duane, and a few others who happen to be in Tegucigalpa-are pleased with what we see and hear about you." My reaction so far was little more than raised eyebrows and the feeling that I was blushing.

"You are self-motivated and industrious. I am going to add courageous to the list, based on what I saw out there today. As of this moment, you are a contract employee of the government of the United States." He looked into my eyes and I saw no room for equivocation. "You will be paid when we decide to pay you, and you will do what we ask of you. I don't want to sound too melodramatic; you won't be killed or anything like that if you show yourself to be less than a team player, but you will be dropped if we feel you can't be trusted. Any questions so far?" he added, leaning back slightly until his back was against the wall. As he swallowed most of his beer, I picked up on the raised eyebrow and the fact that he didn't remove his gaze, at least from the one eye not blocked by the raised bottle.

"What do you want me to do…" I began, "I mean specifically. Am I a spy or something?" At this, the three of them burst into a tension releasing laughter.

"Kid, you are not going to be given a license to kill, and don't expect to be getting a pen that shoots truth serum, or whatever." And this came from Rodney, who had said nothing since we were on the raft. "Here is the straight skinny, as they say. Brian and I, along with some people you will meet on the mainland eventually, are employees of a government agency. The exact agency is unimportant, and you will not ask about it… ever. It will remain an understood thing, just between us girls." With that little statement, Rodney let Brian finish.

"You and Nick are in the same boat, so to speak. We need this expedition to continue. It represents an American presence in Honduras, and justifies our having people in Tegucigalpa, talking with the players that run this country. Fathom, meaning Richard, is supplied with resources of all kinds, including money, to keep this thing alive. Fathom will continue to expand its base here, especially to the keys southwest of Utila. But having a presence on the island here helps satisfy some of the general curiosity of the populace also. We are just a bunch of treasure divers, hoping to build a tourist haven that will benefit the local population." He stopped the revelations at this point and I felt it necessary to change the subject slightly.

"What is it with the Corsairs trying to give us a haircut out there today?" I asked, entirely reasonably I thought. "You guys haven't even talked about it. I'm thinking there is more going on out here than meets the eye, besides what you are telling me, I mean."

Brian appeared to be thoughtful for several long ticks of the mental clock. He then dived into what was to be my current events lesson.

"The conflict between El Salvador and Honduras has come to be known as the "Soccer War," but hostility long predated the soccer games which helped spark the war. Honduras, with a population of about 2.3 million people, occupies some 42,000 square miles. Salvador, with over 3 million inhabitants, occupies only about 8000 square miles. Its population density of 400 persons per square mile is second only to Haiti's in this hemisphere. Inevitably, Salvadorans spilled over into Honduran territory, an estimated 300,000 of them. Most of those were *campesinos*, who have industriously tended plots of land in previously undeveloped areas. They did well, and so did those who found jobs in Honduran factories. Resentment against them developed among Hondurans, particularly in rural areas. Adding to the ill-feeling between the two countries was the fact that certain sections of the border have never been clearly defined.

"Various attempts had been made to control the problem of immigration by agreements between the two countries. There was passage of an agrarian reform law by Honduras, which began taking land away from some of the Salvadorans. When their national teams met for a soccer match in Tegucigalpa; El Salvador lost by a score of 1-0. However, the point was made in overtime, and Salvadorans felt they had been cheated. This became practically a point of national honor. When the Honduran team went to San Salvador for a return match, emotions were running so high that a Salvadoran security unit hid the team at a secret place outside the city before the match. There was rioting in downtown Salvador, and three people were killed, all of them Salvadorans. El Salvador won 3-0." He stopped to take a swallow of beer and look at me.

"You taking notes here? Just kidding," he added, smiling.

"As the Hondurans headed home, a number of their cars traveling through smaller Salvadoran towns were hit by rocks. Honduras was not content to let the incidents go by without retaliation. Exaggerated reports were circulated, and rumors claimed that the Salvadorans were holding Honduran prisoners. For three days, Salvadoran stores and shops selling Salvadoran goods were attacked in Tegucigalpa and San Pedro Sula, the attacks spreading into interior areas. A flow of refugees began moving into Salvador. They told tales of groups of hoodlums who terrorized them. There were incidents of rape and of murder. Many of the Salvadorans sold their properties at low prices and fled to their homeland. A reliable estimate was that over 17,000 refugees crossed the border.

"Honduras broke relations with El Salvador. A few days before the break, El Salvador won a playoff match 3-2, the winning point being made in overtime. The match was prudently played in Mexico City. Later that day, Salvadoran Corsairs, F-51 reconditioned Mustangs, and C-47s with bomb-adapted wings struck Tegucigalpa's airport, which was utilized by both civilian and military aircraft. Salvadoran planes also struck at several other airports. The Honduran Air Force had the edge over Salvador's Air Force, and the raids were intended to reverse that situation. The Salvadorans did not succeed.

"Early the next morning, Honduran warplanes hit San Salvador's airport which is also used by both military and commercial aircraft. Honduran planes also struck at the refinery and industrial complex adjacent to the airport. There were reports of dogfights between Honduran F4U Corsairs and Salvadoran P-51 Mustangs..

"After the Salvadoran planes struck here, their troops crossed the border and invaded. There were two primary attack areas. But these were poorly supplied forces and both sides were running short of ammunition. Perhaps the Salvadoran commanders had not fully understood the logistics problem, or else they had planned on only a brief campaign. In addition, the Honduran attacks on Salvador's petroleum supplies had been effective. The country began suffering a shortage of gasoline, which would eventually force the army to come to a halt. Three days after the raid on the petroleum supplies at Cutuco, one of the burning tanks exploded, setting fire to five more tanks.

"Both El Salvador and Honduras requested United States assistance. Both were turned down. The war between El Salvador and Honduras was a short war, but it was violent. More than 2,000 people died in about four days. Lingering animosities are a natural by-product of the death and destruction seen in this little country."

"And the air show today was the government giving some

Americans the finger," added Rodney. "We did nothing to stop the killing, even when asked. Latin machismo being what it is, the Hondurans couldn't just stop, and neither could the Salvadorans. Not our finest hour."

Brian continued, "Wars are not only waged by large countries. Tiny countries get mad, too. We are lucky they didn't accidentally strafe of few of us out in the middle of the ocean last summer. They were pretty mad at America for doing nothing. But the real danger in this particular conflict was that the war, if it had continued, might have spread beyond the two countries. Nicaragua, favoring Honduras, possibly would have entered the conflict, and other countries might well have followed. Enmities run deep in Central America." Brian paused for effect and to get my attention, looked directly at me and added, "So now we are on a mission. Your job is to be part of the glue that keeps this thing together. We need a believable presence in Honduras and the last thing we need is for the locals to speculate that this whole thing is some kind of United States government operation. So Tommy, with Duane and Nick, you will keep things from getting too out of control out here. That's it Tommy. Just be one of the guys and let us know if trouble is brewing."

"It will be business as usual, then?" I responded with some disappointment evident in my voice.

"That's the ticket," Brian said in a lowered voice. "Business will be as usual."

With my current events lesson concluded, we went through the usual social platitudes and left the cookhouse, going our separate ways.

I decided to visit my hooch and do a little housework, maybe make some claim to ownership of the place that had long ago been ceded to the insects and field mice. I was surprised to find my roommate, Henry Porter, in residence and reading, sitting in our one chair, a nice looking rattan high backed chair looking perfect for a tropical home. Henry looked up from the magazine, Skin Diver, and greeted me with a smile.

"What brings the great white hunter to our humble abode in the middle of the day?" he asked reasonably. I was never in the hooch during the day.

"I just got tired of diving today. I thought I might see what this place looked like in the sun. Sorry I bothered, actually." I looked carefully at Henry and asked, "So are you going to tell me how you ended up this far away from New Jersey at the tender age of fifteen?"

"I wondered when you would get really curious," Henry said with a hint of a smile. "I got into some trouble and my dad has connections."

"Your dad's connections must really be in low places if this is where they got you."

"Yeah, pretty funny, huh? But I had to disappear. My dad heard about Fathom Expeditions from some hardware people he knows. He got in touch with Mr. Dinerman, paid him some money, and here I am."

"What did you do?" I asked. "Kill somebody?"

"I don't think so." This was a surprising answer, so I had to know more.

"What does that mean?"

"It means I was playing around with some fireworks, maybe a little dynamite, you know. Well things got a little out of hand and a buddy and I blew up part of an oil refinery. A big part," he added for emphasis.

I gave a low whistle and shook my head in some disbelief. "Holy smokes, Henry… no pun intended," I added. "That's serious alright. So what does that mean? You're a fugitive from justice?"

"That's pretty much it," he agreed. "Where I come from, you sure don't want to go to juvenile detention, at least not for a few years. So my dad got me out of town and his lawyers are trying to work something out. We send tapes back and forth, I don't write very good, and my grammar is worse," he added unnecessarily.

"Well, kid, there are worse places than a tropical island, and you are learning a trade. I'll bet none of your buddies back in New Jersey know how to scuba dive."

"That's for darn sure," he said with some enthusiasm. "And I owe that to you. Nobody else here hardly gives me the time of day. I guess they think I'm just a kid and not worth the trouble."

"Well, that's their loss." I said this with finality and I meant it. This was a good kid, and I meant to make him see it. "You know, as long as we're telling secrets here, I'm sure as hell no angel. When I was your age, a buddy and I decided that we were going to be rich and famous salvage divers. The problem was that nothing in Indiana ever needed to be salvaged, so we decided to drum up some business for ourselves. One night we went up to a lake that had a bunch of expensive lake cottages. We suited up in full wet suits and scuba gear and got in the water underneath a railroad trestle. We snorkeled out making sure that we stayed a couple hundred yards from the shore. Then we went underwater and headed for a couple of the biggest docks, using our compasses that glowed in the dark. We untied two good looking boats, worked our asses off towing them out to the middle of the lake and sank them by pulling the drain plugs at the transoms."

Henry was grinning in anticipation as I spun my tale, which was all too true, unfortunately. "We didn't wait for them to sink. It would have taken too long. And anyway, we both got to laughing our asses off, about how smart we were and all. Sound carries really well over the water. Even though it was about one in the morning, we sure got somebody's attention, because some dock lights came on and really strong searchlights started flashing right at us. We dove underwater and headed east, using our compasses. We stayed only about ten feet underwater and popped to the surface every ten minutes or so to get our bearings until we got under the trestle and into the little cove where my pickup truck was parked.

"We were as quiet as we could be, putting our gear in the back of the truck. We could hear some boats out on the lake and we were really scared we were going to get caught. I had already taken out the interior light in the cab. You know, the one that comes on when you open the door. This was a really well-planned stealth operation, you know. We were still in our wet suits when I started the truck and we drove away down the only rode that goes right through Rome City, Indiana. I was so smart that I refused to turn on my headlights.

"It didn't occur to me until the next day just how stupid and suspicious looking that must have been, a truck driving right through the middle of town at two in the morning with no headlights." I stopped to catch my breath. By now Henry was laughing so hard that he was holding his stomach and making those snorting sounds. It got me to laughing pretty hard too. I just had to add, "By that time, our brains had finally kicked in and we realized how embarrassing it would have been for us to walk right up to the cottages with the missing boats and ask the people if they needed anything salvaged underwater." I was still laughing and had to catch my breath again before I could continue. I finished with, "the sad commentary on our intellect is that we were going to do exactly that, before better judgment got a hold of us.

"Now that I think of it," I continued, "You are the only person I have ever told about that night."

Henry half fell back into our sole piece of furniture, making it crackle in protest, and continued snorting. "Okay, Tommy, I give up. You win. I may have blown up a few million dollars worth of oil refinery, but you are crazier than I will ever be. And I'm the one that had to get out of the country."

I picked up a whisk broom that was all we had to sweep with and began brushing down the ceiling, walls and floor of our little house. Henry jumped to the project with enthusiasm. In a few hours, we had a pretty good looking hooch, bare wooden floor and all. We went to the cookhouse late in the afternoon and ate fried fish and conch and socialized with a few people that I had barely talked to before. Henry really opened up this day, and everybody took notice of him for the first time. He was one of the gang.

And that was it. Henry and I shared something. Different, but the same. I figured that if he thought I was an okay person, and I had done something so completely stupid, then he could be an okay person too. I never heard from Henry after he left the expedition, but I know he has turned out just fine.

Chapter Eleven

La Ceiba

A trip to La Ceiba, a coastal town with a population of about 25,000, was on for the next week. This was going to be my first return to the mainland, and I was ignorant enough to be looking forward to it. I knew that I was going because at least eight people were signed up on the bulletin board at Fathom House. The most efficient way was to take the *Salva Vida*, and she didn't go anywhere without me. I had made myself invaluable to its operation because I was the only person on speaking terms with the Russian diesel engine, and Captain Mike was getting dependent on my help. None of us begrudged him his leisurely attitude toward work. We just didn't care if a guy worked too much for his own good, and we didn't care if someone was on the island to work on his suntan.

Besides, Captain Mike was something of a legend among us. He was carrying on a torrid love affair with Theresa, the petite, pretty, and new wife of Brian, the owner of the Bahia Lodge. Like a bunch of old fisher wives, we all talked about the latest sightings of the two lovers and clucked our tongues at the inappropriateness of the whole thing. The affair became a Fathom topic mostly because of the exalted status that Captain

Mike had attained in our group. He had a history, and we thought we knew it.

My first Saturday night in Utila Town was spent at the movies, in a manner of speaking. The generator was running, as it always was on Saturday afternoons and evenings, and I was caught up in the throng of Fathom people heading across Main Street for the Bahia Lodge to watch some porno movies. Nick had insisted on my attendance because he was concerned about my general lack of knowledge of women and a serious deficiency in beer drinking talent.

I hated to admit that I had never seen a porno flick, as they are called; but worse, I admitted to this glaring deficit in education to several of the Fathom reprobates. I got the distinct impression that they were more interested in seeing my reaction to the movies than they were interested in watching the movies. I did not disappoint them. I couldn't believe that people did the things that I saw that night, and in front of other people, like the cameramen, for example. I was stunned and tried to be as casual about watching as everybody else appeared to be, but it was to no avail. Loud laughter and crude comments flowed like the beer from the tap.

I occasionally felt myself blush. The comments about the physical attributes or deficiencies of the actors were rich and ribald. Several references to horses and donkeys were made about one faceless actor, whose stamina was a match for his caliber, something akin to a one-fifty-five cannon was mentioned. The awe and appreciation of this group of near castaways would have warmed the hearts of all involved in the production of these cinematic spectaculars.

But I was able to quiet the bunch with one comment. "That sure looks like Captain Mike," I opined when a rare shot of the actor's face appeared for just a split second.

A pin would not have hit the wood floor unnoticed in the silence that reigned for all of ten seconds following my observation.

"What," yelled Jack in a shrill voice? "Run that thing backwards, Ted," he yelled in the same shocked voice. Ted did as he was asked. We saw the thrusting in reverse, which is the same as in forward, we noticed, and saw the flash of face again. Ted ran it normally again and froze on the face for a couple of seconds, being careful to run it soon so as not to burn the film. It was Captain Mike. The shouts and accolades rang out and my discomfiture was lifted. Nobody cared about my reaction now. We had a movie star in out midst.

For his part, Captain Mike took all the comments in stride. All agreed that he was pretty much a god. There was nothing that could be said in the negative. It would have been an automatic "put up or shut up" moment. No one present could have put up what Captain Mike had already "put up," and it was immortalized on film. He was a made man.

And all of this brings me back to why Captain Mike was, without question, afforded grandfather status in being able to beg off to any work detail. This was especially writ large when his affair with the dark beauty became common knowledge. Marriage was more or less a concept of the world, and we could argue convincingly that this place was not of the world.

Any of the sport fisherman boats could handle the eight people, and get there a lot faster, but Sergei was back on the island and watching every penny of Fathom's money. He hated spending money for any reason. The big Mercury outboards burned a lot of fuel on two seventy mile roundtrips. And it would take at least two trips because any trip to the mainland meant bringing back supplies like bags of whole wheat flour, coffee, sugar and the like. And the sport fishermen could not be left overnight in any port on the mainland. Drug dealers, fishermen, or simply opportunists would not hesitate to steal a fast light boat. No harbormaster could be paid enough, or be trusted, to protect a boat belonging to rich Americans.

These were the days when navigating was still navigating. I spent some little time making certain that I knew the speed of the *Salva Vida* and of the ocean currents that we would cross enroute to La Ceiba. I wanted to lay out a course that would put us right on La Ceiba. It just wasn't going to be good enough that I head for the coast and make a right turn until we saw the harbor. We had charts on board, and I spent as much time familiarizing myself with buoys, lights and channels in the approach to the port as I did calculating the headings. Screwing up on my first ocean crossing, with these people as my critics would have found me in the cabin making preparations for Hari Kari. I just couldn't have survived the abuse.

To everybody but me, it wasn't much of a crossing, only about thirty-five nautical miles. I breathed an audible sigh of relief when the light buoy marking the western tip of the jetty protecting the port showed up in my binoculars. I didn't let anyone see me using the glasses, giving all the impression that I had motored right to it with no concern. Hand signals from the harbormaster put me parallel to the correct mooring cleat. I shifted between neutral and forward a few times and let the quartering breeze drift the old girl against the bumpers and the wharf. It was a textbook docking, and it didn't go unnoticed.

"Nice job, Tommy," offered Jack Crabill. "Even we dirt and rock fanciers know a steely-eyed seaman when we see one."

"Not bad, kid," added Duane, nodding his head slightly in approval. "And where does a Hoosier come off driving a seagoing vessel like he has seawater in his veins?"

I was working hard to show no emotion, but I was inordinately pleased with my little day trip, and it was with some effort that I just shrugged my shoulders and answered. "You know what they say about the blind hog and the acorns."

I talked to the harbormaster, telling him to expect us to be his guests for a few days. His English was good enough to get fifty lempira from us in advance, which was exactly twenty-five

American dollars.

I was a follower again, so I followed Duane, at his request. Nick joined us as we cleared the wharf. We walked along the uneven asphalt street, angling away from the waterside. I was not impressed. *This was another sad town of ramshackle buildings and trash-strewn empty lots.* I just didn't quite have it figured out yet that when almost everybody is concerned about their next meals, property aesthetics and community pride go to the bottom of their lists of priorities. Just as I had gotten homesick the first time I hit the Honduran mainland, I was already homesick for the island. It was very telling that I had become so acclimated to the island.

Entering a mostly open air marketplace, we found chairs near a vendor's stand. To one side of the ten foot long counter was a two foot high round chunk of meat, skewered vertically and slowly rotating in front of a propane gas burner. A portly man wearing the most food-stained apron in the free world was half perched on a stool, watching the meat rotate. It appeared to be a compressed amalgam of several kinds of meats. A delicate, black haired girl appeared noiselessly by my side, startling me. She said something ending with *por favor*. Duane spoke to her in Spanish, which meant almost nothing to me, except that I picked up on the "tres Salva Vidas." I was progressing well down the road to being an accomplished beer drinker. It was some better than drinking the water, which usually was not as translucent as the average beer.

"I took the liberty of ordering all of us the only thing they have on the menu," laughed Duane.

"And what would that be?" asked Nick.

"It's kind of like mystery meat on a shingle, but the shingle is a tortilla in this case. It really is mystery meat. You may think I am putting you on, but you won't see much road kill around here. People who have pets keep them in their compounds. These people live in fenced-in areas. If you see a stray dog today, it is a good bet that you won't be able to find it next week."

"You are exaggerating just a little, aren't you?" I interjected. This just seemed to be a bit much, and I suspected that Duane was pulling my chain a little. I had hoped that most of that kind of ribbing was behind me after a few weeks as the new guy in town.

Duane shook his head slowly and continued, "I am just telling you like it is, guys. In some cultures, rats and guinea pigs are normal fare for the table. You may get to Chile one of these days," he said, looking directly at me. "There are bad things happening there and I cannot imagine you won't get to see the world. You are showing some real talent down here. But I digress. In Chile, guinea pigs are raised by just about everybody, and they are only pets like chickens on a farm are pets." I really was starting to feel a little sick as the young girl handed me a plate with a simple thin tortilla topped with sautéed mystery meat, swimming in orange grease.

"Dig in fellas," Duane said with just a little too much exuberance. "It usually is pretty good."

The most surprising thing was that it really did taste good to all of us. The joke would be that it tasted like chicken. It didn't, but it did taste a lot like a fajita you might get at any of the franchises, like Chili's or Applebee's, in the States today. We all had seconds on the food and beer. It was obvious that Duane was expecting somebody. He looked around the plaza just often enough to make me wonder what was on the agenda. I was just the chauffeur, I thought, so I decided to say little and watch.

Within the hour, I had my curiosity satisfied. Two men, whom I took to be Americans even at a distance, walked directly toward us, covering the several hundred feet of intervening plaza cobblestones with the deliberate stride that defines Americans. Hondurans generally walked with their heads down and never in a hurry, never. As they neared, Duane pushed back his chair and stood, shaking hands with each of them. I felt it appropriate to do likewise.

"Tommy," Duane started the brief introduction, "the tall, handsome one here is Allen Grant. He specializes in schmoozing and sucking up to bureaucrats and rich people. The long hair," he swept his hand sideways to indicate the other, "is Paul Larson, the intellectual of our little group here in this tropical paradise. Guys," Duane said turning back toward us, "these two represent us in Tegucigalpa. By us, I mean us." I picked up on the us he was referring to.

"Do you mind if we join you?" Allen Grant asked, with an accent that reminded me of the late John F. Kennedy. It wasn't really a question. "May I suggest we move to a larger table toward the center of the plaza?" And this was also rhetorical in nature. We moved to the biggest circular table and away from the vending area.

After settling in and having more Salva Vidas brought over, we looked at each other for a few long moments. "Tommy," Allen began, "thank you for joining us down here. I apologize for not meeting you at the airport the other day. As Duane so eloquently puts it, I was otherwise engaged in some schmoozing. I intended to head-off Richard and thus allow you to keep your money. I really don't like that guy, and I don't mean that in a catty or gossipy way. I just don't like him. However, he is the only game in town, other than the American Embassy, and that simply won't do. So that we get started off on the right foot, and until you are properly remunerated for my failure, I want you to have this." As he finished his opening statement, and that is what it was, he slid his watch from his left wrist. He casually laid the watch on the table and pushed it past Nick until it touched my bottle of beer.

I stared at it and played the part of a deaf-mute perfectly. I was taken aback by the realization that it was a Rolex. The one with the half blue and half red bezel set around the black face. It is called an Oyster Perpetual for reasons that escaped me, but I knew the watch.

"Just be casual about picking it up. Maybe you could one-hand it with your beer. And this never happened. I guess I can be the dramatist every now and again, but I wanted to see the look on your face." Having said this, Allen leaned back, pushing the front legs of his chair slightly off the plaza surface. I did as he suggested and adopted a casual air that fooled no one at the table. Paul spoke next.

"Tommy, this is not double-naught spy stuff, but Allen and I have goals to meet down here, and it takes all kinds to accomplish these goals. You have now met our little group, the six of you, on the island, and us." He paused to down the rest of his beer. Looking at the bottle, he added, "We never get to drink this with the lace pants set in Tegoose. But I must admit a certain affinity for the local brew. It sure beats the water," he added.

Tegoose was the slang we all used to refer to the capital of Honduras. I thought quickly about the six referred to by Paul. Besides Nick and Duane, he meant Brian, Rodney, Craig and me. No one had yet mentioned Craig to me as being part of what I was beginning to think of as our little conspiracy, but I had heard the talk about Craig having been part of the Guatamalan training camp for some of the eventual Bay of Pigs invasion force. Craig's reputation for hatred of the Kennedy family was no secret. I wondered if he weren't putting himself out for a little too much scrutiny, considering the company he kept. *Back to the present.*

Allen continued with his statements. "You have not disappointed Duane here, Tommy. And that is high praise, indeed. Duane doesn't like anyone naturally." He looked at Duane with one perfectly raised eyebrow, as if challenging him for a response. He received not even a look from Duane, indicating a tacit agreement.

"Your heroic save of Nick, who should know better than to sleep while diving, was good stuff. You also have made yourself an almost indispensable member of the expedition by assuming duties without being asked. I like your attitude." He raised the bottle so that the little girl would see it, bringing her toward us. "Now let's hoist a few."

The next couple of hours were spent drinking beer, eating mystery meat nachos with cheese and hot peppers, and the telling of love conquests and failures. I still had lousy immunity to the very high alcohol content of the beer, and have little more than a hazy recollection of being squired around La Ceiba by Nick and Duane, drinking in at least two establishments, and eating again. The following morning found me hurting and kicking around on a small twin bed, in a very little, but very clean, hotel room.

Nick was recovering, and much faster than I was, in the same room. He was reading a paperback book, lying on his back with his head supported by a pillow folded noticeably carefully. *Navy people.* I tried to talk in a normal voice, but failed. I grunted a good morning and Nick looked over at me.

"Now we know what you will look like when you are dead," he opined.

"Ah… Nick, I don't want to seem ungrateful, but could you turn the volume down, maybe even whisper?" I pleaded.

"This is dangerous work, isn't it? If we don't drown in the ocean, we try to drown in alcohol. Don't worry, kid, I have some sympathy for what you are going through, so I'll cut you some slack. You should be grateful. Captain Mike wanted to take you out whoring last night, but you were hardly able to keep your head up, much less anything else." He then laughed, far too long and way too loudly. I was on the verge of throwing up and my brain was pushing out against my skull with such force that I tried to keep it in check with both hands. I said nothing.

"Just lie still. I'll be quiet," he added.

By about noon, I was able to consider going out in the sun and trying to suppress the gag reflex brought on by the nausea and the headache that was beyond my twenty years of experience. I had a lot to learn about drinking, but I was apparently in the company of experts.

I stared at the ceiling, realizing that I was alone in the room. Allen and Randy had presumably returned to Tegucigalpa. I could not remember seeing either of them after about six o'clock last evening. It surprised me that I was aware of the time that I had seen them leaving one of the bars. I hadn't known the exact time of day, or cared about it, in weeks. I wondered what the purpose of our meeting here had really been about. I looked at the Rolex on my wrist. I mean I really looked at it. It exuded a quality with which I was not accustomed. I wondered if they were trying to buy my loyalty. If it were so, they had succeeded, but not because of the watch. I was, after all, a very private person, a loner actually, if I were honest with myself. I was in no way used to having people appreciate my efforts, much less congratulating me for some small success. I knew that I was going to give my best for these people. I was being treated with respect and it was flattering my ego. *I am so easy.*

I was still dressed, meaning I was wearing a cheap short sleeved shirt and a pair of my white jeans. My tennis shoes were on the floor next to the bed. It already seemed odd to be pulling on shoes. This was all so civilized. I left the room, but not without being reminded to move very slowly. There was an open door at the end of the hall. A toilet that looked to have been manufactured around the turn of the century was pointed right at me. This really was civilization. We had a private bathroom, and right in the building.

Walking carefully down the stairs, I passed an empty office and counter and opened the door. The crashing sound of the unseen bell attached just above the door almost forced me to my knees. A dirt sidewalk was all that separated the front of the little hotel from the street, which was lined with litter of every description. I had no idea where I was, so I turned right and started walking, counting on seeing something that would orient me soon enough.

The seagulls were my first clue that I was heading in the right direction. Soon I saw the rigging of some ships above a concrete wall that was topped with a vicious looking mixture of broken glass, barbed wire and pieces of embedded, rusty metal. I passed along the wall, looking for a way to the harbor, noticing bare electrical wires sticking out from the occasional buildings. Looking up from these primitive electrical distribution points, I saw loose bundles of wires that were haphazardly strung from any available nail or piece of wood nailed to the buildings. It was the work of the electricity pirates.

I had heard stories about the shanty towns being provided electricity by roaming electrical pirates, charging whatever they could get away with to hook the shacks up to the overhead electrical grid. Lights and hot plates in these pitiful dwellings were generally powered with stolen electricity. It was a constant battle between being disconnected by the authorities and being reconnected by the pirate entrepreneurs.

Just the previous afternoon, I had listened as one of our guys was relating a story about an electricity pirate who had been washing himself and the clothes he was wearing by simply walking into the ocean. He was called to by a local woman who was willing to pay to have her house hooked into the overhead electrical wires. A little dickering soon established a fee of twenty-five lempiras. The man had climbed onto the steel roof, feet wet with sea water dripping down his trousers. He touched a hot wire, sending the electricity to the steel roof through his body, which had become an enhanced conductor. He shook almost comically, as it was described, until he was launched off the roof headfirst into the asphalt street. It was not known whether he had died from the electricity or the fall. And it didn't matter, dead was dead. The punch line was that the woman ran up to the body and went through the dead man's pockets. She retrieved her fee and was able to find a few extra lempiras for her trouble. This was really hilarious stuff.

Until you have been to a Central American city, you cannot possibly appreciate the bunker mentality exhibited by the construction around most private property. Virtually every alleyway is blocked by a tall and sturdy gate that was built with the thought of discouraging even a climber. Every single home, or group of homes, is enclosed with fencing, walls and even iron bars that would not look out of place in a prison compound. Whereas an American generally thinks of a city block in a residential area as a place that could be cut across, either through yards or down an alley, such a shortcut is not possible in Central America. I was contemplating this as I looked for a way to get to the wharf area. Years of tramping through cities from Northern Mexico all the way down to Nicaragua and Venezuela have reinforced the impression of "fear as a way of life" that I started forming on this afternoon.

When I happened upon the main route to the wharf, I walked through the only opening of the wall for miles. I was immediately accosted by two seedy looking men, wearing hints of some kind of uniforms and brandishing ancient shotguns. I struggled with getting across to them that I was an American, and that I had a boat moored at the wharf. They were not going to let me in under any circumstances until the harbormaster joined our small confrontation. He yelled at them in fast and furious Spanish that I doubted I would have understood even if I understood Spanish. *How can anybody talk that fast?*

If I expected a chastened attitude from either of the guards upon my legitimacy being established, I was to be disappointed. Each of them stepped back and split apart just enough to allow me through, making certain that I had to brush against the weapons as I passed between them. Swaggering intimidation best describes their body language.

I walked out to the dock and stopped at the *Salva Vida*. I checked her lines for security and proper layout. Being satisfied, I boarded her and made my way below to the engine room. I checked oil, fuel and coolant levels and made a mental note to get fuel. I knew that Duane would pay for anything needed.

For the first time since arriving in La Ceiba, I thought of my own money. I checked my wallet and counted the small wad of play money that constituted lempira. The surprise was that I felt the bulge of another bundle in the same pocket that had contained my wallet. Neatly folded in halves were fifty twenty-lempira bills. Somebody, probably Nick, I thought quickly, had actually given me five hundred dollars. What a strange way to be paid. But this was essentially the way it was for the next two years. Cash was either handed to me or I would find it in my quarters, wherever they happened to be. I sure wasn't in Kansas anymore, Toto.

I felt the boat list slightly, accompanied with a loud call. "Permission to come aboard, Captain?" It was Duane.

I climbed topside and greeted him. "Permission granted, but I'm just the last mate," I countered, keeping up the mock formality.

"Maybe for the moment," Duane responded cheerily, "but I hear what I hear and I see what I see. Captain Mike's dance card seems to be pretty full lately and I'm guessing a promotion is making its way through channels. More responsibility, no respect and no pay will be hard to refuse, as if you will be given a choice." *What was going on here?* Duane was joking, and with me, the new guy?

"Look kid, it's like this. Richard can play with this setup as long as the cash flow works. Without a little help from his friends, it goes negative, unless we really do score some treasure.

Even then, the rats will come out of the woodwork, and both governments. Hell, if we really score, every politician since Isabella and Ferdinand will lay claim to it." Duane looked up toward the harbormaster shack, making certain that this was a private conversation.

"So, Tommy, the three of us talked about you yesterday." I thought about Allen and Paul briefly. "I updated them on the way you have handled yourself. We don't need any choir boys out here, but we need Fathom. You are more than pulling your weight. I think if every player here showed your enthusiasm, and had your talent, this expedition would have been a success long ago. Your quick thinking and immediate action saved Nick's ass, and in front of our people to boot. Just keep doing what you are doing. I'm thinking Captain Mike will become Captain Emeritus or some damn thing. But this boat is now yours."

"Really," I asked incredulously? I could be quite eloquent when I sifted through my repertoire of responses.

"Sure, why not?" Duane said casually. "You know the history of this vessel. We bought her from the salvagers and brought her down to Fathom. Just don't sink her if you can avoid it. Or we'll take it out of your pay."

I knew for certain how the money had made its way into my pocket then. But I said nothing about it. It was just assumed that we didn't discuss most things. It surprised me that I fell into the closed-mouth habit of these people so easily. I had picked up on the fact that many in Fathom knew that American embassy people were around the expedition, but the general consensus of opinion was that they were just interested in the activities and maybe seeking some adventure.

I felt as if I had just been given a field promotion. I couldn't even explain to myself why it made me feel good. I now had to take care of the *Salva Vida*. It wouldn't be something done on a whim anymore, but a chore. Even that thought didn't faze me.

"That is so cool, thanks Duane." I gushed like a teenager. But of course, I actually was, at least for another month or so.

Duane smiled at me. "Nice watch."

We disembarked and went to see the harbormaster about the fuel and some extra oil. Duane put enough money in his hand to assuage any suspicions, which he wore on his sleeve. Leaving the wharf area, I considered glaring at the two guards, but the shotguns were just as big as I remembered and I would need to get back through. I don't know why I always felt the need to get even with people.

We walked down the dusty street, lined with the simple clapboard sided buildings and the wooden walkways. It could have been the Old West. As I considered the analogy, I thought about the dive knife strapped to my right calf, where it always was, but now out of sight.

"This is one ugly, little town isn't it?" was about all I could think to say.

"I'll tell you the truth, Tommy," Duane said with a knowing look, "It looks like every other town in this part of the world. Even the biggest cities have this primitive, hodgepodge look to them as soon as you get away from the downtown areas."

"Creepy and depressing," I said. "Every house has Rube Goldberg wiring, plumbing, just everything. How can these people live like this?"

"This from a man who lives in a hooch, at the edge of a jungle, with no water and not even stolen electricity?" Duane laughed.

"Yeah. But I look at all of that as a kind of vacation thing. I know that I can get on an airplane someday and be back in the world in a few hours. These people are in their world."

"That's why we are finally down here looking around. A Fidel Castro or Che Guevera could turn all of Central America, and probably Mexico, into a Latin Soviet Union, and that's all we need at our back door."

I focused once again on the religious icons everywhere and said, "or maybe an evangelist could swoop down here and start a religious movement that would be just as bad." Duane looked over at me with that statement.

"You know, Tommy, I'm beginning to think you may not be just another pretty face."

"I get that a lot."

We came upon a few of our group at the next block. Duane enlisted them into going shopping and doing some humping of supplies back to the boat. That was how we spent the afternoon, buying the biggest cans of tomatoes, peas and even potatoes. I suggested that we give some things to the harbormaster and the guards. "It might make things easier for us and give them a reason not to sink the *Vida* at the dock," I said only half joking.

It was good to get the chores out of the way. I was all for leaving right then, but Duane decided that we should at least find the rest of the group and eat a little and maybe drink a lot. I couldn't stand the thought of a beer right then, but Duane said that I needed to learn about the recuperative powers of "the hair of the dog." "You should have had beer for breakfast. You would be feeling great by now."

"I didn't have any breakfast, or lunch for that matter," I said.

"Well, that's the reason for your gloomy disposition today. We need to get your head on straight." With that, Duane led our little group off toward the plaza. Captain Mike was holding court at the big table, entertaining two young and very pretty little girls, and showing off more than a little for the benefit of the rest of our group. Other than in the brightest part of the day, it was the custom of just about all Americans to only travel in groups. The fortress mentality of the city made even the dullest person realize that less than friendly forces prowled the streets, especially in the twilight hours.

I was somewhat mesmerized by the beauty of the girls. As I watched them laughing and teasing the men, their liquid black eyes sparkling with reflected sunlight, it occurred to me that Honduras certainly had its contrast in people. So many of the people were the roughest, and even ugliest people that I had ever seen; yet many of the girls were petite, pretty, and had the clearest complexions that I had yet encountered in my long life.

We started eating and drinking in the plaza, and moved as one to a favorite La Ceiba bar, The Pelican, at 7:15, by my Rolex. It cracked me up that I knew the time. The "hair of the dog" must have worked. I felt great.

I took point and found a stool at one end of the bar, where I felt I could keep an eye on the festivities without getting involved. I am not much given to social events, and even sitting there, comfortably drinking a Salva Vida (nectar of the gods, I had recently realized), I mostly wanted to be piloting the boat back home. But when one of the bar girls backed up to me, moving back and forth against me while talking with Nick, I began to think that maybe I could hang around for just a little longer. Nick turned her around gently and wrapped her arms around me. "This one is on me, buddy. She likes you. I recognize true love when I see it."

He was right. At first, I was mostly embarrassed, but the alcohol smoothed that out nicely and I can remember parts of the evening in flashes of color and movements, mostly her movements. I don't remember what I did or didn't do with her, but her love for me was undeniable.

I awoke half-sick again, and in the same room as the previous morning. Nick was drinking coffee from one of those ancient thick mugs that displace more air than they leave for coffee. As I sat up on the bed, he tossed my wallet, hitting my stomach and almost killing me. "I pried this from the hands of your one true love last night, just before you disappeared into the back room and right after you let her look through it for pictures. God, the things I will do for my guardian angel. By the way, I gave her a twenty lempira bill and spent some of your money on me as a reward."

I tried to grin, but failed. I felt something stirring and lurched out of the room, heading for my one true friend, the porcelain god at the end of the hall. My recuperative powers relating to recovering from alcohol poisoning were soon to become the stuff of legend. I had none. I rarely had to pay for a beer once the legend became published in the word-of-mouth free press. Fathom people generally were entertained by the misery of others. I had to fight off the free beers after a while. I suppose it is the same perverse fascination people have in trying to get dogs drunk. I just don't get it.

I pronounced myself capable of surviving the trip back to Utila, and we left in the early afternoon. I was only barely capable of surviving the trip. I got close enough to the course line to Utila that I was able to see it off to our east with the binoculars. Making the needed correction, I steered us into the harbor of Utila Town. The approach to the dock was not as impressive as my stellar arrival in La Ceiba two days before, but this dock was moving.

Chapter Twelve

Whale Shark

Fathom had at least one large and chronic problem. In the midst of plenty the group had always struggled to provide enough food of sufficient quality and quantity to keep attitudes on at least an even keel. The uncertainties of searching, the very hard work involved and the real possibility for disappointment made decent food a necessity. People needed to stay focused on finding and working sites. This was, after all, a treasure hunting expedition. Many of the members were disillusioned, or realistic enough, to realize that there was likely no pot of gold at the end of the rainbow. I was one of those people. But others were completely absorbed by the expectation of riches and worked hard, day after day, to achieve that goal.

Within days of my arrival, in a rare moment of introspection, I realized that getting a share of treasure was not my motivation. I was running away from a too predictable future. I desired adventure, but was I willing to face danger to prove that I had nerve? Being the hunter, providing the sustenance for thirty to forty people, was the basic stuff of survival. It touches the soul. I was young, indestructible and the possibility of danger was not a consideration.

I was very good at spearfishing and the group needed fresh food. And the island was surrounded by millions of perfectly edible fish. Gunter and I assumed the mantles of providers and the rest of the group was glad to let us provide. Almost every day would see one or both of us out on, but mostly under, the ocean and hunting for food. My favorite method of hunting was to snorkel out from a relatively deserted point on the island, by myself and for hours at a time.

It was a typically gorgeous May morning that found me heading west on Main Street from the cookhouse. In this direction there are no side streets. There are only a few intersections in all of Utila Town. The population of the island was estimated to be no more than three thousand. I seemed to see the faces of a more limited universe of only a few hundred. In the same way that high school seniors think they know everybody in school after their few years, the reality is usually that they know fewer than several dozen. The majority of people become background noise.

There was no background noise of people west of our dock. I knew all the people I passed as I kicked up the dust of Main Street with my bare feet. My only clothing was a pair of the white jeans cut off a few inches below the crotch. It was the uniform of most of Fathom. Some shorts had been worn day and night for months, taking on the appearance of loincloths or denim miniskirts that had seen better days. I was indistinguishable from many of the younger members of the group. I had a bronzed lean body, dark long hair and a beard, both of which varied in length only upon infrequent visits to Sadie, an old Honduran native who made straw hats and cut hair. One of the last structures in town was my hooch, which was barely visible behind a line of palm trees and vegetation to my left. I negotiated the hundred feet of path with the usual care. I didn't worry about the snakes, but I wasn't anxious to step on one. After having one drop barely behind me from a palm tree a few weeks before, I had learned to divide my attention up and down as I twisted back and forth, brushing against branches and spider webs.

I visited my quarters, barely noticing the scurrying insects and lizards, just long enough to retrieve the basics of diving. Mask, fins and snorkel, along with my weight belt, were in a bucket of relatively fresh water. I had taken to keeping them in water when I couldn't think of a reason to take them out of the water and provide habitats for insects, lizards and scorpions. I also grabbed a hundred feet of coiled three-eighth's inch manila rope. One end was finished in my signature loop; the other was attached to an inflated bicycle inner tube and wheel. I had dismounted the tire, and then inflated the inner tube around the wheel. It was my invention, or at least it was my adaptation. It wouldn't have worked on a bicycle, but when towed behind me in the ocean, the spokes formed a sieve no kill could slip through and the thing had every bit of eighty pounds of buoyancy.

Gunter and I had an unspoken understanding that spearfishing with scuba gear was now *verboten*. This was not a sportsman's holiday, but spearfishing with the aid of scuba gear is akin to one of those "hunting preserves" in Texas that raise boar and deer in cages to be released for shooting by "hunters" when of sufficient size. In truth, spearing fish when snorkeling isn't very sporting, but it did feed the entire group.

I gathered my gear, eschewing the speargun for a sling spear, part of the "sporting" concessions we were making, and headed back out to Main Street. This time I turned left upon hitting the street. I walked to the end of the street and entered the forest. The foliage in a tropical forest is dense beyond the average American's ability to properly visualize. And I was nothing if not an average American. I loved the desolation and was always a little afraid. Not to admit the slightest fear would be disingenuous. None of us were certain of the denizens of the forest beyond the obvious, meaning thousands of raucous birds and a really huge population of iguana. No more than 5% of Utila was used by the humans, so the potential for a surprise in the forest was great. I stayed near the shoreline, not that I could see it, but the sound of the surf was compass enough. If I kept the sound to my left I would run out of island in about four miles. I made my way through about a half mile of marsh, ancient coral graveyards and fern-covered ground before I turned left and found myself on a coral beach no more than 10 feet deep.

I slipped the eye of the rope into a carabiner, an oval-shaped, spring-loaded metal link, hanging from the weight belt and donned the rest of my gear. Lying face down in all of two feet of water, I kicked carefully out to sea, trailing my bicycle wheel on its leash. I had the rubber sling of my pole spear hooked over the web of skin between my right thumb and first finger while holding the spear shaft in a firm grip. The sea floor quickly fell away and I scanned back and forth, watching from the picture window that was my face mask, getting a feel for the terrain as it were. I swam past fortresses of coral reef, festooned with sea anemones, sponges, brain and elk horn coral. Visibility was slightly hazy at first, but as I left the shore effect, I was able to see more than a hundred feet.

Reef fish were plentiful and active, but I was interested only in game fish, and ignored the usual schools of butterfly fish, grunts, angel and parrot fishes of all kinds. I spied the head of a black snapper sticking out from underneath a ledge of coral, just above the sandy sea floor between coral formations. I took several slow, deep breaths through my snorkel, holding the last and especially deep last breath, before bending into the usual jackknife position, thrusting the heavy rubber fins into the air as I straightened into a vertical dive. I made the thirty foot dive with very little movement, kicking with legs close together and mostly straight. I ran my hand up the shaft of the pole spear, stretching the rubber sling to very near the tip. From five feet above the snapper, I released the shaft. It leapt forward and the detachable faceted point went through the top of the snapper's head and came out its lower jaw. The point came out of the shaft and the snapper was impaled on the steel tether. He never saw it coming.

I ascended slowly, holding the fish and the spear together. I pulled the catch wheel to me and put the fish in the circular walled center. I reloaded and continued my patrol. I shot six more fish in much the same way over the next hour. I let myself go with the prevailing wind, which was moving me away from the island and diagonally across Utila Town. I stayed on the surface gently kicking with straight legs and making certain not to break the surface of the water with my fins. Fins above the water line represent wasted effort.

The other advantage of this quiet motion was that it allowed me to be as much a part of the ocean as any of the larger marine life. It is necessary to move fluidly so as to not bring yourself to the attention of all the other predators in the ocean. I stopped kicking for a moment to turn and check the ride of my bicycle wheel, laden down as it was with at least one hundred pounds of snapper and grouper. As I gently made a ninety degree turn with my head down, I abruptly hit what appeared to be a mountain of sandpaper covered leather. Only it wasn't a mountain. It was what I took to be the world's biggest shark. I was not in a position to analyze its subtleties, but it didn't look right somehow. The mouth was easily four feet wide and in an almost perfectly straight line displaying an orifice that was open about six inches.

I put out my hands, holding the pole spear perpendicular to the line of its wide snout, trying to keep my hands out of its mouth, and pushed off. It continued toward me and I felt real fear for the first time in my life. This was the kind of fear that cannot be rationalized and compartmentalized. In the ocean, virtually every living thing is either the hunter or the hunted, and the roles can become reversed. My initial reaction was that I had just gone from being the hunter to the hunted. But I was wrong. It was a whale shark.

The very large shark as much brushed me aside as it ran into me. It moved in a threatening side to side motion and I was hit from its side with about the same force that it had initially bumped into me. This is the normal swimming motion of the whale shark. Most sharks swim mostly through the movement of their tails, but the whale shark uses its entire body for propulsion. It occurred to me that it had been following me, probably matching my speed, and I had stopped without signaling.

Of course, pulling an open basket of slightly bleeding fish around behind me was chumming for sea life. The great beast had most likely been attracted by the activity near the surface, of the hundreds of fish I was trailing. As my heart rate slowed and my adrenaline high subsided, I was able to watch, and feel its wake as it went by.

It was easily thirty-five feet long and its diameter almost matched my height. It had a near black background color that was mottled with hundreds of off-white spots and splotches. It never looked back and swam into the misty oblivion that marked the edge of my underwater world. It is no threat to humans, but it is the largest fish in the ocean. At least some of them are. In the fish catalog that I kept in the back of my head, I knew that a really big whale shark could be more than forty feet long. This one was probably a teenager.

I looked back at my bicycle wheel and inner tube basket, a hundred feet behind me. It was apparently untouched, but definitely down in the water. I had done enough this day. I turned in toward the Fathom Dock, about a mile away, and kept the course to the dock by establishing the angle of the shadows from the coral buildups. This allowed me to keep my body horizontal and head down, breathing through the snorkel easily, without having to look up frequently. Looking forward is an almost unnatural action when snorkeling. Upon arrival at the dock, I accepted the accolades of hungry fellow expedition members, showing appropriate modesty when I was called the fearless great white hunter of Utila. I completely forgot to mention my not so fearless stare down of the whale shark. I cut all reasonably usable meat from the carcasses and stacked more than seventy pounds of it on my wheel assembly. I was in no mood to support Rosie's fish head stew. I threw the remains into the water off the dock and watched with interest as the sea consumed its own in a frenzy that continued long after I had departed for the cookhouse and the inevitable lecture from Rosie.

She didn't disappoint me. As much as she loved seeing me show up at the kitchen with fresh seafood, she expected to see all the remains also. But her scolding was tempered with a genuine affection for me, I knew.

Rosie lived well because of Fathom Expeditions. She was a big woman. I am being to kind. She was big in the manner of being fat. I cannot stand being "politically correct," so I won't try. She was the spitting image of Aunt Jemima.

"You American mens waste too much food," she said, hoping to start a harangue.

"Rosie," I replied, "I love you like the fat Negro slave I never had, but the heads and backbones of fish do not constitute food. It's what we in *Los Estados Unidos* call garbage." She laughed in the rich tone that made me recall a stereotypical voodoo woman. My irreverence pleased her. Her ample body shook waves of flesh.

"I wouldn't be wasting time this much into the day. Put the fish in the icebox and be out of my kitchen. The working mens will be wanting to eat soon enough." With this dismissal, she pointed to the bin that I knew contained our whole wheat flour.

I had taken to sifting the flour regularly. Unlike the refined and purified white powder called flour in the States, ours was the real thing. It was a rich brown color and real food. The insects thought highly of it also. One of my first lessons in Utila cuisine was that I was eating insects baked into the bread. Rosie considered me to be a prissy, white boy, but I had observed that she didn't mind my sifting out the worms and roaches before she baked the heavy whole wheat bread that we all liked. This was what passed for normal in our group.

In the ensuing years I have demonstrated the difference between white flour and whole wheat flour to anyone interested. Put a scoop of white flour and a scoop of unpurified whole wheat flour on your driveway. In time, the whole wheat flour will be consumed by insects while the white flour will stay untouched.

Chapter Thirteen

Black Coral

Several days later, I was deep into repairing one of the old abandoned launches. Just something to keep myself occupied. I had enlisted Nick's help in mounting an outboard engine and had ensnared him utterly with a variation of the Tom Sawyer effect.

"I'm going to fix the steering hardware, modify the throttle and shift cables so that they can be mounted in a standard Mercury control unit," I said, drawing him in, "then cut a gateway through the transom to a small dive platform.

"That'll work," Nick joined in, taking the bait tentatively, "then we can easily replace this rotted decking and hide the battery and fuel tanks in new compartments. With all the deck space added back and no clutter, this could be a great boat to take lobstering and spearfishing without having to check with any of the crews, because it would be ours." *Hook set.*

"I've needed something in the way of a change of pace around here." He stopped the mental exercise of redesigning the boat, and put a hand on my shoulder while shaking his head slightly. "Sorry Tommy, I have just horned in on your deal. It's a great idea. I wish I had thought of it myself. I've been here long enough. Sorry."

"No, no, that's okay Nick. I could use the help. In fact, we'll tell everybody it was your idea, just in case it doesn't work. With your seniority here, that should keep the wisecracks down."

"Thanks Tommy. What would I do without you?" He stopped and looked down at his feet with pursed lips, lost in a deep reverie. He looked up to make solid eye contact. "I would have died without you, that's what." I saw that his eyes were clouding and taking on a red hue. It was obvious that he hadn't meant to talk about his near drowning. The subject took us completely by surprise. I ran the scene through my mind. I had been labeled as almost a hero, but I knew that it had just happened without conscious thought, and I had felt relief at not having screwed up, more than any particular pride in my actions. Guys just aren't supposed to talk like this. At this odd moment, and long after the event, I felt genuine thankfulness that I had been able to help Nick. And here I was feeling tenderness and concern for another guy. It just wasn't done. I wanted to say something to break the mood, but I felt that I couldn't talk without tears of my own. Being gutless, I turned back toward the little boat.

"That's okay, Nick," I said hoping he couldn't hear my voice crack, "you would have done the same for me."

He moved around my left side, gave me a manly slap on my shoulder to get my attention again, and said with a big grin, "No, I wouldn't have man. I didn't like you the first time I laid eyes on you. You'd be fish food right now." That got us both to laughing and we found a good reason to be wiping tears from our eyes. The male egos had been spared any real damage.

"Hey, Tommy, you interested in making a really cool dive?" Nick asked with a voice rising in crescendo at each word.

"No, sorry, I sold everything I owned and moved to Central America to join a treasure diving expedition. The last thing I want to do, now that I am surrounded by the best water in the world, is to make a really cool dive."

"Man, you can be sarcastic. I like that in a snot nosed kid," Nick retorted, obviously as relieved as me that we had broken through the maudlin mood.

"Seriously," he continued, looking around conspiratorially, "you know about black coral?"

"Sure," I answered glibly. The stuff is pretty rare. I know it's worth quite a bit of money. I remember an article about black coral in Skin Diver Magazine a few years ago. The artsy types swoon over it. They polish it and shape it for jewelry and junk like that." I could be so articulate.

He looked at me as if I were Neanderthal. "Pound for pound it's worth more than gold."

"Are you going somewhere with this, Nick?

"Yes," he said.

"Can you get to the point while I'm still young?"

"I know where some is. In fact, I know where a lot of it is." Now he was grinning like a kid.

"I also remember that it is usually only found in deep water."

"Deep is in the eye of the diver. On the wall of one of the blue holes, we found some at eighty feet. That got me to looking around. Duane and I found more on the drop off on the north side of the island. What say we go treasure diving?"

"Let's take the *Calypso*," I responded enthusiastically. "We can be on the north wall in an hour."

"We should use twins and plan on some decompression stops," Nick added. He was getting into this now.

I put my tools in the cuddy cabin, the protected area ahead of the bulkhead containing the wheel. Heading down the dock, I boarded the *Salva Vida* and retrieved my personal gear. The air tanks were virtually all the property of Fathom. Even if people bothered to bring tanks with them to the island, they were always left behind. We had scores of tanks and an efficient and well maintained compressor. I checked the pressures of two sets of twin 72's.

Non-divers generally ask how long a tank of air lasts. It is affected by so many variables that I could honestly tell you that between depths of ten feet and one hundred feet, anywhere from an hour and a half to ten minutes. A 72 refers to 72 cubic feet of air. Without teaching a class in the physics and physiology of diving I will point out several very important aspects of diving. Every thirty three feet that a diver descends into sea water adds an additional atmosphere of pressure. Simply put, when a diver takes a full breath of air at ninety nine feet in the ocean, he is inhaling four times as much air as he would at the surface. The differing volumes of a diver's breaths and the rate of breaths per minute vary dramatically between divers and even in the same diver.

And here is a revelation meant for virtually every ignorant newscaster in the free world. Sport divers do not use oxygen. This is a pet peeve of mine and I will restate this. Sport divers are not seen wearing oxygen tanks. Oxygen is a very toxic gas at more than about twice its normal partial pressure in the atmosphere. Write this down. Sport divers use compressed, filtered and very dry air. And even air can be toxic when a diver goes deep enough for too long.

Everyone has heard of the "bends." Simply stated, it has to do with the body's absorption of nitrogen when breathing air under pressure. Any diving beyond about forty feet forces a diver to consider how long and at what depth he stayed. If a diver stays at eighty feet for more than about thirty minutes, he has to calculate making decompression stops, usually at ten feet, but sometimes before that at thirty feet and twenty feet. And nitrogen can have another effect on divers. Depending entirely on a person's susceptibility to the narcotic effect of nitrogen under pressure, a diver can suffer from "nitrogen narcosis." It is insidious in that it can affect a diver in any way from impaired judgment, uncontrollable emotions, spasms, to unconsciousness. A real smorgasbord of symptoms is possible when a person suffers from nitrogen narcosis.

With all of that in the background of our thoughts, Nick and I put together the gear we would need to make a deep dive. We stowed the tanks securely, cast off and enjoyed a fast ride out of the harbor and around the island to the north end. We anchored within feet of the drop off to depths that are measured in the hundreds of feet. We suited up, including donning wet suit jackets. It gets chilly below sixty feet or so, even in the tropics. Nick took the lead and we headed down without looking around until we got to eighty feet. Diving next to a wall, hanging over an abyss, is always a humbling experience. Because you have a reference point with the earth, the wall, the realization of depth is most dramatic. It is somewhat akin to standing on the wrong side of a high balcony. Only you don't fall.

Nick pointed ahead and slightly down and kicked more purposefully. It was evident that he had gotten his bearings. I followed and pulled up just short of him as he stopped and reached out to an outcropping of rock with a gloved hand. I did the same. He switched on his dive light. I was thrilled to see several large colonies of black coral. The coral is the exoskeletons of thousands of tiny and carnivorous animals. The colonies looked like the wiry shrubs of a desert landscape; hundreds of branches growing out from central and denser trunks.

We broke off a few pieces that were especially abandoned looking. We had no interest in killing the animals if we could avoid it. We moved on to the west and I saw scores more of the colonies. This was really a surprise. Finding black coral at all is something like looking for four-leaf clovers. It is usually the odd coral in a field of common corals.

Nick looked at his watch and signaled me with five flashes of his right hand. Twenty five minutes since we had left the surface, and we were just below ninety feet. We headed toward the surface, being careful not to rise faster than our bubbles and breathing regularly. We stopped at about twenty feet and loitered for about ten minutes. I was looking at my waterproof decompression table and being very conservative. I then rose to about the ten foot level. Nick and I watched our tank pressure gauges and simply used up the rest of our air. Very boring, but necessary, decompression stops. We exceeded the required times by tens of minutes.

Back on the *Calypso*, we stripped off our gear and examined our specimens. Most were empty, but some had remnants of living tissue. Too bad; the ocean is a cruel world.

"Pretty cool stuff isn't it, Tommy?" Nick asked, grinning broadly.

"Yeah, but I expected it to be smoother and shinier," I replied with some disappointment.

"That all comes out when the jeweler polishes it. All black coral has bristles like these. This stuff shows up in rings, bracelets, and pendants… all that stuff girls get excited about."

"I have just never understood jewelry," I replied. "I can't stand to have junk hanging on me. It is all just something to get caught in tools and machines as far as I'm concerned."

"Yeah, real men don't wear jewelry and eat quiche, right?" Nick laughed at his great wit and I favored him with a wry smirk.

"That about sums it up. What say we grab some lobsters and be the real heroes of the expedition?" I asked. Nick agreed. We weighed anchor and motored toward the island and set the hook again over some likely lobster holes. We equipped ourselves with two foot long broom handles, embedded on one end with a large hook, and secured fish net goody bags to our weight belts.

We spent the next hour snorkeling and diving down to look under shelves and into holes. When a lobster was found staring back at us, we slid the broom handle and hook tool underneath it and snapped it upward. When the lobster exploded into his characteristic backward pulsing stroke, he was caught by the hook under his exoskeleton. Not very sporting of us, but we weren't sportsmen. We gathered more than twenty lobsters in that hour, amounting to at least one hundred pounds gross weight. This was not the Florida Keys. There were twenty pound lobsters out here. They could easily be sixty to eighty years old. I left them alone out of respect for their advanced years.

We returned to Utila as conquering heroes. Captain Mike wrote on the chalkboard in the cookhouse: Great White Hunters 23, Lobsters 0. It was a good day for Fathom Expeditions.

Chapter Fourteen

Tropical Storm

The relativity of time is rarely better illustrated than when we find ourselves living in an environment devoid of contact with the outside world. We had no radios or televisions, and even newspapers were usually days old before we saw them. For the comparative level of sophistication that our group represented in the milieu of a third world country, it seemed incongruous to me that we had no communication beyond word of mouth. As odd as it seems to me now, we were testing and using the latest underwater communication gear on some of the sites, but we had no radio communication ability between even Utila and the several keys we occupied just a few miles away. If anyone on the island had ever made radio contact with the mainland of Honduras, I never heard about it.

Some of us wore watches, but they were little more than affectations of civilization. The exception to this was that we were aware of underwater time, especially if we stayed below about fifty feet. Decompression times had to be calculated if we stayed below that depth for more than about an hour. We simply did not make plans based on the time of day. Such considerations were of the world. We were not part of the world. If a boat were leaving the dock, the most that would ever be said about its departure time would be later this morning or this afternoon. The scale of our surroundings was so small that it was easy to keep up with the comings and goings of others.

Time slowed for us. The responsibilities that I bore, due to a genetic flaw that fueled my enthusiasm, made me a veteran of the expedition in less than four months. I was recognized as a hunter of some renown, the captain of our largest boat and a willing participant to every project that came to my attention. Much can be experienced when there are no demands on our time other than for the activity of the moment.

But this lack of awareness of time and the world could be dangerous. From today's perspective of 24 hours a day of news, weather and access to the internet, it is somewhat difficult to appreciate the sense of remoteness felt by us all. And this was the situation on a windy and cloudy afternoon in July that found most of us in the cookhouse discussing the weather. The wind had been increasing and the cloud ceiling lowering all day. Any thoughts about going out on the ocean were abandoned by mid morning. The wind was blowing palm fronds and branches from the north, right across the island to our position on the southeast end of the island. Word was spreading that a hurricane was coming. It usually happens in a remote community that the facts of any event get blown out of all reality after a few iterations. The story of the coming weather was no exception. The building wind and rain evoked stories from the islanders of the death and destruction that would likely be visited on us all.

Danny, our de facto link to the Utila Town community in general, was sitting cross legged on one of the hand hewn tables and holding the attention of at least thirty of his elders, and Americans to boot. He gloried in the limelight.

"It is true mens," he continued as I entered, brushing water down my arms and legs in the doorway opposite the kitchen and Danny. "This is the same wind direction as when I was a boy. Ahnimals are running into the hills. They are knowing." He looked around expectantly, grinning so hard it looked as if his face would break. This was his moment.

Danny's little drama session did serve to make even the densest of us take real notice of the gathering storm. Being among that group, I began to consider the possibility of some really bad weather. *Same wind direction?* The wind always blew out of the north and the northwest. But this wind did have a feel to it. If we were on the edge of a hurricane, or even a tropical storm, we would need to batten down the hatches, as they say. Severe weather in remote and low lying coastal areas is usually a death sentence for many people.

The trick is not to let yourself become one of those many people. With this in mind, I resolved not to let myself be caught off guard by weather that was broadcasting its arrival so obviously. I began to review our situation. Utila had relatively high ground, with terrain that rises to more than 100 feet above sea level just a few hundred yards to our north, toward the interior. If we were in the crosshairs of a hurricane, there would be a storm surge, the bulge of the ocean surrounding any significant low pressure area. A surge represents millions of tons of water spilling over what is usually dry land. Such a surge would inundate the very low land occupied by our people, the keys. I thought about the keys and remembered that we had two people who had taken to living on Sandy Key, about a month ago.

Pete England, the book loving Pillsbury dough boy of the expedition, had taken to living on the keys. Everybody liked Pete. He was mostly a carpenter, and worked methodically, if not efficiently, when asked to help. And that was the thing about Pete. He would work like a Trojan, and simply did not quit, on any project involving hammering and sawing. But he was not in the least self-motivated and spent his time admiring the ocean and its environs. I had only seen Pete snorkeling a few times, and he had only been sightseeing in those few times, getting pretty badly sunburned at least once.

The other real hermit of our group, Eddie Glackin, happened to be living on Sandy Key with Pete for the last few weeks. They were putting the finishing touches on a new dock and a compressor building on the little island. Eddie was one of the worker bees of our group. He worked in the background; not distinguishing him particularly, but never causing any trouble. For the last several days, he had represented half the population of the island. I knew that the two of them had been working on improving the hooch to live in also. I doubted they had any intentions of returning to live on Utila. They were at their best alone, and we were happy to let them build an off island base, complete with scuba infrastructure, docking facilities and shelter.

Sandy Key was about fifteen hundred feet by seven hundred feet and almost perfectly rectangular. The surface of this coral outcropping was covered in fine white sand, but there was no beach. In fact, the key did not have any slope of land to meet the water's edge. It appeared to have been thrust out of the ocean. The island was little more than a sudden chunk of exposed coral. It surprised me that it actually supported hundreds of palm trees. I suppose that life will always find a way.

Our attention was always drawn to the fact that this key was entirely surrounded by hundreds of feet of very shallow coral reef in every direction but one. The western end of the key could be approached through a hundred foot wide surge channel that was about two fathoms deep. I was reviewing these few facts, I knew, because I was entertaining the idea of mounting a rescue operation. Duane was standing near me at the back of the cookhouse. He was his usual taciturn, quiet self, taking in the reactions of all present. My peripheral vision barely caught him turning slightly toward me.

In a low voice he made an observation. "You are being

awfully quiet, especially considering that you never keep your opinions to yourself." And this was quintessential Duane. He had taken stock of the entire room and had focused on my quiet reverie.

I knew it would not escape his attention that I was studying my tanned, muddy feet, purposefully not looking directly at him. I then spoke softly to my feet, "I was just thinking about Pete and Eddie." God, I hated to be seen as caring and concerned.

I know , kid, that's just what I was thinking too," he responded. "You dropped Eddie and some supplies out there with the *Salva Vida* a couple of weeks ago, didn't you? They don't even have a boat, so their predicament is all your fault, right? Don't worry, I won't tell anybody that a Fathomer is actually thinking about the welfare of another human being. That's the kind of stuff that could turn this place into a convent."

"Yeah, funny how we are all wrapped up in ourselves around here, isn't it?" I asked. "I mean, everybody here is part of the team, but I always get the feeling that if any of us really strikes gold out there, the rest of us will never know about it."

"There are more than a few hidden agendas lurking around this island, I'll give you that," Duane responded, "but I don't think that many here are willing to turn their backs on the others if they are in real trouble."

"You're thinking that Pete and Eddie could be swept off that rock if this blow gets really serious, aren't you?" Duane probed.

"Yeah," I said, looking directly at him, "and I told Pete that I would check up on them every few days or so, and I haven't been back since."

"Okay, we'll chalk this one up to guilt," Duane said, obviously thinking about going with me. "That way we won't be seen as two crazy, altruistic rescuers; just two crazy rescuers. So what boat should we take, Captain? There is no way the *Salva Vida* can get up that narrow channel in this wind."

"Okay, old man, you are crew," I said while turning and heading out the door into the rain. Getting wet meant nothing to me. I had been wearing nothing but my infamous white cut off jeans for months now. Rain meant nothing more to me than fresh water. We barely hunkered down, the wind being at our backs, as we headed for the tool shed on the Fathom Dock. The sharp rain felt more refreshing than bothersome. This would change, and quickly, but ignorance does contain its blissful moments; this being one of them.

Not really running, but definitely making a fast walk of it, we entered the shed and considered our options. It surprised me how much the sky had darkened in the last half hour. The lone window of the eight by ten foot room barely provided enough light for us to see each other.

"I was thinking that we should take the Shark," I half yelled over the din of wind-driven rain hammering the steel roof. "She has the best weather cover of all the smaller boats," I went on. "She has the smallest exposed deck and big scuppers. I don't think she can be swamped."

"That'll work, Tommy," Duane yelled back, "I just wish one of our boats had two engines, though. We could sure use the maneuverability this afternoon."

I at least had the thought of adding one of our ten horsepower Mercury outboards to the transom of the Shark, but with the rain coming down so hard, I figured it would be a good thing to add on another day. I definitely was going to regret my decision to leave things as they were. We gathered some extra ropes, a couple of boat hooks and even some life rings. Pushing the loosely hinged door open against the wind, which was now at least thirty knots strong, was a chore. It slammed closed with such force that more than a few pieces of wood and screws blew into the churning bay, splashing down a long way from the dock. With the strengthening wind nearly blowing us down the dock toward the Shark, I was entertaining the idea of giving up on my mission. Peer pressure being what it is, I pressed on. I half fell onto the deck of the Shark. I stowed my load of gear, and then that which Duane handed down to me, in the forward cabin.

The Shark was a relatively heavy, all wood, twenty foot launch of indeterminate pedigree. I had adopted her, finding her to be unused and in need of many repairs. Weeks ago, I had pulled her up onto a set of wooden rails at the long abandoned boatyard that dated back to at least the turn of the century. In my usual way of creating projects for myself, I had applied fiberglass to her cut up hull, painted her battleship gray and rigged up steering and fuel hardware to accommodate a brand new fifty horsepower Mercury outboard.

I had finished her off with a carefully rendered shark's mouth. It faithfully recreated the look of the Flying Tigers' P-40 Warhawks flown by the American Volunteer Group in China against the Japanese. I considered these men to be the best and the bravest, going to war against the vicious and murdering Japanese even before America was forced to admit that Roosevelt was right about the despots of the time (even though he was a socialist).

I took the usual abuse from my fellow island inmates for the almost presumptive affiliation with the famous group of warriors, but I could tell that they were all pleased with the resurrection of the derelict craft. No one considered taking her out without asking me first. It was a simple formality, but a tacit acknowledgement of my accomplishment. The Shark's most endearing quality was her seaworthiness. She was as slow as cold molasses, but rode steadily through rough seas like an ox slogging through a rice paddy. Her keel was heavy enough, enhanced by my generous and inexpert application of fiberglass, that most of us were convinced that if she were ever to turn turtle, she would continue the roll and make herself upright, especially considering that she was more than half covered with a weather housing. These were the characteristics I wanted to make my way through the heavy seas that were waiting on the other side of the lighthouse.

I started the engine and we motored out into the building storm. With the following sea and wind, making the lighthouse took only fifteen minutes. Turning west around the lighthouse point changed everything for the worse. Instead of surfing down moderate waves, the Shark now confronted five and six foot waves running with a pulse of about three major waves a minute. The work of piloting a boat in heavy seas is a constant left and right spinning of the wheel. I would turn on a northerly heading as the Shark climbed, then make a greater adjustment to the south on the descent. Back and forth for more than an hour was testing my mettle.

Duane, determined and quiet as usual, monitored our progress watching for glimpses of Utila to our right, and holding an arm out in the direction that he reckoned marked the channel between the island and the key. The very shallow reef surrounding Sandy Key was now in sight and it was sobering. The troughs of the waves crashing into the reef exposed the huge brain coral and the jagged, rocky outcroppings. The elk horn coral made the scene even more surrealistic by giving the exposed area the distinct look of a herd of elk standing just beyond a ridge line. I was squinting to see as my face was pelted by the hard hitting pellets that the rain had become. The sun had not appeared this day, but now the light it provided was at best that of late twilight.

I was ruminating on such thoughts when a vicious wave crashed into the starboard side, suddenly rolling the boat on its port side, completely submerging the port rail and throwing the two of us under it, luckily not over it. The engine raced as the propeller was exposed. I crawled across the rolling deck and got a hand on the throttle, pulling it back with such force that the black metal fixture that contained the throttle and shift controls ripped out of the bulkhead entirely. My action was so sudden and rough, because I was thinking only of attempting to keep the engine from over-revving and being destroyed, that the engine throttled back instantly, and quit.

I had been astounded about just how much noise the wind, rain and waves could make. But for some seconds after the engine quit, I heard nothing. I ached for the reassuring sound of the outboard engine, and willed it to life. It was not inclined to acquiesce to my wish. I grabbed at the throttle quadrant. This seemingly simple act became a real trial because I had ripped it from its mount and it was flopping about on the deck of the hard pitching and rolling boat. It was being whipped rapidly back and forth at the end of the cables connecting it to the engine. I trapped it against the starboard rail and pushed the throttle lever forward about an inch. I then held the fixture against my chest and twisted the key to the right. Nothing happened. I looked a few feet aft and saw the reason immediately. The hatch to the battery compartment just forward of the transom was gone, and so was the battery that had never really been secured. It was times like this that made me think of the importance of good workmanship. I should have secured the battery in a snug compartment. I made a mental note to get back to that thought, but not right now.

The very real danger now was that we were quickly being tossed, sideways and rolling, onto the reef around Sandy Key. I heard, and felt, the hull bottom out on the reef with a crunching sound that easily exceeded the crescendo of noise that was the storm. When the boat broke apart, and it surely would, Duane and I would be tossed about and cut to shreds by the millions of razor sharp edges which are the salient recurring features of any reef.

I yelled to Duane, "We are going to have to get restarted.

Right now," I added stupidly.

I yelled over the bedlam that had become our own private storm. It was an event of such ferocity and danger that it perfectly focused my thoughts. I remember clearly that it was impossible for me to imagine that the entire world was not engulfed by this storm. But Duane was gone. I experienced the sickening sense of loss that can only be understood by those who have had a friend violently and suddenly taken away. My sense of loss was instantly overwhelming. And I had not yet had time to consider the implications of my suddenly more precarious situation. Then I heard his voice, composed as always, even when shouted so that it could be heard.

"You don't have to yell, Tommy," he shouted back to me. "I'm right here at the stern."

I looked to my right and saw him wrapped, almost comically, around the outboard engine. "We are going to have to keep her off the reef," I yelled frantically. My mind was racing through the few alternatives available to us. I interpreted Duane's movements after quick consideration. He was trying to get the cover off the engine. Of course, I realized, he had quickly determined that the battery was gone and a manual start of the engine would have to be tried immediately. But I knew that we wouldn't get the chance.

I had spent hundreds of hours diving in and around reefs. They are the most vicious constructs for life and death on earth. Just brushing carelessly against a reef can tear shreds of skin from a body. But there was no time for considering alternatives, of which there were none. I jumped over the port side, knowing I was going to have to push the bow out, and into the wind and waves.

To say that the pain in my feet and legs was excruciating is to understate the truly mind numbing sensation caused by the firing of tens of thousands of nerve synapses, all begging for the attention of a mind suddenly gone mad. I soon enough entered the realm of pain so extreme that it cannot be felt. I was able to see my actions from a perspective removed from danger. I felt as if my body could be controlled by my thoughts, but that it didn't belong to me.

I could hear Duane yelling for someone named Tommy, but I did not associate myself with the name. I was seeing things that were not possible. I was in a field, watching soft clouds drift by an old farmhouse. Birds were singing and a perfectly formed, white, painted fence stretched out to the far horizon. *This must be what it feels like to die.* But the persistent voice reached into my consciousness and pulled me back to reality.

I shouted in what I hoped was a voice of insistence, "I didn't fall overboard Duane. I'm trying to turn the bow into the waves. You're going to have to get on the reef with me to push her into deeper water."

"I can't get on the reef with you, Tommy. I'm not wearing shoes. I'd be torn to shreds."

"I don't have any shoes either, remember? But I can't move her against this wind. You have to get in the water too."

"Oh man. Oh man. Okay." With that I felt the boat rise slightly and it began moving into the deeper water. We had to give the prop some clearance above the reef.

"It's just about clear of the reef now. I can hold it, but not much longer, I think it's going to kill me to stay here very long."

"Yeah, it hurts like hell, doesn't it?" he shouted from around the boat and out of sight. "But keep pushing, Tommy. When we get it into the wind I'll climb back in and try to rope start the engine." I wanted to get back into the boat first, I'll admit here, but I knew that he was the stronger of us and in a better position. I hate being noble; especially when it hurts so much. So I yelled unneeded advice to keep my mind occupied.

"Yeah, it'll probably take a few tries. Don't forget to make sure the switch is on and the throttle needs to be just above idle or it will flood. Hurry," I added unnecessarily.

I had the thought that we were risking our lives. If we died out here no one would ever know how hard we tried. It just seemed so unfair somehow. We were going to die and our story would be lost. These thoughts really do race through a mind in panic. In the same instant that I knew our actions to be hopeless, I committed myself to standing my ground. I looked at the water. Even in the gathering gloom it was easy to see the contrast of the blood against the water.

I felt the weight of the boat change as Duane climbed aboard. I pushed the Shark as hard as I could just behind the grinning red and white mouth. It happened to be a moment of trough in the waves and she swung about smartly. I heard the engine turn through a series of exhaust notes, but no ignition. I tried not to think about the additional minutes needed to hold the Shark in position if Duane had to wrap the cord and pull it through several times. On the second pull the engine roared to life.

"Okay, Tommy, it's in neutral. Get your ass over the stern. Now!"

I scrambled over the transom, noticing that my feet were awash in blood and oddly peppered with black needles. *Oh man, sea urchin spines!* My feet and legs looked like nothing more than bloody pin cushions. The pain of spines breaking off in my feet as I crawled to the wheel was different, but not as bad as being shredded on the reef. Duane had the throttle quadrant clutched against his chest. When he saw me hit the deck, he shifted into forward and gave the engine a careful nudge of power. The thrust from the prop held the pitching boat into the smashing waves, which were driven by a wind that was now absolutely howling.

I walked on my knees to the wheel, trying to keep my feet from touching the deck. I steered the Shark directly into the wind and waves, gradually putting distance between us and the reef.

In a few minutes, I was able to resume the back and forth steering motions that were necessary to negotiate the confused sea. I needed to quarter slightly to the left as the boat climbed a wave, then turn in the opposite direction to quarter down the backside of the wave. A head-on approach would have caused the boat to virtually stall at the peak of each wave. It is possible to actually take one step forward and two steps back if you do it wrong.

I worked my way around the western end of Sandy Key and saw the narrow channel that led to the newly completed dock. Duane had taken a seated position next to me, his back against the bulkhead of the weather housing and facing the stern. I reached under the panel and found the canned fog horn. Every boat in the expedition had one. It could be held underwater to signal divers. I used it to get the attention of Pete or Eddie.

Duane held the detached throttle mechanism against his chest and worked the power, expertly shifting between forward and reverse as we made the dock where Pete and Eddie were waiting with mooring lines. Eddie was a loner, but a seaman of some ability. He soon had the Shark secured with mooring and spring lines in such a way that it could ride up and down between the outposts and the dock, hitting neither.

Pete was a giant of a man, but a gentle giant. I figured his weight to easily double mine, but it was not muscle. He was about to use his six foot three frame and weight to its best advantage. He took stock of our shredded feet and the blood flowing with the water across the deck and out the scuppers. He climbed down into the pitching Shark and took hold of my upper shoulders. I tried to wave him off. "You need to help Duane first, Pete." I looked over at Duane and gave him what remained in me in the way of a grin. "He's a lot older."

"Get Tommy out first, Pete. He's hurt a lot worse than I am. I think he might bleed to death," Duane shouted directly into his left ear to stop him in his tracks.

Pete looked over at me. I suddenly felt myself sink into a deep well. Pete was receding into the tunnel above me. Later, I was told that Pete picked me up in a perfect fireman's carry and climbed out of the Shark as if I were no more than a sack of flour. The wind and rain hit me hard. It brought me back again. I felt Pete duck into the wind and rain as he made his way toward the end of the slippery, windblown dock. With Eddie's support, Duane gingerly made his way after us. I was stunned to find myself at the foot of a shuttered, sturdy little house, nicely anchored on concrete pilings, and obviously wedged between several palm trees for added support.

With Pete still carrying me, we entered a brightly lit room that looked like nothing more than a library with a nod toward being a bedroom. Platforms were hinged into the walls, obviously to be used as beds, and several kerosene lanterns were hanging from the overhead. Pete was already tearing open a medical kit and looking at the curved needles with a practiced eye.

My first words, once having attained this surprising sanctuary on the far edges of nowhere, displayed the heredity that had earned my family the sign of the cringing chicken on its coat of arms. "No, no, Pete, no needles. I think we can just butterfly some of my cuts closed and I'll be fine," I whined.

Pete had a voice that matched his size with the depth of its bass. "You just hold as many of the cuts closed as you can, Eddie," indicating Duane's legs. I'll sew up the biggest cuts on Tommy, first. He looks like he got the worst of it. Nice day for a boat ride," he continued. "What the hell are you guys doing out here anyway? The barometer has been dropping like a rock and the wind speed is at least fifty knots, and we've seen gusts almost to seventy so far." He was looking over my shoulder. I had found that with no weight on my feet, I was almost able to speak like a human being. I turned to look and saw that these two had a veritable weather station built into their quarters. An anemometer, thermometer and barometer were neatly attached to a hand carved board hanging just over my right shoulder.

I looked first to Eddie, who was listening without comment, then at Pete, and said sheepishly, "We came out here to rescue you guys." With that I grinned, grimaced and shifted my feet as I wrapped them tightly with pieces of sailcloth that were folded next to me.

"Yeah... well, you can rescue us as soon as you stop bleeding all over our new floor," Pete remarked, grimacing in empathy.

I looked at him for several beats, felt a wave of giddiness overtaking me, and replied, "I'll be okay, Pete. It's just a flesh wound." We laughed like madmen. Stress will do that, I was learning.

Complete darkness took the island in the next hour. Pete sewed up the major cuts on our legs and feet, which hurt like hell I might add. The next time you get the opportunity to drive a thick needle through your skin, do so about fifty times and you will have some empathy for our plights. Duane was entirely conscious during the whole episode and didn't complain. I took up the slack and commented on each penetration of the needle.

When our limbs were repaired enough that we had stopped bleeding all over the new floor, I fell into a stupor that seemingly kept me suspended between consciousness and oblivion. I watched as if an observer in a dream while Pete and Eddie moved about the small cabin. The tropical storm swept by our enclave, tearing at the well-crafted siding to no effect. The rain hammered at the steel sheeting of the roof, making conversation difficult. But the noise had a way of deadening the pain. It is simply a fact. The unceasing staccato of wind-driven rain distracted my mind enough to dull my senses.

Sometime after midnight, after sleeping very hard, we ate

lobster, conch fritters and drank some warm beer. I still think back on that meal as being one of the best I have ever eaten. Duane and I marveled at the comfortable surroundings that Pete and Eddie had crafted. We again found some sleep as the storm began to subside in the wee hours of the morning.

Up at mid-morning, I was in some pain and barely able to walk. Duane was in only slightly better shape, but we both knew that we were going to heal. Pete was so overwhelmed by the thought of our risking our lives to help him, albeit unnecessarily and entirely without effect, that he made the trip back to Utila with us.

Hobbling and walking down to the new dock, we were pleasantly surprised to see that both it and the Shark were in fine shape. Eddie's mooring had been expert and the Shark was gently riding back and forth on her lines, still not touching the out pilings or the dock. It was a perfect job done under perfectly awful conditions. I was in the mood to bestow some honors and benefits. Being a little giddy from having survived the ordeal, I performed a small rite. Eddie had elected to stay on the key, finish off the conch fritters and make what amazingly few repairs were needed to restore the sturdy little house to good condition. I turned my attention to Pete before any of us embarked.

"If you would be so good as to give me your full attention, Mister England," I said in my deepest voice, "I should like to transfer responsibility for our upcoming voyage to one most worthy." It was supposed to funny, but like so many of my efforts at humor, it was just stupid. It was enough.

"By the power vested in me by no one in particular," I intoned in mock solemnity, "I am pleased to anoint you as captain *pro tem* of the Good Ship *Shark*."

Pete kneeled before me as I spoke and I completed the ceremony by tapping him on each shoulder as if he had just been knighted.

"I accept your charge with humbleness and gratitude, Captain," Pete said in his inimitably deep bass, "I won't let you down."

"Unless we sink on the way to Utila Town," I responded, "there is no way you can." Even Duane, always serious, had to laugh at our impromptu ceremony. Maybe it was funny, now that I think back on the moment.

We boarded the *Shark*, and Pete did a fine job of motoring us back to the main island. When the rest of the group saw the condition of Duane and me, a discussion ensued that the pool should be invalidated. At least that was the general consensus of opinion by those who had bet against our return. Since we had been forced to abandon ship, their argument was that the trip should be logged as at least a sinking with certain salvage rights being acknowledged.

It has always been thus; where groups of men gather, living in too close proximity, and essentially thrown together in an uncertain quest. Seriousness is not to be tolerated. *Gallows and ribald humors only need apply.*

Pete was astounded at the flippant response of his fellow Fathomers to our ordeal. Since he was much given to drama and theatrics, he told a story of heroics and resourcefulness making certain that every member of Fathom knew of our sacrifice. The pool as to whether or not we had sunk was invalidated by general agreement and many questions about our mission ensued. The attention given Duane and me was more than a little embarrassing for me. Duane went out of his way to heap praise upon my performance in the storm.

"Gentlemen, this skinny kid is just about the craziest son-of-a-bitch on the island," Duane said. "If he hadn't jumped overboard when he did, and kept the *Shark* off the reef… well, we wouldn't have been around to let Pete practice his sewing."

"Geez, Duane," I protested, "You were there too. And if you hadn't gotten the engine restarted, that I killed, we wouldn't have had to jump onto the reef in the first place."

Duane shook his head, looking for all the world like an old lion regarding an upstart cub. "You just don't get it do you, kid?"

I have never been able to accept compliments and I did my best to deny anything quite as extraordinary as the picture Duane painted.

Chapter Fifteen

Poltergeist

On one sweltering, humid afternoon in June, I abandoned any real or imagined duties and headed into the jungle north of Utila Town. I enjoyed watching the iguanas and tropical birds. I was particularly interested in finding an anaconda or boa constrictor, I didn't know which type was reputed to live in the jungle, but I wanted to see one in the wild. I never found one of the giant snakes, but I enjoyed the hunt. I was beginning to feel at home with the jungle. Six to eight foot diameter spider webs, reptiles from snakes to frogs, including a few species of vicious looking snapping turtles and scurrying rodents were common and fascinating to me.

After a few hours of my personal safari, I turned to the south and headed for Utila Town. It would be very difficult to get lost on an island only three miles deep, but I had no desire to get caught anywhere in the jungle at twilight or later. You don't know the meaning of the word "spooky" until you have been in a jungle at night. It was not difficult to sympathize with the superstitions of the islanders. Night sounds and sights can be chilling in the primitive and sometimes dangerous surroundings of dense foliage and interminable marshes, complete with water snakes and large snapping turtles.

Fending off the darkness was what drove the efforts of the islanders to install a generator and run the wiring past every building in Utila Town. Electrical power to the island was provided by a diesel-powered generator which was usually started at four in the afternoon and shut down around eleven o'clock. From my first day on the island, I had been impressed and intrigued by the idea of a self-contained community. My background had prepared me to a certain extent for what could be considered an almost primitive lifestyle. My childhood home in Indiana was updated with an indoor toilet only ten years

before, and even that was nothing more than a water closet. What was a closet had been magically transformed into an indoor latrine. There was no room, or plan, to install a sink, let alone a shower or bathtub.

But I had long since moved into more modern digs. I was used to electricity, running water, heating systems and even window mounted air conditioning. To the people of Utila, I may as well have been from another planet possessing superior technology. I spent several hours a week loitering around the few stores and eating establishments, talking about such wonders and generally playing the part of "big man on campus." In rare moments of introspection, I realized that I was feeding my ego more than I was enlightening the masses, as it were.

I finally met the person who took care of the generator. His name was

Gustavo. We met one afternoon at the ice cream shack. Hand cranked mango ice cream was its specialty. I often made my way to the shack which was on one of the few side streets of Utila Town. One lempira bought two triple-scoop servings of the best ice cream. I was notorious for sharing the bounty from my high paying job as a Fathom employee. After all, I made about one hundred dollars a week. Still, I sometimes sneaked in from the edge of the jungle if I didn't want to be buying ice cream for handfuls of kids who had learned to watch for my visits. Being without my usual retinue of young friends allowed me the chance to talk with Gustavo.

He invited me to accompany him to the generator building to show me the operation. Gustavo was probably in his fifties and quite proud of being Electrical Man, as he was called. I had some suggestions to clean up the distribution board and committed some of Fathom's materials to the effort. I had no authority to give away anything that belonged to Fathom, but I was never one to worry about such distinctions. Gustavo spoke in the usual Utila dialect of English that had been morphed into its present form over the last few centuries. Many of the people claim to be descendants of Sir Henry Morgan, the seventeenth century privateer, who was known to have lived on Utila. What must be made clear is that Morgan was not a pirate. He had been issued a paper by the English governor of Jamaica which empowered him to fight the Spaniards on behalf of England. His pay, was, in effect, what he managed to steal from Spain.

Gustavo was surprised that he enjoyed my company. "You are an American," he exclaimed. "Yet you work to make my system better? I am forced to say that I must apologize for the things I have said about your people." I had heard some Fathomers say that we were resented by the islanders, but I had not seen any indication, other than some furtive whispers and pointing in my direction.

"Don't worry about it, Gustavo," I replied." We make comments that are uncalled for too. What do you say we meet back here in the morning when the generator is down? We can get started on repairing Honduran-

American relations by going over to the Bucket of Blood and eating some conch fritters. I am happy to pay if that doesn't upset you."

"Oh yes," Gustavo responded with a wide grin, "the rich American?"

He looked at my shorts and tennis shoes, with some dirty gauze wrapped well above my ankles. My cuts were healing well, but I was weeks away from being barefooted again. "You will not be offended if I state that you do not look so rich to me?"

"It is just a disguise. The money is of no importance," I added in the same almost formal way that he had of speaking. I have noticed over the years that I tended to try to adopt the accents of people with whom I spend much time. It is a silly and probably offensive habit. But it didn't bother

Gustavo, who had no way of knowing what kind of English an American generally spoke.

The generator building was near the end of Main Street, almost to the airport. The muffled noise of the engine and the whine of the generator itself were usually blown away from the town by the prevailing northwesterly wind. It was a good location and it had been Gustavo's idea. It was good planning and I told him so.

The Bucket of Blood was one of two modest sit-down restaurants that also poured both brands of beer well into the evening hours. The other nightclub was The Hernia, but it lacked the ambience afforded the Bucket by a jukebox that could play I Can See Clearly Now and Did You Ever See the Rain. Fathom polling had recently come down on the side of "I Can See

Clearly Now" as being the next national anthem of Honduras. I never heard any other songs emanating from that ugly, nondescript jukebox. Conventional wisdom held that it was brought over to the New World on

Columbus' second voyage; the two 45' s ostensibly not having been installed until well into the twentieth century.

We ate enough conch fritters to sicken a normal human being. I was not worried, I was far from normal. Gustavo and I talked, insulted each other, and descended into conspiratorial gossip the way old friends do. I felt a companionship with him that I cannot explain. It was a good evening for intra-American relations. As I will explain later, it was a friendship that was going to benefit me in a way no one could have foretold.

Some Fathomers joined us and quite a lot of beer was consumed. The casual observer could be excused for assuming that the group was populated with a high concentration of heavy drinkers. With tongue firmly planted in cheek, I can reveal now that our greatest concern was to make at least a modest contribution to the Honduran economy. This was serious work. The entire Central American economy had recently been decimated by the Soccer War. Around eleven o'clock, Gustavo bade us goodbye. We knew that soon the lights would dim, then extinguish completely. My alcohol intake this evening was not excessive and I had no problems walking along the left side of Main Street.

I was in an ebullient mood, a condition not uncommon to most who have just had an evening of food, beer and conviviality. I also had a walking companion. He was only twelve feet away and equally near the curb on his side of the street as I was to mine. I tried to strike up a conversation. "So were you at the Bucket or the Hernia?" I asked reasonably. He kept his head down and said nothing. It was not as if anyone not at one of the two nightspots would have any other reason to be out making his way down a moonlit street in Utila Town. But if this person were one of ours, he was seemingly more obstinate than most. I could not place him. By now I had been around all the Fathom people several times. It was possible that this was a new arrival, a visitor even.

People sometimes flew out to our island on one of the Sahsa Airlines DC-3's. The frequency of such flights to our little airstrip surprised me. The visitors were generally tourists who had been visiting Honduras and had heard about the expedition. They would arrive on the island expecting some kind of resort atmosphere. They were universally disappointed when confronted with our egocentric activities. But some of the more outgoing among us would usually take the opportunities to make a few dives with them and strip them of as much of their money as possible. A simple reason for this guy's dour mood, I thought.

"Could this be a prettier night?" Still no response, unless I counted an even more hang down tilt to his head. This was not a happy person. I felt a sudden chill. Utila was not known for violent crime, but I could not help wondering what was wrong with this guy. A person giving no response to a friendly salutation becomes a potential threat. I had moved my knife sheath to the belt of my jean shorts when I left for my little jungle jaunt many hours earlier. I automatically moved my right hand to rest it upon the hilt. I made an effort to observe him with my peripheral vision so as not to appear too interested. I watched him as he matched my steps. I slowed to an almost uncomfortably slow pace, hoping to let him walk on, but he also slowed. I casually flipped up the rubber loop that locked the knife into the sheath. I thought of the old piece of advice usually given as a jest. Never bring a knife to a gunfight.

Approaching the park, we were surrounded by familiar buildings, Fathom House, the Bahia Lodge and the good old cookhouse. At least six of our people slept in the cookhouse. I knew that this guy would either split off to the cookhouse on his side of the street, or more likely cross to the left, where I intended to make certain that he stayed in front of me as he headed for the front door of the Lodge.

He did neither. He continued westbound, as I was doing. This was ominous. Henry and I were the only non-islanders who lived west of the Bahia Lodge. I wanted to run back to the cookhouse and wake someone. What would I say; I was frightened by someone who wouldn't talk to me? The thought of that embarrassing scenario kept me plodding on. It also occurred to me that there was no way that I could run. My feet and ankles contained dozens of fishing line sutures surrounded by abused flesh. The spines that had broken off into my feet were still being absorbed, and there were scores of them under my skin. My gait was entertaining to watch as I tried to favor the most troublesome muscles.

To my credit, I thought of my young roommate, Henry. He was probably asleep in our hooch. I was running through possible scenarios quite rapidly. We reveled in our remoteness, massaging our egos by bragging about the proximity of the jungle, making us latter day Tarzans. I wanted to know something about this guy and where he thought he was going, late at night and without benefit of so much as a flashlight. There were only Islanders' dwellings ahead of us; beyond that was jungle and nobody went into the jungle at night. We reached the end of the curbed section of Main Street, still matched in speed as if we were marching, although I will admit that my gait was slightly minced.

I had a thought of our two spearguns and where exactly they were hanging on the wall of the hooch. I even reviewed what I knew about

speargun ballistics when fired out of the water. Years ago I had stupidly and experimentally fired a three-rubber speargun on land, aiming at a fifty-five gallon drum. The shaft had jumped up some two feet vertically while covering only about four feet horizontally. Worse than missing the drum was what happened when the rising shaft came to the end of its bungeed tether. It hit the end of the tether and stretched the integral rubber bungee to its limit. Then the shaft headed straight back for its anchor, the speargun and me. I had jumped like a madman and let go of the speargun. The shaft slapped the side of my head on its return. Only luck kept it from penetrating my face.

I was running that old escapade through my mind and pulled up short. When I stopped, he stopped. Worse, he kept his head down, evidently looking at the side of the narrowing street, because he was still looking slightly to his right. I likened his standing there to that of a horse, waiting for its master to make the next move. I had a sudden inspiration. I would kill him.

These thoughts took only seconds and I knew that I would have to cut the tether either before or after locking the rubbers onto the shaft. Then I would have to fire very close to him and even then aim quite low if the distance were more than a couple of feet. The James Bond scenes of people being shot from several yards away with a speargun out of the water were ridiculous. The rubbers pushing forward from notches in the top of the shaft guaranteed the jump.

I decided to give communication one more try. "This is where I get off," I said with a casualness that was entirely out of step with the level of tension I had achieved in the last ten minutes. What happened next cuts to my marrow even decades later. The man, whom I had estimated to be about six feet tall and stocky enough to weigh at least 220 pounds, stopped when I did and turned toward me. I had started a courageous backpedal, intending to keep him in sight, snakes or no snakes. I looked carefully, wanting to be able to identify him the next day and at least dress him down, but in the daylight and in the safety of a crowd. The moonlight shone from over my shoulder directly onto his face. But, he had no face.

His skull was as normal as any other man's, with prominent ears and a full head of hair. I could clearly see the bulge of his Adam's apple, but where there should have been facial features-eyes, nose, and mouth- there were only a few wrinkles of skin. I felt a surge of blood race up the sides of my neck and engorge my ears and the base of my skull. I gripped the handle of my knife in its sheath so hard that it twisted to the horizontal and made my wrist ache. I had the distinct impression that he was studying me, but with what eyes?

He turned his head back to his right and the west, leaving a bold profile in the moonlight. Where I should have clearly seen the outline of a nose and some brow structure, I saw nothing more than the ridges from a few wrinkles. He then squared his body with the direction his skull had taken and walked carefully along the narrowing road that continued into the fringe of the jungle. As he did so, he reached some strands of the overhanging canopy of moss and branches. But I could still see the outline of the fronds as though through a barely translucent glass. The branches should have been brushed away by his head and shoulders. Instead of their moving from his passage, his form melted into them, and he was gone.

I mean he dissolved before my eyes and in very bright moonlight. I walked in the direction of his last steps, thought better of it, and made my way down the path to our hooch. I entered, half expecting to see the man standing inside, which would have surely killed me from fright. I called softly to Henry and shook him awake.

"Henry, wake up and I mean wake up now."

He stirred, "What's going on, Tommy, what time is it?" he asked as he came around. I already had a speargun down and was pulling the rubbers into the notches. When I pulled out my knife and cut the shaft tether, I could hear a certain concern in his voice.

"What are you doing?" His voice was almost shrill. I realized how my actions might have been interpreted. I reached for the other speargun. I handed it to him butt first and thought carefully about what I was going to say. "Henry, I was just threatened by somebody I don't recognize. Just trust me on this. Load the gun and grab your sleeping bag. We need to sleep in the Fathom House tonight, or the cookhouse, but we can't stay here.

Henry sat up on his cot while pushing away the mosquito netting. He looked very serious and much older as he studied my flushed face and shaking hands. I was not making very coordinated moves, but his response stunned me.

"You saw the man with no face didn't you?" I raised my head to look at him straight on.

"You've seen him, too?" I croaked.

"Yeah, I have seen him twice actually," Henry said without emotion. "He seems to be some sad lost soul and I know he won't hurt anybody. I didn't want to say anything, because I can hardly believe it myself and I knew that you wouldn't believe it."

"It isn't every full moon or anything like that, but it seems to be only when there is a good moon. Just go to sleep. We won't see him for months now." With that pronouncement, he stretched back out on the cot and pulled the mosquito netting back into place. Then he curled himself into a fetal position, but still facing me. His eyes were wide open.

"Pretty scary the first time, but the second time he seemed glad to see me and even held out a hand, kind of like a wave. Just relax. I won't say anything and in the morning you will think it's pretty funny really.

For the only time in my memory, I could think of nothing to say. I wanted to push my cot closer to Henry's, but that thought alone got me to laughing, at least on the inside. I sat down on my cot, reached down for the speargun and pulled it inside the netting. Henry watched as I made a concession to safety and released the rubbers. I made sure the shaft point was extended past my pillow and was stuck firmly into the rubber safety cap. I hugged the gun like a teddy bear and tried to sleep. Morpheous eventually found me, even huddled under a mosquito net on the far side of nowhere. I cannot remember even dreaming, but this island was really starting to get to me.

Chapter Sixteen

Mutiny

As captain of the good ship *Salva Vida*, it was my honor, forced upon me by the insistence of the usual belligerents, to make the boat ready for Sunday morning departures. People who work hard usually play hard. People who don't work hard, play even harder, probably secure in the knowledge that they have more time to recuperate, I thought. As loose as the organization was, those who worked during the week, really did work during the week. The assets of the expedition were generally used to advance the goals of the expedition. If you were not working you did not use Fathom assets to play. This was necessary and accepted by us all as a tacit acceptance of a semblance of rules that kept us from descending into complete anarchy. But we all needed to get away from the serious work of hunting and building.

Thus it was that on Sundays, whoever showed up at the dock and wanted to ship out for a day trip of diving, sightseeing and catching some sun out on the ocean was welcomed aboard. I never hesitated to press people into service to load air tanks, equipment, food and liquid refreshments, usually rum and Cokes. The expedition was not a democracy. Whoever took charge of a task was generally allowed to run his operation as a benevolent dictator. It was no different on this bright, breezy Sunday in June, 1970, that I was up at dawn and pumping out the bilge, which was always filling with water. I took pride in the condition of the *Salva Vida*, and when so moved, would make a day out of some select project that always left me feeling better about the old boat. On this day, I was looking forward to doing a little painting of some of the trim around the wheel house. It was this slavish devotion to the boat that was going to get my nose broken this day.

Early preparations for our Sunday "picnic" left me with lots of time to walk up to the cookhouse, just a couple of hundred feet from the dock, and have my usual breakfast of green scrambled eggs and sausage. I never ate anything else for breakfast when I was on Utila. Arriving at the cookhouse I was greeted with the usual warm camaraderie for which our group was famous.

"Hey Tommy, did your scow sink at the dock last night?" called Mr. Sleep. I did so enjoy ribbing from a lazy, drug laden, hippie, who only (and I mean only) emerged from his waterbed long enough to take care of bodily functions and to eat. When I consider it now, eating is a bodily function also, but you get my drift.

"Yeah Tommy, how do you know what size lines to use on the *Vida*, anyway. If you use too strong a line, Sergei will have your ass tanned and hung outside the Fathom House when the old girl sinks and pulls a section of the dock down with her. You need to consider a line that will hold her against the weather, but break away when she goes down," suggested another wag.

I acknowledged the comments with my usual grin. In my best Sergei impression, I hammed, "She is good boat, strong like bull. A fine example of the best that the workers' paradise of Cuba has to offer," I responded.

Peals of laughter and more comments from the even lesser wits ensued. I had noticed that some of the low profile people never made comments unless they knew the general mood was established and a safe environment reigned. These barbs were part of a tradition that must go back hundreds of years, wherever bands of men have been thrust together, alone and co-dependent. I knew that these men respected me and what I did for the team. I had earned the insults. But I was learning early in life that many people are socialist, parasitic slugs. These people, like Mr. Sleep, will take any opportunity to denigrate those who work hard, while gladly accepting the benefits accrued to the group.

The cast of this day trip was assembled at the slip of the *Salva Vida* by about 9:30AM. Captain Mike was already on board. I was captain now, but the title of captain is a sobriquet that once earned, was never taken away. Mr. Sleep, whose given name was Wayne, was making a rare appearance this morning as well. The planets must have been aligned in a particularly rare pattern to let a morning light shine down upon this worthless denizen of the water bed. I had been around Mr. Sleep off and on for some three months by this time and had him pegged as an entirely self-centered, arrogant, suck-up. If he thought he could get something from someone, he shamelessly attached himself to that person until he got it. He constantly congratulated himself on imagined accomplishments. I guess he couldn't help it. He was a thorough socialist. What's yours should be mine seemed to be his guiding principle. I had rarely seen him before noon until today.

As usual, Duane, Nick and Jack Crabill, the geologist, were going with us. I was glad to see Pete England, the overweight, pasty white bookworm from Big Springs, Michigan, who could always use a little sun. I worried slightly that he was not going to survive the expedition. I have a way of underestimating the quiet ones. The introspective Ted Waring, who we all assumed was the oldest member of the expedition, was waiting with snorkeling gear and a pole spear. Ted was accompanied by his mysterious friend Craig, who had been in Central America since before the Bay of Pigs fiasco. I had yet to glean his story from the "keepers of odd knowledge society," but it had something to do with that failed invasion.

"So where are we off to, Captain?" Duane asked me with some interest evident in the speed of his speech. He was usually a slow talker and it had not escaped my attention that he was an accomplished diver and a natural leader on the sites.

"I want to head west, make the turn north and anchor just short of the drop off on the north side of the island," I replied, implying that I had given our destination considerable thought. I hadn't.

"I like it," Duane exclaimed, "I haven't been on the north side of this landfill in months. The wave action can be tough out there at times, but not so bad today, I think. Lots of conch and lobster holes for the lazy bastards here. And you, Ted and I can surely scare up some grouper and snapper.

"The north shore it is then," I responded, warming up to my snap judgement in the face of such enthusiasm. I had visions of our returning with hundreds of pounds of excellent seafood. I descended to the engine room, switched on the electrical system that activated the glow plug, let it warm up several seconds and started the engine cranking by holding down a large, black button. While it cranked quickly with no compression I pushed over the compression release handle that allowed the diesel to make compression. The compression is then great enough that it generates heat sufficient to burn the fuel/air mixture trapped on each compression stroke and, *voila* you have ignition. This was basically great stuff.

Climbing up to the pilot house, I yelled, "Cast off you scurvy dogs, and brace those landlubber legs against the acceleration. Ye be warned...arrgh." Laughter and some rather ugly comments relating to my parentage greeted my order and we were on our way.

The *Salva Vida* rounded the harbor point, with its little lighthouse built by Fathom people some years prior to my arrival. I knew that Shawn Evers, some forty years old now and happily married to a fourteen year old island girl named Esperanza, had designed and built the light house. Shawn was one of the very few people we considered to be an actual employee of Fathom Expeditions. He was a carpenter, without whom some of our building projects would have been little more than shanties. He owned a real house, on stilts, near the Fathom House and I sensed that he would never leave the island. It went unspoken that if he showed up in the states with his young wife anytime in the next four years, he would probably go to prison. Outside of the world, we just saw a happy couple of people. Funny how quickly one adapts.

I made the course west and aimed for the twenty fathom natural channel that I knew to lie between the island and the line of small keys south and west of Utila. We passed Ambassador Key, our name for the little island of some twenty acres, upon which Shawn and others were building a cypress and glass house for the American ambassador to Honduras. I turned north to round the western end of Utila, and another turn in about twenty minutes had us heading east across the north end of the island.

The island looked entirely uninhabited on this side, and made me think of centuries past, when people were scarce on all of these islands and danger surely lurked in the thick jungle, reaching as it did to the water's edge. I cruised along the shore tracing a shelf some three hundred yards out, brought the old girl into a turn to the north and into the prevailing wind of about eight knots. Duane and Captain Mike let go the anchor on my command and I allowed the boat to drift back after feeling it hook something solid. When I had what I estimated to be a scope of about twelve feet to one, meaning the ratio of distance from the anchor to its depth, I had Duane secure the anchor line to a forward cleat. Let the good times roll, I thought.

Some of the guys were drinking rum and Cokes, slowly stretching to unlimber, and generally making headway to getting gear donned and adjusted. The stern of the boat was equipped with a wide, deeply offset and sturdy ladder that was reached from the aft deck through a gate. At the bottom of the ladder was a thick, four foot wide dive platform. This was a great boat from which to dive. Someone had thought to construct a section on the platform that held secure scuba gear and gave divers a hand hold when the boat was pitching and rolling against the waves and anchor. Duane, Nick and I selected pole spears and suited up, making certain that we had two dive knives, one sheath strapped to a calf with a smaller one secured to the weight belt webbing crossing the chest. To a diver, a knife is not a weapon, but a tool. One never wanted to be in a position where a knife could not be reached.

The three of us slipped into the water, quickly made final adjustments to straps and moved snorkels into position. We nodded to each other, jackknifed our bodies by bending at the waist while looking to the bottom, some twenty feet below, and gracefully thrust our legs and fins above the surface. The weight of our legs propelled us under the surface without so much as a ripple. We must have looked like dancers, choreographed in our movements. It was the choreography of warriors. We were not out to rape the reef, but to harvest some of the sea's bounty for our sustenance. The three of us had hunted together many times and two of us took positions behind and above the alternating lead diver. As the lead would go for a jack, snapper, hogfish or grouper, the other two would cover the exodus of fish that always resulted. Within an hour, and rarely getting below thirty feet , we had taken some fifteen fish ranging from eight to thirty pounds.

We snorkeled along the surface to the stern of the *Salva Vida* and shrugged out of our gear, tossing it and our catch onto the diving platform. A few of the others were having some success at gathering conch and a few lobsters had already been dispatched. This was not a sportsman's hunt, I thought to myself, the lobster were probably speared. But we ate everything that we took out of the ocean and that was just the way it was.

Nick and I stowed our gear, after rinsing all of it in a five gallon bucket of fresh water, brought just for this purpose. I watched the snorkeling activities for a while and decided to descend to the engine room and check the engine, along with all the hoses and fittings. I always knew how to have a good time in the tropics. By noon, I had tired of my self-imposed banishment to the dungeon and ascended to the top deck, which was actually the roof of the wheel house. I ate a sandwich and drank a Coca-Cola. Cokes really are all over the world and I had learned that it was practically the law to drink Cokes everywhere in Central America.

Being sober when most about you are drunk is an almost surrealistic experience. I was no teetotaler, but I had not yet learned how to drink. I drank only when it was the dominant activity of the group, with virtually nothing else to do at the time. I still found beer to be distasteful, almost bitter, and rum and Cokes left my head spinning within hours. I was driving and didn't want to join the loud few drinking on the main deck. Captain Mike, Jack and the mysterious Craig Morton were yelling obscenities at each other and occasionally falling down as waves of laughter washed over them. I had found my trim paint and was carefully doing some serious touch up work. My tan was complete by this time and it meant nothing to me to be out in the hot sun, something that would likely have killed me three months earlier.

The raucous laughter approaching the pilot house was my first indication that I was going to be drawn into the revelry. I picked up on some comments being made about my working, when this was supposed to be a picnic.

Captain Mike did the initial talking, or yelling as it happened, "Hey Cap'n," he slurred, obviously affected by who knows how many rum and Cokes, "you too good to have a bit of rum with yer mates?" *Uh oh.* This was obviously a rhetorical question. There had to be an agenda swirling in their alcohol-laced minds. But it was more than just the slurred words that got my attention. He was effecting the quintessentially recognizable manner of speech known as pirate talk. "Yer crew would need to be havin' a word with his royal captaincy."

I sat up as Captain Mike, Craig and Jack came crawling over the edge of the deck. They had me mostly surrounded and were grinning around dive knives clenched firmly in their teeth. This was just too corny for words. "We been thinkin' Cap'n," Mike growled around the ten inch blade of his dive knife. "We be not pleased with the conditions on this scow. We have decided to mutiny." I naively took this to mean, at first blush, that they were going to jump ship with the inflatable Zodiac that was secured upside down just forward of my position. Silly me.

Captain Mike caught me up from behind and under the armpits while Craig held each lower leg in surprisingly strong grips. Jack held up an invisible scroll, one hand over the other in a mime reminiscent of a British court clerk, and read off the charges. "Cap'n Beard," he started, "you are charged with gross negligence in the care and feeding of your loyal crew. How do you plead to the first charge?" Before I could say anything he continued in what I took for a Mr. Christian accent as played by Marlon Brando. "Secondly, you have failed your crew by anchoring us off a godforsaken island that appears on no chart. How do you plead to this charge?" he asked again. As before, I was given no chance to respond. He was on a roll. Craig, who was always a little too serious for my liking, grinned like a drunken maniac from his vantage point at my feet. I was being held horizontally and must have looked like a hammock between these two men. I weighed no more than one hundred sixty pounds and both of them were inches taller and well on the north side of two hundred pounds. "Thirdly, you have been found wanting in leadership skills. How do you plead? Never mind, let us have the decision of the tribunal." He stopped at this point, rolled up the invisible scrolled parchment and looked expectantly at the other mutineers.

"Guilty says I," roared Captain Mike.

"Guilty as hell, I say," added Craig.

"Sorry Cap'n," intoned Jack in his Marlon Brando voice, "but I find you guilty of impersonatin' a captain as well." Jack had the most lucid countenance of the three, but he was obviously well-oiled.

"Overboard with him then," yelled Mike. The two giants swung me back and forth and on the count of three, let go of me at the apex of the swing. I remember thinking I had better twist into a shape that would cushion the blow of the water, a good twelve below me. As later related to me by Nick, who had started aft to see what all the yelling was about, if I had stayed horizontal just a little longer, I would have easily cleared the gunwale, the wooden railing surrounding the first deck.

Instead, upon release I twisted around, trying to effect an entry that would avoid a back slapping entry into the ocean. What I achieved was a momentum killing maneuver that left me hanging in space like Wylie Coyote running out of dirt off a cliff. I then started a headfirst dive directly onto the top of the gunwale, which happened to be about three inches of solid old wood that was very unforgiving. My nose apparently took the entire weight of my body hitting the rail, snapping my head back viciously and flipping me into a couple of loose cartwheels before hitting the water in a particularly bad entry.

The three mutineers roared their approval of the whole

thing. Everybody on the boat looked overboard at my face-down body, making its way past the stern due to the action of the wind and waves, as a blood slick grew around my limp body. I would not want anyone to think that we were particularly worried about sharks. We saw and dove around sharks virtually every day. The media frenzy about the danger of sharks in general is the most overblown crap that has ever been foisted on an ignorant public. But sharks are scavengers. We had attracted a few curiosity seekers from the shark community with our previous spearfishing activity.

Of all people, Pete England was the first to react. It was said he just threw his pasty Pillsbury doughboy body into the water. That action seemingly awakened the others, and he was quickly followed by Nick and Duane, who actually reached me first, spinning me face up. They pulled me back to the boat and rolled me onto the dive platform. Apparently that action started me breathing again. Later, we figured that I had stopped breathing because I didn't spit up the first drop of seawater.

I was drowning in my own blood as I came around to some level of consciousness. I kept bringing up clots of blood in alarming quantities. Nick, competent in his Navy first aid, cut up thin strips of cloth from a shirt found below. He reached into my nostrils and pulled my nose from its perch against my right cheek. It didn't hurt at all, the pain was still hours away as I enjoyed the false bliss of shock, but everybody else winced at the sound of cartilage cracking. He then pushed several feet of the thin strips of cloth as far back into my nostrils as he could, even pushing the first sections deeper with a ball point pen. The bleeding slowed, inside as well as outwardly, and he pronounced me fixed. I climbed and crawled my way up to the first deck, stumbled through the companionway to the cabin area and curled up into a fetal sitting position, then passed out.

Duane took command and pronounced the outing over. Even the mutineers were in accord with this decision. They didn't feel any particular remorse, but one just didn't argue with Duane.

The event was to become known as the Great Mutiny and it made me something of a celebrity as even the people I barely knew took stock of my hugely swollen face and great black eyes. Rocky Raccoon was the most common appellation given me by this motley group of wits. Sympathy and understanding of my ordeal were out of the question, save from Jack, who actually suffered a pang of regret for his part in the mutiny. I have never been able to hold a grudge; this was no exception. I considered the entire thing to be just the result of too much rum and even a touch of ancient times.Captain Mike and Craig never mentioned the episode in my presence, much less apologized. This was a tough crowd.

Chapter Seventeen

Jack and Jill

As unsettling as meeting the man with no face was for me at the time, I found that Henry had been right. It is popular to say that time and distance salve all wounds. Time and daylight were sufficient for me. Utila was becoming a mystical place. The island was soon to affect me in a way I would never have expected. She was about to usurp my abilities as a spearfisherman of any particular value to the expedition. I could still kill or capture any underwater creature I decided upon, but I lost my motivation. I fell in love with a fish.

One doesn't have to go far to kill fish, one only has to go underwater. The fish will come. A few days after my moonlight sojourn down Main Street, I decided to spend the day harvesting fish. And that is what I did. There was no sport in killing an animal with no expectation of danger. Gunter and I had some time ago decided the difference between fish living in a dangerous natural environment and our entering that world with weapons were not remotely analogous situations. We knew that we were not sportsmen.

Neither were we sightseers. Donning my mask, fins and snorkel, I took up a shallow position on the reef not more than

100 yards from my hooch. I was in no mood to put up with kicking the fins for hours, knowing full well that the rubbing of the stitches, to say nothing of moving the sea urchin spines around inside my feet, would be more than I could stand. Holding onto a branch of staghorn coral with my left hand, I was able to steady myself enough to semi-float in a seated position. I held the pole spear with my right hand and became part of the reef. At least that was my intent. I had never really thought about it so philosophically before, but that became my objective. For once, I was spearfishing with almost no intent to spear fish. I rode up and down with the gentle wave action, breathing shallowly through the snorkel and viewing the sea life as if through a window. It always felt that way to me. I never felt as if I were a part of the ocean; just an observer.

I watched as the tiniest of animals emerged from hiding. Adjusting to my surroundings so intimately allowed me to notice the slightest movements. Shrimp came out of hiding, clown fish darted around tiny pillars and striped grunts schooled in huge numbers. I became one with the ocean.

It was a revelation for me. Because I was part of the reef, the smallest of the creatures began to seek shelter on my body. Some took refuge under my mask, others hid in the small folds of my cutoffs. Nibbles and brushes against my ears were more difficult to ignore, but I did not move. When the smallest of fish are at ease, the larger fish must sense a relative safety. Larger species of fish visited our area. Squirrel fish, sergeant majors and butterfly fish abounded. I studied the butterfly fish with more than idle curiosity. Ichthyologists have opined that the symmetry of its body, front to back, and its markings, provide for a unique protection. It has a circular black and white tattoo near the tail that mimics the look of the eye on its head. It is said that a predator cannot tell front from back, giving the little fish an added 50% advantage in avoiding being eaten. The predator cannot know which direction it will dart.

I was lost in these kinds of thoughts and observations for hours. I had nothing else to do. It would be difficult to overstate just how startled I was by the intrusion into my little world of two very large fish. My first impression was that they were dolphin fish. Many people are confused by this designation. Contrary to what many people think, the Flipper of television fame is not a fish, and it is sometimes referred to as a bottlenose dolphin. Flipper was is in fact a porpoise, but these were neither.

After their initial pass, it appeared that curiosity got the better of them. I watched as they moved in unison, making a large, sweeping arc to my right. Continuing their turn, they came directly at me, appearing for all the world like fighter aircraft in formation. Streamlined in frontal profile they gave only a hint of their bulk with significant bulges in the middle regions of their bodies. I estimated them to be between 80 and 100 pounds. They swam to me and stopped not more than three feet away. We studied each other in the almost perfect quiet of the underwater world. I remembered that I was spearfishing.

I pushed the shaft in my right hand back while holding the sling in the web of my thumb and forefinger. Thus armed, I could have easily sunk it into either of the fish. I decided that they were of the jack family, something like a tuna or a permit. I waved the shaft within inches of their nostrils and they made a perfectly choreographed turn to my right. This showed their tall nearly flat sides and five foot length nicely. For the first time in my memory, I hesitated, but let go of the shaft nonetheless. It entered near the tail of the lead fish, when I had meant to hit the gill plate of the second.

Not surprisingly, the fish exploded into movement. The spear point detached as soon as pull was applied to the shaft. It was connected to the shaft via a thin steel cable. I was connected to the shaft via a looped cord, the loop being around my right wrist. The fish, which I later identified as a Crevalle Jack, was hardly hurt and he proved to be a powerful swimmer. He dragged me like a horse with a fallen rider caught with a foot in a stirrup.

Time, of course, is relative; it seemed that he pulled me for every bit of fifteen minutes before showing a real sign of tiring. His first powerful pull caused me to be pulled horizontal and streamlined. I offered little resistance, but knew that I would win. When I did win, it surprised me more than I can convey. I found myself in three feet of water, feet hurting, with the Crevalle virtually beached. I kneeled in the water and got some purchase on the fish by grasping around the thin tube shape between the body and the tail fin. I began to drag him out of the water backwards. It was then that I saw his companion. There was no doubt about it; the other fish had followed us on our journey. His (or her, I thought) dorsal fin was well out of the water. My fish offered no resistance, but was making pitiful grunts. I looked at the spear point and cable. Without making a conscious decision, I knew what I had to do. I stood on the shaft of the pole spear and held the detachable point in my left hand. I snapped the retaining ring of the knife sheath from the handle of my dive knife. I turned the blade up and underneath the cable and snatched it upward quickly. With the cable cut, it slipped easily through the wound in the base of the fish's body. I turned Jack upright (what else would you name a fish that was obviously of the jack family?) and pointed him out to sea. I duck walked him into deeper water and steadied him. His mate swam to us and brushed against me as she nudged against Jack. He shrugged as if shaking off a chill. I stood transfixed as the pair moved off, displaying little more than indignant wags of their tails.

I removed my fins and walked out of the water. I carefully made my way down the rocks along the shoreline and returned to my hooch. I left my gear and headed for the Fathom House and its small library. I quickly found a photograph of my friends in a book of fishes. Not really, but you know what I mean.

The next day found me back out on the same shallow reef. As silly as it seems, I wanted to recreate the magic of the previous day. I had not slept even my usual four or five hours. My head had been filled with regret, recrimination and guilt. I sat in the same position, watched as the sea life grew accustomed to my presence, and waited.

I didn't even want to admit to myself what I hoped to find. Of course, I wanted to find Jack and Jill (what else could I name Jack's companion?). For the second time in two days, and for that matter my life, I calmly rested in the water and paid real attention to my surroundings. Things happened faster this time. I held a muslin bag filled with lobster and shrimp. The natural dissolution of the fish meats created a chum cloud, attracting thousands of fish and unnamable sea creatures to the particles. And then they appeared. At the limit of the underwater visibility were the tall, thin shapes of my new acquaintances. The bulges of their bellies further confirmed their identities. I was incredulous, but expectant, as I watched their approach. It was circuitous, but inevitable.

As they neared, I pulled loose the drawstring on my goody bag. I withdrew several pieces of the lobster and shrimp and floated them in the water in front of me. A feeding frenzy of small fish engulfed me. The curtain of fish was drawn only by the presence of Jack and Jill, who once again idled to a stop directly in front of me. I softly floated large chunks of lobster and whole shrimp. Like living vacuum cleaners, they inhaled the food. I moved methodically and without threat, I hoped. I wondered at their trust.

As I watched, I felt the ocean. I was not viewing through a window now. I felt Jack and Jill as they swam around me, brushing against my body to get the scent and feel of me. I had some difficulty with my emotions. I could see the wound on Jack too clearly. The exit side was ripped and shredded. Strands of white meat co-mingled with remnants of torn skin. I didn't delude myself with the idea that the fish were giving me a great deal of thought. I did think that my pointing Jack back out to sea had made an impression. I don't even care if I am wrong. What I can tell you is that over the next several months I visited with Jack and Jill every day that I could, which was every day. I know enough about Pavlovian conditioning to make astute arguments against my observations. But these two fish knew me and looked forward to my visits every bit as much as any pet with whom I have shared my life.

I found that Jack and Jill were particularly partial to fresh lobster. If bits of fish flesh more than a few hours old were offered, they would suck the pieces in, and then flush them back out at me. We became such friends that I would cut two and three inch pieces of lobster just so that I could hold the ends in my mouth to entice them. I found that lobster had a much longer shelf life than fish. Not only could they discern the difference between fish and lobster, but they would push each other, and me, out of the way to take the strips of lobster from my lips. It became habitual, and expected, that they would hit me hard enough to knock my mask askew. I regularly would reach out to them and slide my hand across their dorsal fins. They grew so accustomed to the gesture that they would relax the muscles of the spines, allowing them to lie down ahead of the stroke of my hand.

Years later I read a serious study about fish behavior that froze me to my seat. The author of the article held forth in all seriousness that many species of fish were given to behaviors that suggested more social adaptation than could be explained by simple mating behavior. She wrote that the Crevalle Jack in particular appeared to mate for life. When one was killed, the other was often observed to return to the location of its mate's disappearance, circling the area for days, even weeks. The behavior that I knew to be fact was validated. Crevalle Jack lived in pairs. For me, the recognition of personality in fish was devastating. I knew that my days as a serious spearfisherman were being threatened by this intrusion of compassion.

I was such a wimp.

Chapter Eighteen

Shark

The Sunday after I met Jack and Jill, I arose early as usual and made preparations for a day of picnicking on the water. I made the usual checks of the *Salva Vida*. I had so much time that I even walked down to the ice house, trailing our old Radio Flyer wagon, and brought back two 50 pound blocks of ice. I broke them into enough pieces with my dive knife that I was able to half fill two coolers. Wanting to be a good host and especially wanting to keep busy, I filled both to the brim with beers.

The cookhouse was next on my list. I banged around while I cleared out the debris of the previous night's drinking and card playing. I wanted to waken all of the troops within. One of my many faults is that when I am ready to go, I want everybody to be ready to go. I banged pots around and fumbled with the big coffee urn. I drank coffee because all the men drank coffee and I was one of the men. It was impossible for me to learn the right way to make coffee because I had no idea what good coffee tasted like. I did succeed in waking people.

"Hey Tommy," someone growled from the main room, "stay where you are. When I wake up I am going to come in there and kick your scrawny ass around for my morning exercise."

"It'll be too late," Captain Mike's unmistakable Missouri drawl intoned, "he'll be dead by then. But you can help me break him into smaller pieces and bring the gruel pot up to speed."

"Yeah, good idea," the first voice responded. "It would be a surf and turf gruel. I like the sound of that already."

While the wits of complaint tried to one-up each other with *bon mots*, I left the kitchen through the back door, carrying a flour sack. It contained several pounds of Rosie's gruel. I had rolled the bag down to near the bottom and sunk it in the large pot. Using it as a sieve, I strained out at least half the chunks of sea food surprise. My inspiration had come while I was fumbling around with the coffee urn. If Jack and Jill would eat this stuff, I could dispose of some of the toxic waste while making Rosie think that "her men's" were finally eating responsibly. And that was the way things transpired. Rosie actually started cooking better from this day onward, spurred on by the belief that the spoiled Americans were not wasting any part of the fish.

We had talked about throwing out some gruel every day, but had decided that it would be too obvious when the iguana and trees began to die off. One of our guys, Shawn, was a real life Vietnam deserter. He had deserted during an R and R trip to Australia. It was his feeling that our spreading the gruel around the island would bring UN environmental watchdogs down on us. He joked that he didn't want any government people finding him. *Little did he know.*

I walked westward toward our hooch. I retrieved my dive gear and entered the water just out from my seaside home. I stretched out in the few feet of water and began making clicking sounds. I was hoping to train my new acquaintances to listen for the clicks. When Jack and Jill arrived I rolled back the bag. A rich cloud of fish parts spread out before me. Jack and Jill inhaled the larger pieces and hundreds of smaller fish and creatures took care of the rest. I touched Jack with no small regret, thinking that I would make it up to him and his mate. I then kicked off to the east, watching the fish, lobster and a host of other sea floor denizens going about their early morning lives. I left the water at the stern of the *Salva Vida*.

Every day went pretty much this way. Spur of the moment activities, entering and leaving the water at will, and drying out while starting other activities were the norm. I rarely saw anyone with so much as a towel. You sure weren't going to stay wet long, not with the Honduran sun and heat. I returned to the cookhouse via the Fathom dock, hoping to confuse the conspirators of my doom.

My disruption of an hour ago was long forgotten. Rosie was frying eggs and meats, people were milling around, and talk about a day of recreation was the salient recurring theme of the breakfast hour.

More people than usual showed up for the *Salva Vida* Sunday Soiree, as Jack had dubbed it some weeks before. Even Mr. Sleep, Wayne, the dope smoker who rarely left his water bed before noon, was in attendance. With gear stowed, rum and Cokes already in the hands of most, I started the Russian diesel engine and headed to the east after clearing the harbor. I had identified a large underwater plain of white sand bottom, broken by occasional oases of sea grasses and hundreds of holes. The holes would contain lobster and the grassy area would likely be hiding spots for many conches. Reaching the plain, I swung the Salva Vida into a gentle turn to port and made a little seaway up the wind line. I shifted into neutral, allowed the boat to drift back from the push of the modest breeze and gave the command to drop anchor. Nick let go the line from the belaying cleat and we were soon hooked.

Being ever mindful of the recent mutiny, I weighed my

words carefully. "Okay you clowns, the bow, that's the pointy end for the nautically impaired, is pointing directly at the airport reef and all those surge channels. Directly beneath us is fifty feet of water, interrupted by sand and grass. When you are buzzed enough to consider diving, you are on your own. I have all of you on the manifest and I will make some effort not to leave anybody this afternoon, but not much," I added. Catcalls and chunks of precious ice were quickly tossed my way. We were such an amicable group.

I know all the recriminations and warnings that leap to mind in the average modern diver. Just as we hadn't taken to flotation devices in this, the Bronze Age of diving, neither did many of us give a whit about those who wanted to drink and dive. Our group included people who would likely consider diving sober an act of desperation.

"One more thing," I called out to those who cared to listen, "If anyone casts a fishing line, it will be found trailing off the stern. Anybody catching a diver will be on his own when it comes to the gutting and filleting; unless it is Sergei or Richard, and then I will help." Some laughter drifted up to me from the deck. The slightest chuckle from this group indicated a hit.

We had a good day. A few snapper and grouper were taken, many lobster and conch as well. I had installed a propane stove in the galley and it held a large pot, filled with boiling sea water. I didn't hesitate to take lobster, but I could not stand to throw a live animal in a pot of boiling water. Like any good hypocrite, I would let others do the killing, then eat the spoils.

It was a good several hours of eating, drinking and lying about. Life was good. Nothing could go wrong on such a beautiful day. I was actually asleep when I was startled into consciousness by a hoarse shout.

"Shark!"

Everyone's attention was focused on this word. We saw

shark on just about every dive. Not one of us was particularly concerned about sharks being in the vicinity of any dive. All the self-aggrandizement, spewed by people wanting to make themselves out as heroes by creating tales of personal courage in the face of shark attacks, made me want to gag. I was repelled by the image of some buffoon, shooting or butchering a shark for the amusement of his friends and admirers. I had long ago considered some revenge on behalf of the shark population. But this was different.

Not one of us would consider yelling a shark warning without a real threat being attached. The abuse to be heaped upon such a person would be life threatening. I snapped to a sitting position and looked out upon the water from my lofty perch atop the wheelhouse. About fifty yards out, on our starboard side, I saw the gray hair and yellow mask of Ted Waring. The water was churning around him. As I watched, I saw the body and dorsal fin of a shark break the surface, then another.

Incredibly, Ted yelled the word again, "Shark!"

I leapt to my feet and clambered down one of the stanchions holding the roof over the wheelhouse. Heads were popping up on deck. Yelling and pointing was the order of the moment. The comments were almost surreal.

"Hey, look at that, some sharks are after Ted."

"Yeah, man did you see that? His mouth was wide open. You could see the gum line for about a foot. Ted is history man."

I caught glimpses of at least eight people standing on the fore deck, pointing and yelling. I snatched my pole spear and snorkel gear from the bulkhead pegs just inside the wheel house. Taking only seconds to snap the heel straps of the fins in place, I caught sight of Mr. Sleep climbing over the transom, with mask, fins and snorkel in place.

"Wayne," I yelled, even though he was not ten feet away, "Ted is being attacked by sharks. Over there." I held out my pole spear at arm's length while pulling my mask and snorkel down into position over my head with my free left hand.

"Why do you think I'm out of the water?" Wayne responded. For the second time in my life, I was completely at a loss for words. What an asshole I thought, probably too doped up to be of any use anyway. Climbing onto the gunwale, I felt someone else's weight making the big old boat list a little more. Next to me was Gunter, my spearfishing companion from the early days on the island.

As if we had rehearsed our moves, we both grabbed our masks, keeping our pole spears pointed upward, and stepped off the boat, keeping our fins slightly in tandem. As our legs hit the water we each kicked in a powerful scissors motion. The immediate kick allowed us to stay at the surface. In unison we put our faces down and kicked smoothly and hard, making certain to keep our fins completely underwater. We wasted no energy flailing at the surface.

Within seconds, looking ahead and down through the clear water, we both saw sharks. These were not the curious and lazy sharks that I had seen hundreds of times before. These sharks had arched backs and were twisting their bodies back and forth, looking for all the world like an angry pack of hyenas, bent on getting some of the kill, while making certain that the others did not. I later realized that this infighting was what saved Ted. Like most of us, Ted had gone off by himself. I had weeks ago decided that Ted was the oldest guy in the expedition. He was every bit of fifty years old. He was still pretty nimble I noticed from my vantage point of youth and immortality.

The sharks were a very dark gray/green, with splotches of white mottling their backs. Tiger sharks! Funny how one stops to analyze even in the middle of a crisis. There was no doubt that this was a crisis. Ted had made hundreds more ocean dives than I had and would not have mentioned the presence of the sharks if it were not an emergency.

As I approached, I saw a pattern developing. The sharks

were making passes at Ted from below, and there were four of them, little ones actually. Only appearing to be about six or seven feet in length, they could be more than twice this long and four times heavier. Not that they weren't dangerous in this situation, it was just an observation. I could clearly see the source of the trouble. Ted had a very full stringer of speared fish hanging from his weight belt; probably ten fish in the neighborhood of eight to twelve pounds each, a nice neighborhood if you are killing for food. So Ted was chumming for shark. I could see that the sharks had already taken chunks out of the fish. This accounted for their excitement.

Small rivulets of blood were expanding from the fish and being diluted by the water. This was a fully developed feeding frenzy. Like fighter aircraft, the sharks were making vertical passes at Ted's fish, then heading back down to turn and make another pass. I saw that Ted's knife sheath was empty. Just as we got to Ted, Gunter and I realized that we had now become targets too. We all had turned our pole spears around, apparently thinking as one to avoid hurting the sharks. They might get mad, I thought. I watched as one lined up on me from below. As he ascended, he opened his mouth, wide enough to take in a leg or two I noticed dispassionately. I saw his eyelids close with the action of opening his mouth. I instinctively pointed the blunt end of the pole spear at him and waited.

At what I hoped was the last second, I twisted hard to my right and pushed against the head of the shark with the pole. Because his eyes were closed, he missed me even with the violent side to side slashing movements of his head. Seemingly for some seconds, the shark seemed to hang in the air. Then he crashed back into the water next to me and headed back down for another pass. I guess he figured that time was on his side. I was certainly thinking so. I studied Ted's weight belt. I remembered that he had tied the damn thing on that morning, because the buckle had worn to the point that it didn't grip the webbing very well. The stringer was integral to the weight belt because he had years ago sewn the stringer to the belt with a wide piece of canvas and scores of fish line stitches. It was a very secure attachment, which happened to be stupid beyond description.

I pulled my knife out of its sheath and yelled in Ted's ear to keep an eye on the sharks. Ted and Gunther took defense postures. Somewhere in the activity, Gunter had acquired my pole spear also. As they pointed downward, I took a handful of Ted's weight belt and inserted the blade of my dive knife between Ted's body and the belt. With the heavy sharp blade toward me, I pulled and slid the knife down. The belt parted and fell like an anchor, headed for the bottom. One of the sharks caught the fish and belt. Holding his catch like a dog with a bone, he headed for the sandy bottom some fifty feet away. The last we saw of them was almost comical. One shark swimming away across the bottom, evidently hoping to get away and eat in solitude, while the other three chased after him snapping at the trailing fish and weight belt.

We swam back to the *Salva Vida*. Hands reached down and pulled the three of us up onto the stern diving platform. Congratulations and backslapping was bestowed upon Gunter and me by every one of our shipmates, with one notable exception. The general consensus of the group was that Gunter and I were steely-eyed masters of the ocean. I will admit that their approbation meant much to me, but I thought it was a little overdone. After all, it had never occurred to me that I could have been hurt, much less eaten. From my present perspective, some decades hence, it is obvious that I was simply young and immortal.

It was all good fun until we heard from the last of the group, "Man that was the stupidest thing I have ever seen in my life." It was Wayne, Mr. Sleep, still wearing his fins and talking directly to me.

"Thanks for the help, Wayne," I responded, wishing my

stare could make him wither and die.

"The day you see me risk my ass for anybody, you will know the end of the world is near." I had not yet been the least bit contentious with anybody in the group, but I decided that it was time to make an exception. "If you represent the future, Wayne, then we have nothing to look forward to." I regretted saying it as soon as the words were out of my mouth.

"I'll try to live without your approval," he said with a smirk.

I let it go. I looked over at Gunter and Ted, "Sorry, just a little philosophical difference."

Gunter grinned at me, making certain that he could be heard over the slap of the water against the underside of the dive platform. "Mr. Sleep has been calling me the Nazi since he got here. I think today he has shown himself that he is a coward. It is an honor to be serving with you, even if you are a Nazi sympathizer."

The three of us sat on the platform, legs swaying in the water with the wave action. Ted looked back and forth, seated as he was between Gunter and me. He reached out with long muscular arms and hung them over our shoulders. "Anybody you know ever need killing," he said, looking over his left shoulder and up at the assembled crew, "just let me know. I'll take care of it personally. Seriously, thanks for saving my stupid ass…you two," he added for effect. He was still looking at the assembled crew.

"Hey Ted," a voice from one of them came back, "didn't you get any fish? You were gone for hours man."

With that, the great shark attack was over. We weighed anchor and made a course for Utila. I started drinking in earnest on the way back. I may have touched the dock a little too heavily upon our return. No one said a word.

Chapter Nineteen

Mr. Sleep

The Wednesday after the incident with the tiger sharks, Duane made a point of seeking me out when I was alone. That was not difficult. I had begun to scrape old paint off the *Salva Vida*, with a plan to repaint her from stem to stern, while replacing rotted or beaten up wood wherever found. My plan was obvious. Like Chicken Little, I couldn't buy a friend, lest he be sucked into my project.

"Permission to come aboard, captain," Duane said with mock solemnity.

"Permission granted," I replied. It was a mock courtesy, but I had learned that even in our little group, people respected the command of a boat. Since I took the *Salva Vida* seriously, I was taken seriously. The formality of the request may have been parody, but the meaning was the same as for any naval vessel; one did not step on a man's vessel without his assent, even if it were as subtle as a nod.

"Captain," Duane said as soon as he had made eye contact as I leaned around the companionway bulkhead, "you and I are taking the Aztec to Tegucigalpa on Friday."

"Sure thing, Duane. I'm flying, right?" That is what

passed for humor these days, I thought. I was a regular riot.

"I'm counting on it." I locked eyes with him. He was serious.

"Pull back to go up, right?" I asked rhetorically.

"Pull back even more, and you go down."

"Yeah, that's what I hear." Somewhere along the line, just thinking about things, I had learned not to ask questions. I was either going to fit in, or I wasn't. And I was, I decided.

"I'll meet you at the airport," he stated matter-of-factly, "let's say about oh seven hundred hours, give or take a hundred hours." With that he smiled broadly, stepped through the gangway and strolled down the dock toward Fathom House. He was laughing to himself and said in the softest voice, "I really like this kid." He shook his head slightly, and said again, "I really like this kid."

I had no idea what this was about, but I figured that "in the fullness of time," it would be revealed to me.

I returned to my scraping and didn't think about the reason for the trip with Duane nearly as much as I thought about the flying. The Aztec was an almost, ugly twin-engine plane, but very capable of actually flying after filling the six seats while still having enough payload to carry sufficient fuel to go somewhere. I knew that Duane intended to let me fly, and I had just about no time at the controls of any airplane. I didn't want to make a fool of myself. I am practically gifted with the ability to make a fool of myself. I was lost in thought about flying and scraping away at paint almost mindlessly when I felt the *Salva Vida* list slightly. I hadn't heard anyone approach, but someone had boarded the boat. *So much for marine protocol.*

I stood to look out the dock side glass of the wheel house. The person standing on the deck between the cabin and the gunwale was the last person I expected to see on my boat. And the *Salva Vida* was my boat. Mr. Sleep was looking fore and aft.

I called out to him. "Permission to come aboard granted,

Wayne," I said by way of subtle reproach. The meaning of my gentle rebuke was lost entirely on this dullard. He was the one person in the expedition I didn't like in the least. I had found him to be arrogant without any reason to be so. I didn't care in the least that he was mostly a loner and not at all a team player. We were all here for self-serving reasons of one kind or another. He was simply lazy. I didn't look forward to any conversation with him and expected this time to be no different. He surprised me.

"Hi Tommy, I mean Captain Tommy, I guess," he began. "I know that we haven't exactly been friends, but I wanted to change that and even ask a favor of you, if you will consider it, I mean." Mr. Sleep was stammering around as if he were an inarticulate kid. *This should be interesting.*

"What I mean is, everybody here likes you and I have heard them talk about your diving and all as if you were some kind of damn fish or something." I was not at all flattered by the way he was backing into whatever it was he wanted to ask me. He pressed on. "Well anyway, I haven't done much diving and I wanted to come out here and apologize for anything I may have said in the past that might have come out wrong. And I wanted to ask you if you wouldn't mind working with me sometime and giving me some pointers on real diving, I guess you'd call it. I heard you were an actual scuba diving instructor, too."

"Actually, Wayne, I am just a YMCA certified assistant instructor. You can't be an instructor until you are at least twenty one. I just turned twenty last month."

"Yeah, I heard that Brian's mom nailed you. What is she fifty-six, now? Good God; that must be like robbing the crypt or something." This guy was really charming. I began to wonder about the combative nature he exuded, and decided that it had to be a defense mechanism. He may not have known the nuances of the English language enough to make himself sound sincere, even if he weren't. It was an art form with which I was particularly familiar. I could be disgustingly ingratiating when I wanted to be. I figured I would give him the benefit of the doubt.

"Yeah well, stuff happens you know? This being a bit of a remote island and all." I wanted to change the subject, so I did. "Look Wayne, I've seen you dive. You look like you know what you are doing. You probably should dive a little more often though. It's the kind of skill that needs pretty constant reinforcement."

"I know it looks that way, but I really don't know any of the book learning stuff and I have never been deeper than about thirty feet. I haven't ever told anybody this, but I'm kind of scared every time I go underwater. You tell anybody and I'll kick your ass." He stopped himself, grinned a little too menacingly to successfully pull off an apologetic mien, and added, "Sorry, I didn't mean that the way it may have sounded." It sounded exactly like he wanted to kick my ass. But I am a sucker for helping people, and I decided to let this pass also.

Against my better judgement, if I ever had any, I heard myself say, "We can work on some stuff right now. Any excuse to get away from real work is okay with me."

He actually smiled, beamed really, and said, "That would be great, Tommy. By the way, I know everybody calls me Mr. Sleep behind my back, but I really like to be called Wayne.

"Wayne it is then," I replied. "What do you want to work on first?"

"I saw some of that black coral that you and Duane brought up. I know that it isn't super valuable or anything, but I would like to be with a guy like you and make a deeper dive and maybe find some, you know?" And there it was, the real reason for all this dancing around. Wayne had heard about the real value of black coral and had decided to use me as his transportation and guide to getting some, maybe a lot, for himself.

Well, who cares? I had certainly thought about getting some more and possibly making a little commercial effort myself. I certainly had nothing against free enterprise.

"Okay Wayne, let's go over some of the decompression basics and scare up some gear. We'll take the *Shark* and let's shoot for at least an eighty foot dive with some decompression thrown in for good measure." I was contemplating our going out to the wall, but away from the really big area of black coral that Duane had shown me. We could explore the wall east of there and surely run into some. The coral animals tended to propagate downstream and the prevailing currents ran from the northwest to the southeast.

As unlikely as it would have seemed even that morning, Mr. Sleep and I were going to go diving together. I figured him to be only a few years older than me, but he sure acted and looked a lot older. It was no secret around the expedition that he was a dope smoker, but that hardly put him in a select group. Many of the islanders and some of our group were regular users of marijuana. I had tried it a few times myself, but it left me mystified as to what was the big deal. I had gotten rather sick each time. Certainly no feelings that would make me spend good money to get the stuff and than make a day of it.

I watched his reactions as we talked about deep diving and he looked fine to me. When we anchored over the wall some two hours later, he looked to be in good shape and I was even starting to enjoy his enthusiasm and company. Who knew?

I was careful not to be condescending as I played instructor. I didn't want to treat him as a complete neophyte, but wanted to make certain that he understood all of the hazards and even the simple changes brought on by a relatively deep dive. He didn't take umbrage as I covered basic things like the compression of the wet suit and its associated loss of buoyancy that we would experience as we went deep. He did not once say something that would have indicated that he was offended by the simplicity of some of my instruction. I wondered if he knew less than I had expected or was just being polite. I reflected on his personality and that made me suspect it was the former, more than the latter.

And thinking about the problems of buoyancy, I decided to expand on that somewhat. "It is strange that none of us has a buoyancy vest," I began. We have all had trouble staying down or up and back in the States it is becoming a required piece of gear to have when you go out on a dive charter. We are being unnecessarily primitive out here and I am going to look into our getting some vests."

"So how much weight do you think we should use?" he asked reasonably.

"Well, I have taken to wearing booties, because of these aching feet of mine. What with the wet suit jacket and all, even though we are using twins, I am thinking about using twelve pounds. Remember, we'll lose a lot of buoyancy when the suits compress to about a third of their thickness at eighty feet, but as we use up our air we will gain back at least ten pounds of buoyancy. It's a real crap shoot without buoyancy control."

He looked at me and said, "Hell, Tommy, you can't weigh more than a hundred seventy and I weigh more than two hundred pounds. I am going to wear at least twenty pounds or I'll never get down."

"I would recommend that you start out light and work to get down," I replied after a little thought. "By the time we get to sixty feet, you will feel fine."

"I'm wearing twenty pounds." He said this with a finality that left me with nothing to add. I just shrugged my shoulders.

"Suit yourself." Then I added, "Suit yourself up while you are at it. Let's get this show in the water."

I had decided to bring two single sets of gear, complete with regulators and hang them from the anchor line with snap links at about the ten foot line. I didn't think they would be needed, but one never knows.

He looked good in the descent, we went down a little too quickly by my standards, but it was fine. I dove virtually every day and clearing my ears and blowing bits of air into the mask to equalize pressure were effortless and second nature. I noticed that he seemed to really work at clearing his ears, but I let him set the pace and he kicked powerfully and smoothly down.

He sure doesn't dive like he's feeling any fear, I thought. We reached eighty feet so quickly that it took me by surprise. By the time I read the depth gauge, caught up with him and grabbed a fin, we were through one hundred feet. Man, we really needed to slow things up here. Being heavy on air, scuba tanks weigh six to eight pounds heavier full than when near empty, and wearing a wet suit squeezed down from three eighths of an inch in thickness to about three thirty-seconds of an inch, I was working my fins to maintain the depth.

I shook my head back and forth at him and pointed at the depth gauge on my left wrist, strapped on just above my beautiful Rolex Submariner watch. I signaled up and over with an index finger and swam to the east. I was surprised once again by this wall as we soon found a growth of black coral that was at least three feet square and stuck out from the wall more than three feet. It was some ten feet below us and we descended to it for a closer look. This single clump of hundreds of pieces of black coral, taken in total, polished and marketed, could easily have been worth twenty thousand dollars. And there was more even deeper, easily in sight in the dimming light.

It is not bright at one hundred feet, no matter where the sun is or how clear the water. I was contemplating the wonder of tens of thousands of dollars of black coral, considering the irony of being with a treasure diving expedition looking for man made treasure, and finding absolutely natural riches. It was most attention-getting when a large shadow moved over me. My first thought was to get oriented to the source quickly. I was thinking fast and my first mild concern was that of a curious shark, or possibly a harmless, sometimes very large, manta ray, or just about anything. Nothing in my experience could have prepared me for what I confronted. My diving partner was descending toward me with his dive knife in his right hand. He held it close in and had the sharp end pointed at my mask.

Being the ever-trusting fool that I am, I swiveled in the slow motion that water forces upon us, looking for the threat, obviously something behind me. There was nothing more than the void of the abyss. I looked back to Wayne, recalculating the threat. I must have had a "who me?" look on my face, because he grinned enough that I could see the smile lines spread out from his mouth, past the obstruction that was the mouthpiece of his regulator. He was upon me before I was convinced that he was threatening me. The knife was barely visible, pointed directly at me as it was. I saw that it was going to enter my neck. I reflexively thrust my right arm up, somewhat blocking my view, but taking the blade on the underside of my arm and just above the elbow.

A dark liquid suffused my vision. Now isn't that interesting, I had black blood. Wayne pulled back his thrust and crouched against the wall. He coiled against it and sprang out and away from it. All moves are necessarily telegraphed underwater. One cannot move with the speed one might wish to find in a situation like this. It is a slow motion activity at its fastest. I easily pirouetted away from him. I saw him look back at the wall after his missed attack. But he wasn't looking at the wall. He was watching a fin fall away. He was wearing wet suit booties also. I considered quickly that he may have tightened the rubber sling against the bootie on the surface, but failed to appreciate how much slack it would acquire as the wet suit material compressed. It is easy to lose a fin when wearing booties because of the lack of tactile feel.

In any event, I now had the advantage. I considered my

options. I could pull out one of my knives, and we could engage in an old fashioned knife fight. But my right arm was starting to hurt, and I am right handed. Besides, I just didn't have the passion in me needed to stab anybody, even someone who had just stabbed me. Staying relatively calm, and trying to be reasonable, I suspected that he was suffering from nitrogen narcosis. I was still negatively buoyant. I brought my fins together and let myself sink. It was easy for him to go down too, especially head down. I gathered speed in the descent, and he came after me. I backpedaled with my hands as he neared me again. Because we were both very negatively buoyant we continued to descend. I spread my legs and flared the fins out to steady myself. I then brought them together in as powerful a stroke as I had ever performed. I breathed out gently as I rose at least ten feet initially. Wayne turned to press his attack, but with only one fin and being very heavy, he continued his descent. *Release your weight belt, dummy.* That must have been the instructor in me; it was not something I really wanted him to do.

I gently kicked upward, breathing regularly. I lost sight of him as he descended feet first into the dark void. By the time I looked at my depth gauge, I was just passing through one hundred feet, but ascending. I must have been down to at least one hundred thirty feet at the low point. I looked at my right arm. The wet suit had a "v" cut into it. The "v" was formed by two inches of gash in each direction. I clamped my left hand around the wound and continued the ascent. I had to surface to find the boat, then descended again to the ten foot level and swam in its direction. I found the anchor line and the waiting cylinders. My tanks were down to about four hundred pounds of pressure now. A lot of air for a calm diver at ten feet, but I was going to have to get calm first.

I used most of the air in my twins, then switched to one of the singles and breathed out of its regulator for at least another half hour. Convinced eventually that I had decompressed enough to avoid decompression sickness, I let go of the spare regulator and put my own mouthpiece back in place. I clambered aboard the Shark and shrugged out of all my gear. Apparently Mr. Sleep wasn't going to be joining me. I knew that my wet suit was helping to keep my wound closed, but I wrapped a piece of cloth around it anyway and tied it roughly with my left hand and teeth.

As I motored back around to the south side of Utila, then eastbound to Utila Town, I thought about Wayne and the real possibility that he had been motivated by a natural greed, exacerbated by the effects of nitrogen narcosis. I was in excellent shape, accustomed to diving every day, even deep dives. Wayne was a regular drug user, did not dive more than about once every three weeks or so, and then it was only shallow stuff. The very high partial pressure of nitrogen at one hundred feet and beyond is certainly capable of causing terrific changes in one's ability to think. The high concentration of nitrogen dissolved in the blood impairs the conduction of nerve impulses and mimics the effects of alcohol or narcotics. Apparently Mr. Sleep had died the way he had lived. *So much for the drug culture and diving.*

My return to the Fathom Dock caused quite a stir. Several people had just returned from two of our working sites and I had to look for somebody to tell my story. I found Nick and Duane together, obviously discussing some aspect of the dock's construction. I strode up to them and stood too close to be ignored.

"Hey Captain," Duane said, looking at my crudely wrapped and blood spattered arm. "Out fighting sharks again I see. It looks like they scored this time.

"Worse than that, Duane," I responded, suddenly feeling very old, "I just killed Mr. Sleep…., Wayne," I said finally.

"Whoa, that's a new one, even for this place. You want to

expand on that?"

So I went through the whole story. As I talked, a crowd gathered. No one said anything through the entire recantation of the trip, dive and ensuing attack. There were a few low whistles and some head shaking, but not one question was raised. When I finished with all I wanted to say, Duane looked around at the group, maybe fifteen guys by now.

"Well guys, I don't know how you all feel about it, but if Tommy says that's the way it happened, then that's the way it happened." It had not occurred to me until then that anybody would have thought that I was telling anything but the truth. *Now what*?

"Why didn't he just release his weight belt?" Peter England asked, more to himself than to the rest.

"Because he was a damn pot head hippie," Jack answered in a much louder voice. "Any of you ever been to San Francisco?" he asked, looking around at the group. "Those commune people all belong to the church of 'If It Feels Good Do It.' About half of the people work and the other half takes half of their money. Bunch of socialists. And they smother their french fries with mayonnaise." For Jack, that seemed to be the most outrageous thing of all.

"Jack, what does mayonnaise on french fries have to do with Wayne attacking Tommy and not releasing his weight belt when he was sinking like a rock?" asked Brian with a grin. At that, all of us laughed, albeit somewhat nervously. My arm was beginning to hurt with a throb by this time. I felt my legs getting rubbery and I went down a bit too hard on my knees, still holding the rag on my right elbow.

Gunter was standing a little off from the group, and was the next to speak. "I sure am going to miss that set of twins and that adjustable Scubapro regulator." Most of the assembled engaged in a few more nervous laughs, then gallows humor, and talk of dividing Wayne's effects.

"Tommy," Duane said, making certain to make eye contact, "we'll fly down to Tegoose in the morning and make a formal report to the embassy. It will be just a formality really. Don't worry about a thing. Let's go find Shawn and get some stitches in that wound. You do seem to have a black cloud over you at times… and maybe a guardian angel," he added.

Having made this assessment, he walked down the dock, obviously expecting me to follow. A couple of the guys half picked me up. They touched me lightly on the shoulders first to let me know they intended to help. With their help I was able to stand while hugging myself. "Thanks," I muttered, "I'll be okay now."

"Nice job, Captain," someone called after me as I unsteadily made my way down the dock.

I caught up with Duane just as he stepped onto the island. "Duane," I said, "do you remember the first time we met and you told me that you were aging in dog years?" This stopped him utterly. He turned and faced me, looking at the blood soaked rag I was holding against my right elbow.

"Yeah, I remember," he said simply, looking fully at me.

I looked back at him, just as fixedly and said, "I get it now."

Chapter Twenty

Tegucigalpa

Duane took pity on my lessened capacity, what with my body having acquired another twenty stitches. But we did leave on the following Monday for Tegucigalpa, the capital of Honduras. I had packed very lightly, but was wearing my signature white denim pants and white cotton shirt.

Duane flew the Aztec off the very short (two thousand feet long) airstrip, then told me to try to keep the wings level and maintain eight thousand five hundred feet. I have to tell you, with everything working, flying in good weather is not at all difficult. Make little corrections and stop bad trends before they develop. That's about it. If something went wrong, the airplane was all Duane's I figured.

The navigation was as rudimentary as it gets. We tuned the automatic direction finder into the most powerful AM radio station of Tegucigalpa. We listened to the lousy Latin music that hasn't changed in decades and followed the needle which was pointed right at the transmitter. When the mountains and sprawling, ugly city came into view on the horizon, Duane contacted the tower and we were cleared to land immediately. He handled the throttles, told me to maintain ninety knots on final and I was able to make a decent landing. It was exhilarating.

Duane taxied in to the customs area as previously arranged. Dour looking soldiers met us as we climbed out. Duane spoke to them and they relaxed a little. Allen Grant, the man from our "public relations department," strode out to meet us before we reached the customs shack.

"Good to see you two again," Allen gushed. He was about to go on in a chatty ramble when he was brought up short by the sight of my bandaged arm. "Tommy, you look like something the iguanas have been chewing on. I know about the reef you guys damaged, but what's with the arm."

"We'll talk about that later, okay, Allen?" Duane looked toward the armed soldiers as he spoke. "There has been an incident, but we need to talk about it in private."

Allen became all business in a moment. "My car is at the curb, let's go to my office and have some coffee."

I don't know what I expected Allen to be driving, but a yellow 1957 Chevy Bel Air would not have been on my list. I would soon get used to seeing almost nothing but old, American iron, no matter the city.

I was feeling somewhat anxious. I did not quite believe that Wayne's drowning could be dismissed as easily as Duane thought and I wondered what the primary reason was for our visit. I rode in the back seat and fretted. I have always been able to make the anticipation of a bad thing much worse than the reality. It's a gift. As we drove the very narrow streets, lined continuously with parked cars on both sides, I marveled at the speeds everybody maintained. It was my second lesson in Central American driving protocol, which was apparently based on giving no quarter and taking every opportunity to cut off the other guy. It worked with no accidents on our drive to the city center. I did notice that there were no undamaged cars to be seen.

We parked underneath a three-story office building that

reminded me of a rundown medical building. Allen's office had a frosted, translucent glass door, complete with block letters proclaiming this to be the office of Fathom Expeditions, Inc. Allen started a pot of coffee brewing and opened the conversation. "What's the incident Duane?"

"Tommy here lost a diver last week," Duane said, pointing at my arm. "It seems that our resident hippie lost his dive knife. Tommy retrieved it with his elbow, then lost track of the guy. He could still be swimming around on the north side of the island, but I doubt it."

"So you never saw the guy actually die, Tommy?" Allen asked, turning his attention to me.

"Well no sir, but he was sink…"

"Ah, let's just leave it at that then," he interrupted. "Until we get proof otherwise, this guy is just missing. You get my drift here, son?" He stared at me. If I didn't get the drift, I would have had to have been the densest log in the forest.

"I understand, sir."

"Good, now let's get down to business. Tommy, to put it bluntly, things are going well here in Honduras. The politicians down here are cooperating and we are going to be holding joint military exercises soon. I know you have only been down here for about six months, but you have become one of Duane's anointed few. This has worked so well as an intro that we are going to do it again, south of here. Any questions?"

I stared at Allen. "I'm guessing you want me to be part of this new operation, right?" I asked, just to get the obvious out of the way. "You do realize that I'm just a diver don't you? What do you expect out of me, south of here."

"Tommy, Duane tells me that you suffer from low self-esteem." Then he laughed. "Dr. Duane, eminent psychiatrist."

Duane shook his head. A slight smile appeared, then he shrugged his shoulders. As he took a cup of coffee from Allen, he collected his thoughts. "Sorry, Tommy, Allen has such a way with words. He's in the right field. The State Department shredded his application years ago. All I mean is that you don't realize that you display a rare talent. You are self-motivated and you adapt well to situations in the field. Remember me? I'm the guy who was out on that reef with you. You put yourself in harm's way, got hurt and we completed a tough mission. In fact, I'm losing track of the heads up things you've done so far. Face it Tommy. You have talent and we need you."

"Who are we?" I asked. I watched with some amusement as Allen and Duane exchanged glances. I knew the answer.

Allen was definitely the man in Honduras. "Tommy, we will just call it the Company. You will never call it anything. An Act of Congress established a formal agency in 1947 and it was signed into law by President Truman. We collect information and write reports that allow the decision makers to make policy as regards foreign governments. We answer to the NSA, the National Security Agency. I asked Duane to bring you down here so that we could formalize this a little."

"We will pay you in cash. How you handle that is your problem. You will start at one thousand dollars a month. For now you will have to trust me to keep track of that. If you need something, let me know. We mostly talk only in person. I'm sure you have noticed that communications down here are nonexistent."

I decided to get a little historical perspective. "So Honduras specifically has something to do with the Monroe Doctrine, I guess?"

"You see, Allen," Duane interjected, "this kid has some depth. The gears are always turning."

Allen thought about this perspective a bit before answering. "That's not bad. It is official policy that an attack on this hemisphere is an attack on the United States. Attacks do not always come as military actions, not any more. We have ignored Central America. We take it for granted. The Panama

Canal is here and we just assume that it belongs to us. With Cuba being just up the road, we cannot afford to operate in a vacuum here. And we definitely got screwed to the wall on that. If you are a Kennedy fan, you are welcome to your opinion, but keep it to yourself."

"Yeah," I said, "I have caught some of Craig's feelings about the Kennedy family."

"Craig has some issues. He is going to have to learn to keep his mouth shut." Allen suddenly looked hard.

I looked at them both, tried the coffee and said, "I'll try to get over this self-esteem thing, guys. I'm having a good time in between half-killing myself every now and then. But I don't have any anything else to do. I'm in," I said simply.

"Alright, Captain," Allen said, extending a hand. "I'll say it again. Welcome to the clan." I shook his hand with my left hand. Allen remembered my right arm at that and laughed. "Let's go find some lunch. Our work here is finished. I want to hear the details of that arm."

We went to one of the common outdoor eateries of the kind that proliferate from Mexico to Argentina. Allen asked me to give a detailed explanation of the incident with Wayne. I went into my oral saga mode and gave a spirited rendition of the whole thing. I summed up by opining that I doubted that he had attacked me with premeditation. Duane disagreed.

"Wayne was in love with drugs. I had talked with him about it a few times. There is a permissiveness that fits in perfectly with the whole hippie movement. Wayne wanted money. I think he looked at the black coral as a way to finance a little export business. You may be right about his being a little narc'd out, going that deep that fast, but the intent was there. You ever notice the little spear pistol I never dive without? I don't take it to shoot fish. I'm sure not going to miss the lazy son-of-a-bitch."

Allen took us back to the airport. He paid for the fuel and

the various fees that get attached to everything in Honduras. I noticed how discreet he was and that he showed little extra money. I got another flying lesson from Duane. The Aztec was easy to fly, I thought, but Duane disagreed with me again.

"You just don't get it, Tommy. You have some real natural abilities that most people just don't have. Learn to expect that you are above average and you are going to kick ass in life." I had never had my ego massaged before. I wasn't used to compliments. They embarrassed me. I still don't take compliments well.

Duane talked me through another landing on the short airstrip of Utila and pronounced me a pilot.

Chapter Twenty One

The Sinking

I visited Shawn, our official corpsman and US Army deserter, a few times over the next two weeks. He poured acid into the wound regularly. His theory evidently being that if it didn't hurt, it wasn't doing any good. The wound would actually smoke. He told me to keep it clean and to stay out of the water. I ignored his advice and the thing healed, leaving an ugly scar.

I checked on Jack and Jill almost every day. They were obviously monitoring the area just off my hooch, because it never took more than ten minutes to find them. I fed them chunks of lobster and whole shrimp. It was good to have pets, but it wasn't enough. I had a sense of foreboding settling over me. Being told that I was going to be pulling up stakes had made all my efforts on Utila temporary and unimportant.

I had offered to take a few guys out to one of the sites that we were excavating. I never got excited about working an excavation. Spending hours underwater and moving the business end of an airlift around was mind numbing work. I understand that some people are excited by the prospect of imminent treasure. More power to them. I don't buy lottery tickets for the same reasons that I couldn't get excited about scraping away layers of sediment to see what is underneath. My cynical mind assumed that the treasures were going to be found by someone else and my trusting mind assumed that if riches were found, I would get my share.

An airlift raft had been anchored over the site for about a week when Sergei decided that we should bring it in and replace the rear main bearing seal on the diesel engine. We had been leaking oil for days now and all it would take for us to get caught was to have a single flyover by the Honduran Air Force. Contrary to conventional wisdom, an oil leak in the ocean is a nonevent, unless it is truly a large leak. The ocean disperses oil spills with an efficiency that is completely misunderstood by a gullible public. But it would be all the Hondurans would need to create an international incident. More importantly it would be all the Honduran government would need to get more American dollars.

The *Salva Vida* was the logical choice to tow the replacement raft out to the site and bring the other one in for the needed maintenance. Eddie Glackin was one of my three passengers. He actually enjoyed using the airlift and spending hours underwater, barely moving. The other two, Greg Newell and Ernie Padgett, were relatively new to the expedition and were excited to have the chance to go treasure diving.

We met on the Fathom Dock on a typically sunny day, which happened to be a Friday morning. Greg was so excited about the possibility of finding treasure that it was easy for me to get him to do almost all the line hauling and the humping of supplies that we were taking with us. *Ah, youth.* Ernie was not nearly so pliable. He was a quiet kid, maybe twenty-two years old, and followed my every move, asking questions about everything. I was twenty now, but I was aging in dog years.

I generally could not abide having someone shadow my every move, but I was in my instructor mode this day. I explained almost every move and was most pleasant, by my standards anyway. This alone should have alerted me to my impending doom. I pressed on. "Okay, Ernie, let's see if the old girl is going to start before Greg gets all the gear on board." I was being a regular tour guide.

Ernie looked around the wheel, obviously expecting to see an ignition switch or at least a starter button. "Do you have the keys, Captain?" he asked. This gave me the chance to roll my eyes and be condescending, a perquisite of being an old salt.

"This is an old boat, Ernie, and it's a diesel. We need to go below." I was in rare form and wondering if I could impress him with some nautical terms. He followed me through the companionway and we duck walked through the hatch to the engine compartment.

"Since it's an old diesel," I continued my lecture, "we need to release the compression with this lever, and then hold down the starter button to get her turning over. When she is cranking, we push the lever down, causing compression and she fires." I demonstrated as I talked and the engine rattled to life.

Once topside, we helped Greg stow the rest of the gear while the engine reached operating temperature. Four more of our Fathomers had shown up while we were in the engine compartment. Being in an expansive mood, I invited them to join us, which they did. I ordered Ernie and Mr. Glackin, as I called him today, to cast off the lines. I motored the *Salva Vida* slowly away from the dock and let her drift perpendicular to the raft. I held position with fore and aft shifting at idle and the tow lines were secured.

My ego was in overdrive as I magnanimously turned to my awed understudy of the day. "Take us out, Mr. Padgett. Make it two knots." He was so excited, he could barely contain himself.

"You're going to let me drive?" he gushed.

"It's known as taking the helm, but it's all yours," I sniffed.

Eddie and I shared a knowing look, being the old veterans that we were. I was Captain Bligh today, and he was my Mr. Christian. Besides, we had an audience.

The ocean was a spectacular blue. I stood in the wheelhouse with my binoculars swinging from their lanyard, which was secured about my neck. Where did this attitude come from? I was showing off and it was going to cost me.

It took most of an hour, but we rounded the lighthouse and made a westward course in the middle of the twenty fathom channel south of the island. I should state here that Ernie had taken it upon himself to speed things up by advancing the throttles, but he didn't. I did. My thought was that since the raft was riding the waves so well at two knots, what harm could another knot or two do? The raft plowed under the surface almost immediately.

The increased pressure tore the sideboards completely off and the raft began a spectacular sinking. It went down like an anchor when a few of the fifty-five gallon drums let loose, easily tearing away when the sideboards departed. Each drum represented more than four hundred pounds of buoyancy and like everything else we did in this outfit, the raft was loaded until it was barely floating anyway.

As the raft sank, it turned turtle, heavy side down, like a piece of bread with lots of peanut butter, heading for the kitchen floor. But that wasn't the worst that could happen. I knew what the worst could be. With a boatload of gawkers moving to the stern, yelling and pointing, I shifted the *Salva Vida* into neutral and pulled my dive knife out of its sheath and sprang from the wheelhouse. I leaped over the ledge between the first and second decks holding the knife over my head. People scattered at the sight of a mostly naked, somewhat muscular madman wielding a large dive knife and screaming at them to get out of the way. Just as I reached the stern, the raft hit the end of the towing lines. It now weighed probably fifteen hundred pounds and every fifty five gallon drum left to the raft was exploding to the surface like a depth charge in reverse.

I felt the boat going down at the stern when I cut the port line with the hardest stroke of a knife that I will ever make in my life. The one inch line parted is if it were a thread. I had hit the line so hard that the knife twisted back and out of my grip. It clattered to the deck and out of my reach. The reason it slid out of my reach so quickly was because now the very heavy raft was hanging from only the starboard stern line. The *Salva Vida* was going down by the stern and at an angle. If this had a saving grace, it was that it threw me into the corner next to the remaining line.

The stern was now awash. I saw people jumping overboard. I had the sudden thought that maybe I should go down with the ship. This was pretty funny stuff, for about a moment. I couldn't find the knife. I always wore two knives. I took the other knife from my leg sheath and hit the second towing line. The *Salva Vida* took on a more level attitude almost immediately. I looked around sheepishly. I was alone on the deck.

In just those few moments the *Salva Vida* had taken on hundreds of gallons of water. Each gallon weighed six pounds I thought to myself. There were only two small scuppers on the big boat. Scuppers are the holes you see at deck level on any boat of more than about thirty feet. They are meant to allow the deck to drain whenever water is taken aboard, as can happen in rain or heavy seas. Damn Cubans. They hadn't allowed for the amount of water that can be taken aboard when the boat is dipped stern first into the ocean. My mind was racing. I had another problem.

Before this much water could drain out through the scuppers, it would head for the lowest points in the boat, down the companionway and into the small engine room. Oh man, I should have gone down with the damn boat. I was thinking that it would have been a sad thing then and I wouldn't have had to listen to the laughter that was already rising from the surface of the ocean. As I listened and considered my few options, the engine shuddered to an ignominious end. I knew instantly that the water in the engine compartment had just risen to the top of the diesel engine. The engine room had been closed in by added bulkheads over the years. I had once considered knocking down or opening at least one of the bulkheads there, just in case we ever got caught shipping water in heavy seas. I just never got around to doing it.

Within minutes, all seven of my shipmates were back on board. It was humiliating, but I started laughing too. My hubris had sunk a raft that had been equipped with what was easily ten thousand dollars worth of engines, compressors, scuba gear and associated hardware. Then it started.

"Hey Captain," one wag started, "you want I should throw out the anchor? We are over a great salvage site."

"Maybe we could build a memorial here. You know, something like the Arizona in Pearl Harbor. Tourists will come to pay their respects. We'll charge admission. We'll all get rich."

I wanted to point out the obvious, that I had at least cut the lines to the raft, keeping the *Salva Vida* from sinking, while they had all looked like rats abandoning ship. I knew instinctively that any attempt to salvage some dignity was just going to subject me to more abuse. Besides, this really was funny stuff. I entered the wheel house, found a couple hundred feet of eighth inch nylon line and a bleach bottle. Ernie, bless his heart, didn't make me explain what I was doing, for once this day. He went to the foredeck and returned quickly with a weight belt. We started to unthread some weights when I realized what a waste of time that was. I cinched the weight belt up into a snug loop, and then tied the line very, very securely to the weight belt. With the bleach bottle at the other end of the line, I threw the weight belt overboard. Site marked. I then retrieved the artillery compass and took bearing sights from the lighthouse and the tallest tree of Pumpkin Hill, the highest point of the island.

"Okay guys, I know you are all having a good time, but let's bail out the bilge and see if I haven't ruined the engine. If it's toast, I'm swimming for the island."

Eddie Glackin, the quiet hermit, evidently took pity on my situation. "Get those plastic buckets from the forward cabin. Let's set up a relay line from the engine room and get the ocean out of our boat."

Everybody hopped to it and in about fifteen minutes the bilge was down to a couple inches of water. Good enough. With everybody willing the engine to run, I pulled the compression release lever and let the engine spin up for at least twice as long as was normal, hoping to clear any water out of the combustion chambers. When I pushed the lever down, the rugged, beautiful, overbuilt Russian diesel engine went through its usual gasping and rattling as it came to life. I made a course for the harbor and Utila Town, thankful for the noise of the engine and the temporary respite from the helpful comments of my companions.

Explaining the event to Sergei was excruciating. But the nasty monster showed the only glimmer of compassion that any of us had ever witnessed. He growled, threatened and cussed at me for a few minutes, got that out of his system, and shifted into salvage plans for the lost equipment without seeming to take a breath between the two trains of thought. He knew that time was of the essence if we were going to save the gear. It took us one day of diving in one hundred ten feet of water to bring the raft up. Amazingly, the stuff was almost all still together. Of the nine fifty-five gallon drums, we were only able to find three. Another couple days of hard work and we got the engine and compressors working. Nick worked with me the whole time and even Duane came out to our workplace at the old shipyard.

"Captain Conklin," he called out as he approached, "you feeling old enough now to be a Tom?

"Duane," I answered after letting out a heavy sigh, "I have lived right through Tom and made it to Thomas."

"Dog years," Duane said with a big grin. "Dog years."

As awful as I felt at the time, the whole incident became one of the great legends of Fathom Expeditions. My attitude mellowed with time and I look back on it now as one of my better moments. My place in the history of the expedition was assured. It wasn't much of a legacy, but I was doing the best I could with what skills I had.

Chapter Twenty Two

Indecent Exposure

The day I was arrested was so routine, as days on the island go, that I did not even have my usual premonition that something was about to go wrong. Not that I consider myself to be psychic, but over the years I had developed a relatively effective trouble detector. Looking back on the accuracy of my premonitions, I suspect that I could generally foretell an impending problem because it was a safe bet that I would soon enough do something to make it happen. But I got arrested by doing nothing wrong.

I had just docked the Shark. I had taken our corpsman, Shawn, and Jack Crabill out on a lobster hunt. I usually didn't play hunting guide, but the two had massaged my ego at the breakfast table, telling me that my ability to find lobster and game fish was uncanny. I was vain enough to be swayed by their compliments. Jack was a hard working guy and educated way beyond my twelve years of primary schooling, but he had no hunter's instinct. Shawn spent his time, and money, taking care of anybody on the island who got hurt. I didn't know that he even knew how to dive. Their talk of lobster had gotten the attention of several others. It got my attention, too. I agreed to take them to a likely spot that would result in enough lobster for a good evening meal for everybody.

It was not yet noon when we returned. Shawn and I were carrying a four foot long cooler between us. It was almost filled by the twenty lobsters from our little foray. We hardly ever tried to bank seafood. We were surrounded by the stuff. Having only iceboxes to store perishable food simply did not work. If anything spoiled and we could not detect it, we would almost certainly get food poisoning. It would be an ironic way to die, I thought, what with all the hazards that we faced almost every day. But this was a relaxing interlude and we were headed down the Fathom Dock for the cookhouse. I saw the town constable, Lewtie was his name, coming toward us carrying his trademark machete, flat side of the blade against his right shoulder. The clown had the edge turned toward his neck. What with his being almost always drunk, or stoned on the ubiquitous exotic tobacco, I wondered how he managed to survive such simple and deadly hazards.

"Good morning, mons," he said as he stopped in front of us, "I must be telling you that you are under arrest. All threes of you."

"Under arrest, Lewtie? What for, expired lobster permit?" I countered, showing great wit.

"Yeah, Lewtie," Jack joined in, "What is this, some kind of shakedown for beer money? All you have to do is ask. Or is there some kind of ticket quota on the island now. That crazy broad, Elyria, put you up to this?" Jack had lived on the island for two years now. He was of an intellectual bent and was one of the few among us who actually took an interest in the dynamics of island politics. I had no interest in the subject of island politics. How could that affect me? But I did know Elyria.

She was the head of the local Church of God. The consensus of opinion held that she was probably a snake handler at least. My only interaction with her had come months before, when she had managed to chop part of her left thumb and forefinger off with a machete. I happened to be in the area of her house, on my way to get some mango ice cream, when I heard her yell. She hadn't really screamed out in pain as much as she poured out a steady steam of invectives at the devil and other demons in that rich, difficult to understand, Creole-like language that the older islanders spoke. I had been so rash as to burst into her house uninvited.

She had been chopping up at least two chickens with a machete when she made a small miscalculation. I had cajoled and half-dragged her down to Fathom House. Shawn had performed a near miracle by actually sewing the severed pieces back on her. He had half knocked her out with ether or something, and then gave her a shot of morphine. I am guessing at the chemicals he had used on her that day. I represent the antithesis of pharmaceutical thought. I don't even trust aspirin.

I didn't stay to watch. I hate the sight of other people's blood. I am not too thrilled about the sight of my own. Elyria never forgave me for entering her house and dragging her away for medical treatment. More than one islander had told me that she considered our intervention to be blasphemous. She had yet to forgive me or Shawn for our hateful actions. Go figure.

"How could Elyria get you to arrest us, Lewtie?" I wondered out loud. "Did she threaten you with a curse or something?"

"She is the new police chief of the island," Jack stated from behind us. I half-turned to look at him, incredulity evidently writ large on my face, as they say. "Don't look at me as if I'm crazy, Tommy." Jack responded. "If you guys would pay attention, you'd know these things. There was an election, or at least a vote, and she was put in charge of Lewtie here."

"I am not the one happy here to be telling you this, mons, but you will have to come with me to the courthouse. Mrs.

Morgan is awaiting your arrivals." Lewtie was clearly not the one with whom to take issue in the matter of our arrest. But that piece of good self-advice was ignored by the recipient.

"Lewtie," I said in a voice that was much too loud, and I hoped intimidating, "this stinking island doesn't have a courthouse." Affected by my charm, Lewtie drew himself up to his full height of five feet, six inches, and even took the machete down from his shoulder, holding it diagonally across his chest with both hands.

"This is not a stinking island Mr. Captain Tommy, sir. You three mons will be coming to the schoolhouse with me."

"Or what, Lewtie, you going to cut our heads off?" I yelled back at him. I have been told over the years that I evidence a certain resentment to authority. To this day, I cannot stand morons being given authority. I haven't changed much in that regard. I may be ranked a few notches below tolerant.

Jack was shaking his head as he walked around us and signaled that we should follow. "You really need to work on your people skills, Tommy. You keep this up and we'll probably be stoned. You know; some kind of Old Testament punishment. Let's just go see what we have done this time that offends them and pay the fine."

I looked over Lewtie's shoulder and saw Nick just stepping on the dock. I purposely yelled right through Lewtie, as if he weren't there and hoping he was suffering from the usual hangover. I would show these pople a thing or two. They just didn't know who they were messing with. "Nick, would you take these lobsters to the cookhouse? We have an appointment with the snake handler." I just couldn't stand to keep my mouth shut when an insult was appropriate. I remember that Shawn never said a single word. Things were to work out better for him. There is probably a lesson there somewhere.

Lewtie had the temerity to get behind the three of us and march us down the dock to the cabana. I had an image of the scene in the movie *Wizard of Oz*; the one where the ugly apelike guards marched Dorothy and her companions into the fortress. I was about to make a reference to it as a further insult, when I realized that there was no way Lewtie would have any idea as to the reference. Damn, it would have been perfectly good insult wasted on the ignorant.

The cabana, or schoolhouse, was one of the two buildings on the government park property. The other building was the jail. None of us had ever seen it occupied. That was about to change.

We could hear the voices of many as we approached the ramshackle, unpainted two story building. Ramshackle is the only word that could convey its condition. It actually leaned, like one of those last century barns seen all over rural America. I grew up in rural Indiana. I had been a kid with a thousand questions. I flashed back to having asked my good ol' Uncle Jim Porter why those barns were never torn down. I remember him telling me that the farmers had something like State Farm Insurance, hence the name of the company. A grandfather clause relating to farms allowed the farmers to declare a loss only if the barns fell down of their own accord. This being the way my mind worked, those were my thoughts as we ascended to the second floor. I was somewhat cowed by the spectacle that we beheld. I should have been speechless, but you know me.

I couldn't believe what I was seeing. More than a hundred townspeople were crammed into the undivided second floor room. This room should not have had more than possibly forty or fifty people in it. Low rising bleacher seats had long ago been built along the lengths of the room. To say that the benches were packed would be to understate the case. Children were perched on the shoulders of parents and most people were standing. The building was vibrating from their movements. In the center of the room was a table and chair. Seated in the chair was Elyria.

"Tommy," Jack said, holding a palm out to me, "let me handle this. You are in a bad frame of mind already. The last thing we need is to say the wrong thing."

The room quieted quickly when Elyria hit the table with a wooden meat tenderizer. I saw the cross-hatch pattern when she raised it. It was generally used to pound conch meat into submission. Elyria made good conch fritters. I had given her scores of conchs.

"This is a court and it is now in session," she declared. I just looked around, recognizing most of the faces in the crowd. Jack took the lead.

"Your honor, my name is John Crabill (*I didn't know that*). Your constable says that we are under arrest, but he hasn't told us what we have done to be arrested."

"You have been arrested because I told him to arrest you," Elyria replied, looking haughty. I looked at the scarred finger and thumb of her left hand. They looked pretty good, considering.

"But what is the charge?" Jack asked in a quiet and reasonable voice. I should have been taking notes right here.

"You are arrested for not wearing a shirt."

"Not wearing a shirt?" Even the reasonable Mr. John Crabill was taken aback by this assertion.

"You are violating the law that I have written into the laws of the island," Elyria stated flatly. "I am the chief of police."

"And you can just write a law and put it on the books?" Jack asked. My lawyer was obviously treading on new ground.

"I have done that because the Americans are showing no respect for the laws of Utila. They are always not wearing clothes. I have been giving sermons about this for many months and now it is a law. Americans have to be fully dressed whenever they are on the island."

Jack immediately seized on a loophole. "But we were diving, your honor, and not on the island. And we didn't even know there was a law."

"There is a law, and you will all pay five lempira." I had to hand it to the old broad. She wasn't going to get into a debate. This had been set up in advance, hence the audience, and she was in high dudgeon.

Jack turned to Shawn and me. "We should just pay the fine. We'll get the law thrown out, but it will take something from Tegucigalpa to get it done."

"How do you plead?" Elyria demanded. She must have been reading Perry Mason books, I thought. "Each one of you must plead guilty."

"I plead guilty, your honor." It was Shawn, finally saying something. Elyria couldn't help but look at her hand at this. "I hope your thumb is feeling better," he added, sucking up to her.

"My thumb is not the law we are showing to be the reason for this court. You should have paid a fine for doing the devil's work. And you," she was looking at Jack and me now, "you will plead guilty, too. You need to say it out loud so the court is hearing."

Jack capitulated with a firm, "Guilty."

I was glowering now. Fathom had done much in general to help these people, and I, in particular, had gone out of my way to be nice to every islander with whom I had come in contact. And now I was being railroaded in some kangaroo court? I had to put in my two cents. "This is crazy," I blurted out. "Half the kids on this island run around wearing nothing but a shirt." I looked around the room. There were people in the room not wearing shirts, and some of the kids were wearing shirts and nothing else.

"This law means that Americans must wear shirts. It does not mean that Honduras people must be wearing shirts," she shot back in the twisted vernacular used by the islanders. "You will now be pleading guilty."

"The hell I will," I said, my voice rising. "People all over the island run around half-naked and you come up with some crap that only applies to Americans?"

"Shut up, Tommy." It was Jack, warning me. "This isn't the place to debate."

"Americans will be full dressed all the times." Elyria matched me for volume. "If God had meant for peoples to run around naked, they would have been born naked. And Americans do not look good being without all their clothes." This is where I snapped and showed just how stupid I could be, given the right circumstances.

"I may not be looking good without a shirt, Elyria, but you look like hell with all your clothes being on." I had shrewdly adopted her use of the language as a way to mock her. It probably helped my case.

"You are swearing in church? (*church*?) You are being arrested and put in jail."

The room erupted in shouting and I was grabbed by somebody from behind first, then more hands upon my arms. I had a great comeback, but wasn't given the opportunity to make my carefully considered legal retort. I was marched downstairs and taken the few hundred feet to the jail. Lewtie opened the steel door and I was pushed inside. The door was slammed shut.

What a joke, was my first thought. I'm an American. They can't do this to me. My second thought, what a hole. The room was six feet by six feet and had a dirt floor. There was a small barred window in the back wall and another in the steel door. The sills of the windows were about five feet from the dirt. I could just look out.

For the next few hours, I was the center of focus of the entire island, including my fellow Fathomers. I was encouraged by promises from the guys that they would straighten out the whole thing quickly, and I would be out before nightfall. I wasn't.

Duane and Nick stayed around the jail building for several hours. They brought me some lobster and Salva Vidas and we laughed about the entire situation, except I was the one in the cell. Drinking too much beer in a cell with nothing more than a dirt floor presents its own problems. Jack brought a couple of grass mats and my sleeping bag.

When it was apparent that Elyria wasn't going to change her mind about my being jailed, I began to think more pragmatically about my situation. First there were the spiders. They had set up shop here years before. This was an insect rich environment. I asked for a broom and some cardboard. It wasn't too long before I had the cell pretty much to myself. Nick proved to be resourceful and loyal. The insect problem seemed intractable until I got to thinking about the small lizards and chameleons around my hooch. Nick got the word out and within hours I was sharing my cell with several chameleons and other small lizards.

Once I was in the jail, there seemed to be no rules. Lewtie certainly wasn't going to play guard. My only contact with Lewtie after his locking the cell door was later in the day, when he stopped by to have a beer with us. We considered a jail break, which would have been laughably easy, but the consequences of such an action were too unpredictable.

Sergei was livid. Jack had thankfully chosen not to tell him that it was my mouth that had gotten me thrown into jail. He just knew that a silly and unfair law had been foisted upon one of his people and that I was the one being punished. I thought it was pretty funny stuff and I was almost enjoying my status as a martyr. That would change.

I spent my first night in the cell. It was a very dark night, indeed. Nick brought me a kerosene lantern and some books. I didn't sleep much, but it wasn't too bad. I knew that Elyria would have to let me go sometime. My reasoning was based on the premise that one cannot be given years in jail for not wearing a shirt. I am not that naïve now, but I still had much to learn when I was twenty years old.

My first week in jail was spent making a home of the cell. Book shelves were added. The lanterns were hung from the beams. Homes were made for my lizards, complete with imported insects because the native population had been eaten in the first days. The islanders were mostly sympathetic to my plight and Fathom people took my incarceration personally. I had so many well-wishers coming by with books and advice that I actually longed for a little privacy.

It didn't take long to figure out that Elyria had no interest in my fate. She had made her pronouncement from the pulpit of power, not mentioning a term of sentence, and essentially ignored me. Lewtie gave Jack the key to the old padlock, so we soon had it polished and oiled. Then we simply hung the padlock in place so that I could leave the cell at night to "use the facilities." The same dockside privies that I had so long ago decided I would never use. If you have ever wondered if crabs sleep at night, I can tell you with certainty that they never sleep.

Pete and Eddie came in from the key with a load of wood and built a wooden floor in the cell. Then we became entirely brazen and knocked down the wall, or part of it, between the two cells. Our decorating spilled over into the other cell and the lizards had new hunting grounds for a few days.

The second week was to see a mini-revolution against authority. An impromptu parade of hundreds of shirtless islanders and expedition members formed at the government park. The participants walked the length of Main Street, making a point of detouring up one side street, stopping only to hoot and perform in front of the home of one Elyria Morgan. It was a circus atmosphere for several hours. Jan Maresak stopped by to take my picture. I grasped the bars and centered my face between them. A good picture, all things considered. Posing for that picture was a mistake that was to take on epic proportions in my life, almost ending it. But I get ahead of myself.

Gustavo, the town manager whom I had befriended at the ice cream store, came to see me every day. He brought me mango ice cream regularly. He had appointed himself as my lawyer. As such, he made frequent visits to Elyria to plead for my pardon. I had suffered enough, he had argued consistently. It was Gustavo's idea to start a personal war of civil disobedience.

The generator and its diesel engine suffered massive mechanical problems in the third week. Gustavo made it clear to Elyria and the entire Church of God congregation that the system was beyond repair as long as I was still in jail. No ice from the icehouse, no lights to ward off the spirits and no washing machines. As primitive as the island was in 1970, electrical technology had become a necessity. The privations forced upon the pious proved to be too much to bear. Seven days of inconvenience drove Elyria to scripture and soul searching. Without ever laying eyes on me after my sentencing, she found sufficient reason to rescind the new law and to order Lewtie to release me. I took lobster, conch and fish to Gustavo for the next couple of weeks, until I got arrested again.

I never learned how, but the picture of me in the cell, taken by Jan, found its way to the mainland. A newspaper in San Pedro Sula ran the photo on the front page. It was accompanied with an article attacking Fathom Expeditions. The gist of the story was that a colony of foreigners, mostly Americans, had taken over Utila and its keys with the intent of stealing Honduran national treasures. The article never mentioned that I had been arrested for not wearing a shirt. It described my crime as indecent exposure. The phrase sent shock waves through the citizenry.

I became the most talked about person in the country,

seemingly overnight. Within days of the first newspaper story, every newspaper in the country had rerun the photo and embellished the story. A Honduran Navy patrol boat, once a US PT-boat, was dispatched to Utila, complete with a complement of soldiers. They had no trouble finding me. They had my picture. I was on the dock watching the boat cut through the harbor. It would be difficult to overstate the surprise between us all. I was the first person to greet them as I finished securing the mooring lines. As usual, I was just being helpful. Without saying a word, the officer in charge pointed at me. Two of the troops moved toward me without comment.

I would like to say that I was treated with respect and escorted to the boat. But that wasn't at all what happened. I was roughly spun around and handcuffed. Once onboard, I was chained to the deck. Lines were cast off and I was treated to a scary, lonely boat ride of several hours. Two soldiers, armed with World War II vintage M1 carbines sat on the aft deck beside me. They didn't speak or take their eyes off me. We headed west and I knew that we were going to Puerto Cortes. My mind raced. I thought of parodies of Central American firing squads. This was not my finest hour. I was scared sick.

At the wharf in Puerto Cortes I was unchained from the deck cleats and half pushed and half carried to yet another vestige of American military influence so ubiquitous to Central America. I was chained again; this time to the side rails of an Army truck known as a deuce-and-a-half. Each side of the truck bed was lined with a wooden bench. The vehicle was filled with smartly uniformed and armed Honduran soldiers. I was evidently in some serious trouble. I thought of the eighteenth-century wit who was once tarred and feathered and run out of a New England town on a rail. He later became a respected author and wrote of the event. "If it weren't for the honor of being the center of so much attention, I would have just as soon declined." I had always loved the quote, but I couldn't recall the name of the man. It'll come to me, I thought. It is possible that I was becoming slightly irrational.

There is a state prison in San Pedro Sula. In the last few years, it has become somewhat infamous. In May of 2004, a deadly fire caused by the explosion of a refrigerator killed at least one hundred three people. It has been reported that more than three hundred inmates were living in an area intended to house about fifty. Most were burned to death, but some were lucky enough to expire from smoke inhalation. The sewer system was said to have been entirely clogged and methane gas was likely an accelerant to the fire. A few years before, some seventy inmates, guards and visitors were killed when a riot erupted over the alleged torture of scores of inmates. It may have helped that starvation tactics were used by the authorities and generally rotted and fetid food was provided when they were allowed to eat. This was the prison I was taken to in 1970.

I was lead down fungus encrusted, concrete corridors, the walls of which were festooned with odd strips of rusting, iron hardware. Indescribable heaps of garbage and waste were interspersed along the way to break the monotony of blackened concrete. I splashed through puddles of dark water and felt odd masses of material squeeze between my toes. I was to learn soon enough that the liquid was not water. It was almost a relief to be shoved into a six foot by eight foot cell, decorated with a stinking, heavy, stained mattress which was stuck to the floor. The only other accessory of interest was a galvanized bucket, which didn't look to be in such bad condition, all things considered.

I would have more than a little difficulty conveying the feeling of living in a small cell with a bucket for a toilet and a mattress that was a colony of symbiotic and parasitic animals, more than it was a bed. There was no electric light. Three walls had no openings, but I could see high, small, barred windows down the corridor. I was given green scrambled eggs every morning, speckled with what I hoped were bits of bacon and sausage. Since I cannot convey the feeling, I won't try.

This incarceration was serious. I was allowed no contact with anyone and was not allowed out of the stinking cell. Not once. Even the water I was given to drink emitted a stink. And there is no other word to describe it. To call it an odor would be to praise the darkened, cloudy liquid. I went in well-fed and in excellent health. In little more than two weeks, and helped by an incredibly painful chronic and acute case of "abdominal distress," I was reduced to an almost emaciated state.

I felt abandoned and lost track of time. The Rolex watch was an early casualty of my imprisonment. Getting so sick sent me into a world of despair and hopelessness that transcended the fact that it was only a little more than two weeks of such treatment. I was learning more about the relativity of time. It was a crash course. The dysentery (I diagnosed it only years later) could either cure itself or kill me. I have always been essentially resistant to contracting most diseases, and I think my inherently strong constitution probably saved my life.

My salvation came from, who else, Allen and Duane. One day they simply showed up at my cell, accompanied by some uniformed, non-verbal thugs. The cell door was opened for the second time since my arrival. I was a leaner, long haired and more heavily-bearded person than they remembered.

"You look like a survivor from the holocaust," he said without preamble. I considered his wit to be without parallel. I thought his observation was hilarious. I thought everything was hilarious. We were allowed to walk down the only corridor I had seen in the cavernous, ugly fortress, through the several steel-barred doors and out into the sunlight, which nearly staggered me after who knew how many days of only indirect and dusty light.

Allen's yellow 1957 Chevy Bel Aire awaited. I marveled at the beautiful countryside and my plush surroundings. We talked about the weather. Just kidding. I ate tortillas with mystery meat and tomatoes and drank too many Salva Vidas. My taste for beer had finally blossomed into a full blown love affair. We were on the best rode trip of my life, and I mean to date. I had to beg that we pull off the road several times. I threw up everything that I ate and drank, but felt better than I had in at least two weeks. Everything, not just time, is relative.

Allen started the real conversation.

"Tommy, you are one tough nut. You move to the mainland, leave no forwarding address, don't call, don't write and make new friends. You just shut Duane and me out of your life. We missed you." Allen was looking over his right shoulder and grinning while he talked. "It took a week just to find out and confirm that you were in the San Pedro Sula Howard Johnson. Then it took another week, and some help from the ambassador himself, to convince the government to release you to us. A few more days to work out the details and bribe the local politicians and here we are." Allen took a swig of beer and continued. "They want you to stand trial in Tegucigalpa for, as of yet, unnamed charges. We agreed," he added, "and here you are."

"Oh no," I whined, feeling doom close in on me again. "I am going to jail again; and all for not wearing a shirt?"

"Well," Duane drawled out somewhat ominously, "that and insulting the Right Reverend Elyria of the Church of God, while spitting on the sacred laws and testaments of the sovereign state of Honduras." Then he drained his beer, dropping the bottle into the cooler next to him and retrieving another for himself and me. I was washing out my polluted system.

"Don't worry about it, Captain Conklin," Allen said, beaming like a schoolboy at recess. "This is working out just fine."

"Don't get me wrong here, guys. But it is freaking me out that you guys are in such a good mood at my being sacrificed for the good of the State Department, or whomever. Right now

I would do anything for you guys, no matter how perverted, just to show my undying gratitude. But I cannot imagine going back into one of their jails, or prisons; whatever that place was back there."

"Oh, you were in a prison, Tommy," Allen intoned in a quieter voice, "and the worst. People rot in that place. But you did very well. You kept your mouth shut and caused us no trouble."

"How could I have caused any trouble?" I said too shrilly, "No one talked to me and they never let me out of that cell, not once."

This seemed to surprise Allen, because all he said was, "Really?"

"Yeah, really," I said in that still too shrill a voice. "And now you guys seem pretty happy that I am going to be put on trial." I was whining like a baby. If they were looking for heroic stoicism when they chose me, they were going to be sorely disappointed, I thought. Didn't they know about the symbol of the cringing chicken on my family's ancient coat-of-arms?

"Oh, haven't I mentioned yet that you aren't going to stand trial for anything?" Allen said, still looking back and forth between me and the narrow road, "You are going to the mountains, to ride horses and stay in an actual mansion on an actual estate."

"Huh?" I could be so eloquent when I pulled out all the stops.

"Sure," Allen said gaily. "We are going to hide you and use your situation as an excuse to funnel money and wampum to the politicians. This is perfect. They supposedly have something we want, your sorry ass, and we definitely have something they want, mainly American dollars. I intend to see to it that we make reparations for the insult to their sensibilities that you represent. Some payments will be made public. We are, after all, a legitimate American company just trying to right a wrong.

Some gifts will be given. You know that Rolex watch you used to have?" That was the first moment I realized that I hadn't gotten it back when we left the prison. Well of course I hadn't. "Well..., a lot of those are going to be sprinkled around, even the gold ones now that I think about it," Allen added almost parenthetically. "This is one of those rare win-win situations you hear about every now and then. "I'll get you another watch, too, for all your help. Hell, take this one."

With that, he stripped off his Rolex Submariner, exactly as he had done a few months earlier, and handed it back to me. "Now, Tommy, I'm sure that you realize by now that your usefulness in Honduras has come to an end, but not your usefulness to us. There are other places and tougher situations where people who can think on their feet and be trusted are most helpful." I took the watch numbly and without even a thank-you. I was just waking from a bad dream and social courtesies were beyond my ability at the time. I wasn't going back to jail? I was going to the mountains and live in a mansion? Is this a great country or what, I thought? And I wasn't thinking about Honduras. We drove on, stopping a few times to water the vegetation. Several Salva Vidas later, we arrived in, and more importantly, passed through, the sprawling and suddenly not-so-ugly metropolis of Tegucigalpa, and drove up into the mountains to the west.

The old Chevy handled the switchbacks and hard climbing of the mountain road with some strain at times. That got me to thinking. "Allen, if we can get some points and plugs and maybe find the tools, I wouldn't mind tuning up your car. It's the least I can do to thank you for getting me out of prison and probably from being in front of a firing squad." Weeks later, Duane and I would think back to my offhand comment about the firing squad. I had it right, just the wrong country.

Duane grinned at Allen, "You see what I mean, the kid is

always just jumping into things, and there isn't anything he won't try or do to be helpful."

"He does seem to be almost a one-off kind of guy doesn't he?" Allen asked rhetorically. "I wonder what he'll think of Chile?"

I was a little uncomfortable with the talk about me being in the third-person. I talked to remind them that I was right here. "So what do you say, Allen, can I work on the car. It probably has a 283. Unless it has had the engine replaced sometime. I will figure it out though."

"I think something can be arranged kid. You may not know it, but this is Friday. You know the nice place I promised you? Well, it belongs to a friend of mine, and Duane and I will be staying the weekend if you don't mind. Monday will mean descending into the bowels of Honduran bureaucracy for me, but you will be staying here." With that, the gravel road through the heavy canopy of trees opened into a wide vista of a courtyard, fields and beautiful buildings. It really was a mansion. There were guest quarters, outbuildings and barns. The quality of all the buildings and the obvious high level of maintenance were stunning to someone coming from a one room hooch in the jungle, not to mention a prison.

We spent the weekend in an almost drunken state. At least I did. My drinking lessons had taken hold nicely. Nick would be proud of me. That was what got me thinking about the island. I wondered if I would ever see it again. I had a vision of Jack and Jill swimming around the harbor, looking for me to show up and feed them. I missed the early morning dives, the mango ice cream and even the mood swings of drinking. I was in the best of surroundings, living a life I could not have imagined a month ago, and I was feeling sorry for myself. I could be so pathetic at times.

I learned to live with the wonderful surroundings. It happened that the house came with a full-time cook, two groundskeepers and even a stableman and horses. I still know nothing about horses. I don't even know how to start the things. But I let one of them take me around the grounds almost every day for three weeks. The air was cool, being far above sea level, and the afternoon thunderstorms arrived as if on a schedule. I found a large collection of albums and an elegant Magnavox, console-style stereo system. I used to work for Magnavox, you know. It made me feel a little homesick.

While I played, Allen and others prowled the corridors of power in the capital of Honduras. Buying a country takes a little luck and a good sense of timing, I decided. By the end of the second week, the justice system of Honduras was willing to compromise with my being deported "for no less than sixty days." The decision was reached after much deliberation and consultation of the time, as kept by some recently acquired gold Rolex watches.

Chapter Twenty Three

Border Guards

The day I left the mountain estate was depressingly perfect. Allen arrived in late morning, driving his signature, yellow 1957 Chevy Bel Aire. I was sitting on the veranda, as a porch is called if you own a fancy house, swaying back and forth gently in a white wooden swing. He braked a little too hard for the gravel and dirt courtyard. As he emerged from the car, the dust kicked up by the locked wheels caught up with him. He emerged from the dust cloud choking on the dust and laughing.

"Tommy," he called out while brushing himself with hard slaps to his clothes, "how you doing, kid? See, I told you there was nothing to worry about. We greased the usual palms, the politicians look good with their deportation order as punishment for your heinous crime of not wearing a shirt while swimming, and you get to see more of the world. Funny how things work out, isn't it?"

"Yeah," I responded, standing up and reaching out to shake Allen's hand. "Just hilarious."

"Ah, don't take it so hard. It's just theatre. It really works out for us. We have a good reason to buy the bastards off, which puts them deeper into our back pockets. And they get to lie to themselves that they deserve the money for giving up their right to keep you in jail, something they really didn't want to do anyway. Not when you were a poker chip just waiting to be cashed in. Quid, Pro, Quo, you know?"

"Yeah, I guess so." I mumbled more to myself than him. I was feeling sorry for myself again. I would just have to learn to lighten up a bit. *That which doesn't kill you, strengthens you, right?*

"Sure you do. Okay, let's get your things and get back down in the city. Gonna feel pretty good, you know? No Federales waiting to handcuff you and toss you in jail. You and Nick are going to have a good time." He walked back toward the car as I picked up my duffel and followed him. I tossed it in the back seat. This seemed to bring Allen up short.

"Hey Tommy," he said looking at me across the roof of his car, "how long has it been since you've driven anyway?" That brought me up short. I hadn't given it any thought. I considered it for a few moments.

"About seven months, I guess." I grinned back at him. "You thinking I have forgotten how to drive?

"No, no, not exactly, but maybe you would want to drive us back into Tegoose. You know, take a little practice." He punctuated this by lobbing a set of keys in a high arch and somewhat behind me. I stepped back, lined up the arc of the throw perfectly, made the subtle calculations that allow for a perfect catch and saw them sail past my hand and drop into the gravel. Allen came around the car.

"Yeah, a little practice, that would be good," he said as he climbed into the car on the passenger side.

I drove down the mountainside, being careful to not ride the brakes. The old Chevy had a two-speed Powerglide transmission. Low was just too low, but I was not going to rush it. It was a real hassle keeping the car slowed down without running the RPM's up too high or using the brakes too often.

Allen had been right. I needed some practice.

Getting into the much lower hills of Tegucigalpa was a relief. I followed Allen's directions and we snaked around through shanty towns and suffered the horns of the impatient drivers; all Latin Americans are impatient drivers, no exceptions. I know it sounds arrogant of me, but I couldn't imagine why all these people drove so fast, and hard. When they got to their destinations, they were still in Tegucigalpa. If that is indicative of my American inbred arrogance, it is just too bad. This place sucked canal water, to use the line of my old buddy, Greg Fox.

Generally following Allen's directions (I missed several turns due to my hesitance to push my way into the right or left side of the seemingly innumerable one-way streets), I found myself parking underneath the nondescript three story building that was the Honduran home of "Fathom Expeditions." I negotiated the tight confines of the building without running into the concrete supports. This must have impressed Allen, because he mentioned my not wrecking his car. Piece of cake.

I will be the first to admit that I was relieved to see Nick as he emerged from the stairway. I had come to realize that having a friend could smooth out the lumps in life. Not very manly stuff to admit, but there it is.

"Hey Tommy," Nick gushed, evidently as glad to see me as I was to see him, "great to see you, and not in jail too."

"It's good not to be in jail, Nick." I know that I looked as curious as I felt, because I had my head cocked slightly as I regarded Nick, wondering if I should shake his hand or really commit a social *faux pas* and give him a hug. He and Duane had emerged from a sea of people as the only two friends I had in the world. It was my fault that I didn't have many friends, I knew, but that only made their helping me the more remarkable. I was most comfortable only in my own company. It was my good fortune that Nick and Duane had seen something of value in me; although I couldn't imagine what that would be.

"It could have been me as easily as you." I wondered exactly what he was thinking. "I mean if that old broad had laid that crap on me, I would have gone off the deep end. That island is out of my system. You know that we are going on a road trip, don't you?"

"We are?" More of my eloquence.

"We are." Nick parroted. "You have been formally asked to get the hell out of Honduras, heavy on the asked," he added for effect, "and I have asked to get the hell out of Honduras. It's a perfect fit. We have a place in Tampico, Mexico. I've been there. That's where I drove from in the stake bed truck I told you about. I told you I drove down from the States, because that's what I told everybody, if you get my drift. I brought a bunch of gear down here, just before you got here, as a matter of fact. They want the truck back in Mexico, and a Volkswagen minibus too."

"I'm driving out of here?" I asked stupidly. "I mean we're driving out of here?" That was much more intelligently asked.

"Sure, except that we are going to put the minibus on the truck. And Duane is going with us. That's the only reason we hung around to get you out of jail. We need you to drive, because you have impaired drinking abilities. We'll work on that in Mexico. Much better selection of beer there."

As if on cue, Duane appeared, driving the stake bed truck, carrying a Volkswagen minibus. He rumbled around the corner of the building and stopped short of trying to enter the parking area, which would have been a mistake.

Duane climbed down from the cab and greeted us. "I see you guys are ready to go. What say we leave before we get all choked up at the thought of leaving this hole?" And that was the extent of ceremony that we attached to leaving Honduras. Nick and I stowed our meager possessions in the back of the minibus, climbed into the cab of the truck, with Duane driving, and headed out of the city. Duane knew how to connect with the Pan American Highway, and that was all we needed to know about getting out of the country.

I had never driven a truck before, but I told Duane that I had a great deal of experience. I always lied about my ability to do just about anything. I have noted this flaw in my character all my life. I just couldn't say the words "I don't know how to do that." I knew that if I had told the truth, that I didn't know how to double clutch between gears, when and how to engage a two speed differential, or how to even find the "gate release" to get the thing into reverse, I would be subjected to instruction. I don't like to be taught anything. For my entire life, my mother has been telling anyone unfortunate enough to get ensnared in her web of motherhood stories, that my first real phrase was "I do it myself." I didn't invent trial and error as a method of learning, but I certainly was a devotee of the concept. And I had the scars to prove it. I watched Duane carefully and knew that I would be able to hide my ignorance once again.

Some months before, I had given up any attachment to a civilized life. As such, I spent almost no time reflecting on what lay in store for me. My conversations reflected this. The deepest thoughts that I entertained as we turned onto the Pan American Highway had to do with the route that we would take.

"Where exactly does this highway go, Duane?"

"Technically, we could stay on it and make our way to Alaska, but that's not what you are asking is it?"

"Hardly."

"You know where we are, Tommy, I mean in relation to everything else in Central America?" This put me in my place. My fear of displaying ignorance kept me from answering. My silence was answer enough. "What I mean is, we are in the thick of Central America when we are in Tegucigalpa. From here we can turn south and in a day be in Costa Rica, Panama, Nicaragua, or even Colombia. The way we are headed takes us through El Salvador, Guatemala and Mexico. We could head northwest instead of west and take in British Honduras."

"I hate to admit that outside of the charts on the Salva Vida, I haven't given the layout of Central America any thought." I may as well admit my pitiful lack of geographical expertise, I decided.

"Few Americans give any thought to countries south of the Rio Grande. You realize that Brazil is bigger than the lower forty-eight?" I sullenly shook my head. Answer enough. Duane just laughed easily at my unease. "Don't worry about it. When we get to Tampico, we are all going to have a little strategy session. You are a tiny cog in a big machine. We all are, but some of us are on the front lines. This road trip is going to give us about twenty hours to sort things out."

The twenty hour estimate was not even close. We were headed into a gathering storm. I was just hours from a life-changing event. There was no way that we could have foreseen any of what lay in store for us. A quiet settled on the cocoon of the cab as we gave ourselves up to personal reveries. Duane drove, Nick leaned against the window and I slouched between them, arranging my thoughts for the upcoming geopolitical lesson.

I remembered a geography textbook from the fifth grade. The cover photo was a beautiful signature shot of the Matterhorn, with a spray of powdered snow blowing from the famous wedge shaped peak. I often arranged facts this way. It seemed natural to me to associate items with the source of the information. Anyway, this was the book from which I had learned all that I knew of the great Pan American Highway. An entire chapter had been given over to touting the route's potential for bringing the Americas together. As I compared what I was seeing to what had been stored in my mind's eye, I realized that the geography book's descriptions had been more than a little overblown.

This wasn't a highway by any standards that the average American would use as a reference. It was just another asphalt route, barely wide enough to qualify as a two lane road. No white lines along the edges. No yellow line, dashed or otherwise, to separate opposite direction traffic. Every oncoming vehicle represented more than the usual trust in faith that the other driver would remain on his side of the road. And our truck was more the norm than I would have suspected. I would concede the commercial aspect of the road.

Trucks were the rule, not the exception. And almost every truck sported a large, sometimes ornate, structure of steel on the front end. These were called nerf bars when added to custom cars of the fifties and sixties back in the world. Except that these were not meant for show. They were designed and built to deflect errant vehicles and animals. Some years later, I would see the movie, *Road Warrior*, with an unknown actor named Mel Gibson, playing the protagonist. The fixed stares and malevolent intent of the drivers of the post-apocalyptic world portrayed in the movie would make me flash back to these drivers and their trucks. Didn't anyone relax down here?

A few hours of defensive driving brought us to the border between Honduras and El Salvador. We were stopped first by Honduran soldiers, manning a checkpoint. Our passports were perused and the truck was examined thoroughly, including the underside. The Volkswagen minibus presented another problem for the bureaucratic sides of the guards. They needed more documentation before passage of the vehicles could be granted. Papers in the form of American dollars sufficed.

Duane was a gifted speaker in the Spanish language. I still hadn't acquired enough Spanish to talk my way out of a barroom fight, and this guy was mesmerizing these clowns. I felt bile rise in my throat as one of the guards took an especial interest in me. Apparently I was somebody special. My name was on his list. Not surprising, considering my recent tour of the

Honduran penal system and subsequent official deportation, but disquieting nonetheless. The guard wore a neatly pressed uniform of a solid gray-green color. His brass hardware was polished and he wore a peaked, billed cap at a low forward angle, just covering his eyebrows. I thought of just about every World War II movie I had ever seen. Here was the quintessential Nazi officer demanding papers. I saw his gaze fix upon my shoes. But he wasn't interested in my feet. He reached down and pulled the right pants leg up slightly, exposing most of a leather knife sheath. He backed away slightly and brought the little carbine up just enough to indicate his displeasure at the sight of a knife. He spit out some invective in Spanish that left me clueless, but I noted that it didn't end in *por favor* (please).

Duane heard the tone of the verbal ejaculation and confronted the guard without hesitation. There was a brief staccato of words exchanged. Duane turned to me and said, "He wants your Buck knife. I told him he could have it if it would get us on our way." I was so thoroughly cowed by the thought of the prison that I handed over my beautiful Buck knife without comment. *Just get me out of this stinking country.*

A few more American dollars were added to assuage the offended delicate sensibilities of these guardians of Honduran culture and we were allowed to proceed. We crossed an obvious no-mans-land between the Honduran check point and the next one, manned by Salvadoran border guards. This was just a year after the Soccer War and we were on what had been the front lines. More than a thousand soldiers and civilians had been killed in the fields and forests around us. The tension was palpable, as they say. Still, my ignorance allowed me to feel relief at escaping Honduras without further incarceration for any crimes, real or imagined.

Duane ground the gears as he double-clutched between first and second. "This transmission just about refuses to synch no matter how carefully I try to get it in line between shifts. It could use a little work." His words were prophetic.

The Salvadorans were not happy to see us. We were visiting their country from the wrong direction. Anybody coming from the Honduran side of the border was evidently still the enemy. Almost worse than being fresh from Honduran soil was the fact that we were Americans. It was no secret that the *Estados Unidos* had sided with the Hondurans more than El Salvador after the cessation of hostilities. The truck and minibus were searched even more thoroughly than before.

Duane was in his element, exchanging money and ideas without showing the least concern. He even displayed confidence. I was being transformed in a more subtle way. I hated the way I feared these people. I didn't hate the people; I hated myself for feeling the fear of what they could do to me. As is my custom, I got angry. When my passport was demanded, I threw it across the counter of the guard shack, bouncing it off the ample stomach of the Salvadoran soldier. He regarded me from beneath a furrowed brow that brought me to my senses slightly. These people could cause us a lot of trouble without answering to anyone. I chickened out yet again.

"Sorry," I mumbled, "it got away from me."

For his part, the soldier studied my photo and me, making me conscious of the fact that I barely resembled the pale little boy grinning out from the photo. I now had very long curly hair and a nicely trimmed, but very full beard. My skin complexion was close to scarred, tanned leather and I sported a very broken nose. My upper and lower jaws were no longer in line and I couldn't have replicated the smile in the photo if my life had depended upon the task. Rubber stamps flew. From Mexico on south, immigration people are evidently required to have a rubber stamp fetish. They stamp several pages with barely intelligible imprints, generally making certain that previous entries are obliterated in the process.

Things were moving along, though, until I heard the word

seguridad (police) hang in the air. It was hung there by Duane, and the question mark appended to it particularly got my attention. Duane turned to Nick and me and shook his head to display his disgust to the Salvadorans "We have to pay for a soldier to ride with us through the country. He is supposed to protect us. This is just another excuse to extract money."

"Duane, it strikes me that these people don't need excuses, they just demand money." I quickly realized that my opinion didn't mean squat down here, but I argue logic without regard to race, religion or sexual orientation. Duane stared at me, lost in thought.

"You are absolutely right, Captain," Duane responded in that mock formality that always amused me, this one time being the exception. I could feel my mood souring again. "They are doing this as pure intimidation."

"I should have mentioned this before," Nick joined in. "We brought a soldier through El Salvador when Brian and I came down here last year. He was a nice guy and even spoke pretty good English. I thought we were just doing them a favor. It was no sweat. He rode in the cab and talked about his thirteen brothers and sisters. He got out right here and that was the end of it."

"Alright, alright," Duane capitulated, "I know there's nothing I can do about it. I'm just letting off some steam here I guess." I could feel the stress in me too. The catharsis of the mountain retreat had evaporated. I was back in the real world of Latin American machismo and intimidation. Duane reentered discussions with the main bureaucrat in charge of the station and fees were paid.

The "guard" assigned to us was almost laughably unthreatening. He appeared to be at least sixty years old. He had a Pillsbury Dough Boy physique and the countenance of a subservient gardener, more than that of a soldier. He wielded a gun, such as it was, and his uniform was too small and hadn't seen an iron in weeks. Without a word to us he climbed up into the bed of the truck and squeezed into the Volkswagen minibus by using the sliding door.

"Okay, Captain," Duane addressed me, "you have the helm. Take us out of here. Set a course for Guatemala… Engage." *Captain Kirk?*

Chapter Twenty Four

The Firing Squad

I climbed up behind the big expanse of steering wheel. I felt more like a toddler in one of those car seats with the steering wheel and horn arrangements than I felt like a truck driver. I started the engine and checked the fuel gauge. Like every truck in Central America, the thing had twice the fuel capacity of the average stateside rig. No worries. The three of us turned as one to look back at our protector. He was now seated in the passenger seat of the minibus. He was looking around from his high perch. I noticed that he did not make eye contact with us; as if it wouldn't have been appropriate. This was not a warrior.

"Man, he looks like my uncle's golden retriever, sitting in the pickup, waiting to stick his head out the window to bite the air." Nick had been somewhat morose, but clearing out of Honduras had a way of elevating one's mood. I clumsily ground the gears in the transmission just getting the thing into first gear, and we were on our way.

This was the moment Duane and Nick had been anticipating for hours. Nick had actually scrounged some ice from who knows where in Tegucigalpa, and stuffed it into his duffel bag. Luckily, the ice was not bruised too badly, its fall having been broken by contact with many bottles of Salva Vida. I was out a Buck knife so far, but thankfully no beer had been seized.

Night fell within the hour, but the twilight that prevailed at first allowed me to make myself familiar with the modest complement of controls. More importantly, the fading light helped me get a feel for the unmarked, highly crowned and too narrow blacktop road that was the Pan American Highway. I found that I had to concentrate on what was illuminated by the headlights, reminding myself to look past the beam of light and rely on my peripheral vision to keep the big rig aligned with the edge of the road. Driving out of the almost interminable canopy of trees that had marked the beginning of my first night driving in many months was a relief. I caught glimpses of open fields. This was an area free of forest, the first truly open, grassy land that I had seen since arriving in Central America.

I also noticed that we were elevated several feet above the surrounding terrain. The height of the road presented a new concern. There was no shoulder wider than a couple of feet. The slight shoulder sloped almost vertically some eight to ten feet on either side. I took to driving down the middle of the road. The little moonlight that I had enjoyed soon disappeared behind thickening clouds as we plunged into the darkness. I began to calculate the width of road afforded us and the implications of sharing that with an oncoming truck. A light drizzle began to spot the windshield. I had resorted to driving within the beam of the headlights when an indefinable shape on the road ahead took me by complete and utter surprise.

I wasted precious seconds attempting to identify the obstruction. When I realized that it was a cow running ahead of us, I did the worst thing I could have done. I stomped both feet on the brake pedal and held it down. A real driver would have tapped the brakes repeatedly, not letting the brakes lock on the slippery asphalt. The slightly wet road provided no purchase for the tires, locked up as they were. Time slowed as I took in the building disaster. The cow was running hard, its fat body swinging back and forth ungracefully while the bony hind quarters stood out in bold relief against the generally wide mass ahead.

It seemed to me that the truck was picking up speed on the slick surface. As the big grill engulfed the animal, I lost sight of all but its head, which was turned toward me. I made eye contact with the beast just as the truck achieved some traction and slammed to a stop. I heard voices, probably mine included, yelling unintelligibly. I watched as the body of the animal went airborne. Now that time had slowed I was able to analyze the situation. The greater speed and weight of the truck, complete with a Volkswagen minibus, Salvadoran guard and three wide-eyed Americans, had imparted a great deal of energy into the mass that had been a living animal.

The truck had taken on a left turning drift as it skidded to a halt. Imparting its direction to the cow, I watched for what seemed an impossibly long time as the animal's legs splayed out, and then tucked in as it completed a graceful and acrobatic, complete roll to the left just as it reached the acme of its climb. It made a noiseless and incredibly slow descent off the left side of the road. The lighting was excellent, I thought, because the truck had parked itself with a perfectly situated left cant. When the cow disappeared below the road level, time returned to my world.

Being a coward by nature, my first impulse was to run. Not a noble first thought, but there it was.

In the way that I have of reviewing my options while living a building disaster (I have had my share), I thought about the ramifications of driving away. Putting a voice to this idea first, Duane looked across the cab of the truck and around the still wide-eyed Nick and said, "If we try to drive away, that damn guard will probably shoot us, starting with you." I quickly canceled that course of action. For a few seconds, I entertained some wishful thoughts, hoping that our guard hadn't seen the cow, just some really bad driving.

"Let's go back and see what our buddy has to say, okay Duane?" I was too much a coward to go alone. Besides what good would it do? I sure couldn't talk to him in Spanish.

"Maybe he didn't see what happened," Duane thought out loud, "and we can make our escape." I liked the way this guy thought. We needed to avoid controversy right? It was just good diplomacy not to let these things get blown out of proportion.

I was entertaining these thoughts as I climbed down from the cab. The fantasy ended when I saw the first peasant. A bent old man wielding a machete stood looking at me, not ten feet away. *Where did he come from?* More peasants appeared. If this is not a politically correct description of the scores of people who seemingly materialized out of the mist, it is simply too bad. They were peasants. There were scores of them. They surrounded the truck, and us. Not one of them said a word, Spanish or otherwise. But the real menace stood away from the crowd.

Three smartly dressed soldiers, wielding larger than average weapons and not smiling, were taking in the scene. I watched as our guard exchanged a few words with them. I noticed that the uniforms of the three newcomers were markedly different than our guard's. It was also evident that the guard seemed intimidated and nervous. He shook his head back and forth several times, and then moved off, not to be seen again. The scene was almost surrealistic, the figures silhouetted against the black sky by the beam of the truck's headlights.

Being compassionate, and stupid, I decided to check on the cow. I hoped that it hadn't been killed by the collision. I slid down the wet embankment, almost landing on the cow. It was lying on its side, but definitely breathing. I looked around, wondering if one of these people knew something we could do to help the cow. The animal raised its head, emitted a long and baleful mooing sound and laid the long head back down in the wet grass. The exposed side no longer moved. It was dead. And I wasn't feeling so well myself. I felt regret at killing the cow, but I felt much worse about my situation. I scanned the scene along the roadway, some five or six feet above my head. I could hear Duane's voice. He was alternately speaking Spanish and English. Nick was nowhere to be seen.

I couldn't help but feel sorry for both of them. My actions had once again put me and others at the center of attention. Then I got mad at the cow. What the devil was the damn thing doing in the middle of the road at night anyway? I was busy formulating excuses when I was grabbed by my left arm and spun roughly around. I was stunned to see a man with one arm cut off at the shoulder. The beam of the headlights shot out directly overhead and provided enough illumination to take in the hollowed socket and even the man's demeanor. Not that I could have mistaken the fusillade of Spanish for anything less than extreme anger.

He called out over his right shoulder, which did have an arm attached, while not taking his eyes off me. I picked up the words *undulay* and *vamanose*. The three soldiers came walking purposefully out of the darkness parallel to the road and straight at me, following a natural depression that formed a wide, shallow ditch. One was wielding a knife, with his large automatic rifle slung over the opposite shoulder. The other two were carrying their weapons with both hands and the barrels were pointed at a slight downward angle, but in my general direction.

I stood transfixed as I watched the first soldier reach down near my right side. He grasped the rope halter of the dead cow with one hand and quickly cut the line in several places. By this time, obviously taking orders from the one-armed man, the other two had shouldered their weapons and forced me down onto my knees while bringing my arms painfully behind me.

The rope was looped around my lower arms several times and I felt the jolt of a knot being cinched over my hands. I reflexively clinched my hands into fists and bent them somewhat backward. I tried to stand, but both soldiers at my side pushed me back into the soft ground. All three walked away toward the darkness from which they had appeared seconds before. Great, I was a prisoner again. But I dully realized that I was not going to be a prisoner for long when the soldiers stopped and turned back toward me.

This was a firing squad.

My mind raced as it went into slow-motion. The dichotomy of that description did not occur to me until years later.

Time entered the zone with which I was becoming all too familiar. I could hear the voice of the one armed man, but it was drawn out into long low syllables and his backward movement, away from me, was too slow to be possible. I was about to be shot and I could feel nothing. I had no emotion. My natural instinct to survive was gone. I thought about being slammed by a World War II fighter aircraft, my feet being cut to shreds on a reef, having my face smashed into the gunwale of the *Salva Vida*, being knifed by Mr. Sleep and being thrown into prison for not wearing a shirt. I was tired.

I took careful note of things that meant nothing. The three soldiers were lined up in order of descending height, tallest to my left. As the weapons were raised, I saw the glint of the gold belt buckles. Then I corrected myself. *They would be polished brass, silly*. I began to rise in the slowest movement of my life. I remember thinking, what did it matter that it was taking so long to stand? I had the rest of my life to accomplish the feat. If I could ascribe any emotion to my last moments, it would have to be the humor of that thought.

I achieved full height in a synchronized motion with the raising of the rifles. We all made eye contact in the moment I could feel my trigger finger flexing. The world had melted to the four of us. I wondered if it would hurt. I tightened my chest muscles. Just when I expected (and wondered if I would hear) the crack of the rifles, I heard a startling yell.

From my upper left I saw a figure suspended in mid-air. It was a man I vaguely remembered. His arms and legs were spread-eagled, making me think of a granddaddy long legs spider spreading his many legs when tossed into the air. Time exploded in a crescendo of noise and movement when the man/spider crashed into my firing squad, roughly destroying the poetry of the moment. Then another figure was briefly illuminated in the beam of light, caught in a graceful arc that ended in another rough crash. People were yelling and arms and legs were flying.

As my brain began functioning, I realized that Nick and Duane were fighting for me. I pulled at the ropes. Because I had made fists and flexed my wrists, and because only one knot was evidently thought to be needed, I was easily able to get an arm free as I ran to the pile of fighters.

My first action was to grab a uniformed leg and drag a soldier out of the fight. The bastard was doubling up on Nick, and hitting him while he was occupied with one of the others. Now we had a fair fight. As I dragged him through the wet grass one of his legs was twisted back and underneath him. I jumped forward and kicked him between the legs as hard as I possibly could. I decided to kill him. I kicked him again as his hands reached the spot. It was the middle height soldier I noticed. I fell onto him and hit him as hard and as often as I could. For once in my pitiful experience of fist fighting I did not punch once and wait for my opponent to react. I really wanted to kill this person. But the rain was ruining my chance.

The rain increased in intensity as if in concert with our rush of movement. Punches began glancing off and it was impossible to achieve any purchase on the now slicked vegetation and exposed muddy ground. We found ourselves falling into each other and the hilarity of our ineffectual fighting got the better of us all. We quit fighting as suddenly as we had started. We helped each other to our feet and began laughing. The release was contagious.

"You *gringos* fight good," said the soldier I had tried to disable. "The rain caused us much trouble, but it was a good fight." I jumped when the shortest of the three slapped me on the back. For their part, the other two were laughing and making their views known. The mood was broken. They had decided not to shoot me.

I looked at Nick as the tallest of the soldiers turned a flashlight on him. He looked the worst of us. Besides the clumps of mud-encrusted grass attached to him, he was bleeding. He had used the weapons to break his fall. My attention was drawn to the rifles as I thought about Nick and Duane. In a moment of uncomfortable silence, the rifles were retrieved from the wet ground. The one-armed man was talking to the soldiers.

They listened, but were more attentive to the guns. Initially, they held them out to the rain, which served as a welcome shower for us all.

"Nick, you crazy son-of-a-bitch, that was the bravest thing I have ever seen," I said to the darkness in general. "I don't know what to say." I felt a choking sensation and couldn't talk.

"Ah, forget it; you would have done the same thing. Hell, you did. Remember the Corsairs? I owed you." I just untangled the rope from my arms and shook my head. Not the same thing, I thought. What do you say to people who have just saved your life? Thanks?

Our spectators began to laugh and a virtual circus atmosphere ensued as we tried to climb the rise back to the road. My climb was made possible by taking the sling of a reversed automatic rifle, held down to me by the soldier whom I had so ungraciously tried to kill with a field castration.

Duane launched back into diplomacy mode and entered negotiations with the one-armed man.

"Tommy, this guy is the foreman for the ranch we are driving through. It extends for miles in every direction. That cow was his responsibility. He wants us to pay for the cow, but I told him we didn't have much money. Just go along with me on this. We cannot have money. Not out here. You understand?"

"Yeah, I guess so," I responded stupidly.

Nick shook his head and I could see the logic in this. We had hidden almost all of our money under one of the stakes that made a fence around the truck bed. That stake had been cut short and a t-shaped piece of steel held the wood up to the proper height. It was a stash.

Duane grasped the back of my neck. "Sorry we lost track of you kid. If Nick hadn't yelled, there is no way I would have seen that these goons were going to shoot you. These people are very high strung. They are national guardsmen. They actually work for the hacienda. It's the only way they can get paid right now. Why don't you turn the truck around since it is almost pointed the other direction? Jorge, the foreman, says the hacienda road is just a mile back up the road. We need to get away from here. Bad karma, you know? I'm going to ride in his car and keep him calm. Follow us."

Duane was the penultimate leader. I have never known anyone else as capable in my life. He adjusted to situations and made plans without the usual human trait of assigning blame and mulling over the inconsequential. Somehow, I had managed to make this trip with the only two people who could have saved me. I may have a black cloud over me, but over the years, I have been fortunate to have just the right people around me to provide the silver lining.

Nick and I climbed into the truck and kept the little car in sight. We all stopped on the road to the hacienda and worked out a plan. Jorge shook hands with me and said sorry several times. I couldn't believe it. Duane had put him on a guilt trip. We all agreed that as soon as we got back to the States, we would send him $240 for the cow. To seal the deal, Jorge pulled a newspaper from the car, tore off a small section from the front page, and wrote "$240 for a cow" across the newsprint and handed me the piece of paper and his pen.

"He wants you to sign it since you were the driver," Duane said seriously. "Then he wants you to keep the paper as proof that you owe him the money." That didn't make any sense, but I did as I was told.

We all shook hands, said goodbye several times, and got in our respective vehicles. The interior light was illuminating the cab just enough for us to see each others' expressions. We were soaked and grinning. We laughed and punched each other in the way males do when sharing a special moment. Relief washed over me in waves. I had felt nothing during my brief stint in front of the impromptu firing squad, but now was on the verge of fainting. Instead, I ground the gears, putting the truck into first gear and drove slowly up the drive, looking for a place to turn around.

"Turn into this field on our right," Duane said casually, "we can back up and get the hell out here. I don't want to see the hacienda." I didn't think we should get off the pavement, considering the rain, which had stopped just as we had turned back to this road, but Duane was the boss. I turned into the field and we were all surprised to see that we were almost hard up against a barbed wire fence. No sweat. I only had to shift into reverse and we were gone. Only the truck wouldn't shift into reverse. The shift lever simply jammed. We were stuck in the very low first gear known as the granny gear. We weren't going anywhere. This was to become a very big problem. I didn't know it then, but I was well on my way back to a Central American jail.

Chapter Twenty Five

La Libertad, El Salvador

Because the truck could not be shifted into reverse, and the fence was within a few feet of the grill, we were trapped. We all three in turn tried to force the long gear shift lever to move. We had a lot of leverage, because the stick was about three feet long and very solid. I found that to be the most ominous portent as to the nature of the problem.

"This just isn't happening," I said as much to the truck as to my companions. I quickly abandoned any thoughts of whining. It was time to show a little courage. "Don't we have some tools in the VW?" I asked, looking at Duane.

He looked at me as if I were crazy. "We have some wrenches and screwdrivers, but nothing that is going to fix a gear box. This is bad."

"I think we should drive right through that fence, make a big circle, and get the hell out of here," Nick opined.

I just shook my head. "We can't do that Nick. I mean, you're right, we could drive through the fence and probably rip it down for a half mile. Then those national guardsmen will be here to shoot all three of us."

"You don't think they wouldn't have shot us after they shot

you, Tommy?" Nick rejoined. "They wouldn't have left two American witnesses. They were just going to start with you. I thought about that briefly. I knew that he was right. But that wasn't the problem at hand.

"Well, right know we need to stay focused. This thing is stuck in granny gear. There is no way we can do more than about fifteen miles per hour without blowing the engine. I'm going to get the tools and take the top plate off. There is a kind of swivel attached to a steel ball under this rubber boot. I know how the stick is attached at the top of a manual transmission. I think we can pry the gears back out of whatever jam they're in." With that I was out of the truck.

Without getting into the ugly details, I got the top of the transmission open after some hours of work, but it was all for nothing. Each of us tried to move a few of the gears that slide on the shafts near the top of the transmission. Nothing moved. The dawn came and our hearts sank with the rising sun. I will never forget the sight that spelled my doom. I was keeping a wary eye out for the reappearance of the national guardsmen or the one-armed foreman, Jorge. The big multi-story hacienda of the owner of the ranch was less than a quarter mile up the drive and to the east. As the sun rose fully above the horizon, I stopped just one of many times to look for signs of movement in that direction.

With the moving orb of an orange sun as backdrop, I saw the tallest and the shortest of the three national guardsmen descending the steps of the front porch. They were walking across the horizon, from the left to the right. Their body language was quite telling. The gait was more of a shuffle than a walk; certainly not the purposeful strides they had displayed the previous night. Their heads were down and the rifles were carried low and held by one hand. While I was trying to interpret their mood, I saw both heads turn in our direction. Their relief at seeing the truck and us was electrifying.

They almost leaped into the air. They each shouldered their rifles and ran to us. Knowing that Duane spoke Spanish, they engaged him immediately. He told them of our problem and the shorter of the two trotted off to get a tractor.

A tractor was driven out from the general direction of the hacienda and was easily able to pull us out of the field. While this was being accomplished, Jorge drove up in his battered Toyota. He told us that the owner of the ranch had spent several minutes berating him and the guardsmen for their stupidity in letting us get away. The cow was, in his opinion, worth at least a thousand dollars. The master of the manor made it clear that he was going to make the four of them pay for the cow, because the crafty Americans would certainly never send a dime, much less two hundred forty dollars.

But none of that was going to be necessary now, because the police in La Libertad had been called and there was a bulletin out that essentially said that I was to be arrested on sight. And here I was. We were told to get back in the truck. Jorge would lead the way to La Libertad, about thirteen miles away, where a judge would sort out the details.

With a guardsman on each running board, and guns once again pointed at me, I drove the truck to La Libertad at an average speed of about ten miles an hour. It was as fast as I could go without risking over-revving the engine. Once in La Libertad, arrangements were made to get a local garage working on the transmission problem and I was marched off to jail. I was to be tried the following day on charges to include killing a cow, failure to report an accident and flight to avoid prosecution. Of course all of this was relayed to me through Duane. I spent another night in jail, fighting off insects and thinking about a swim in the Pacific Ocean.

As one might expect, the trial was a joke, but not a funny one. The judge made it a point to rail against *Los Estados Unidos* in general and the arrogant American… me, in particular. I sat in a chair and said nothing, which was exactly what was expected of me.

It didn't take long for the judge to extort $500 from us. Duane was able to get the money. His performance was most moving as he made it clear that we barely had enough money to get to the States. The truck was repaired under Nick's watchful eye. Things were moving toward my release, but the owner of the hacienda still had not been paid for the cow.

After much haggling and a visit from the all-powerful hacienda owner himself, we were able to negotiate a settlement. I was surprised to learn that he was an American, or more accurately, a Texan. There is a town there which bears his family name. I will not mention it here. My life has had sufficient trials without my purposely inviting trouble. He really wanted the truck as payment for the cow, but even I went through the roof at that suggestion. He settled for the Volkswagen minibus. I wanted to argue, but didn't. We had no idea who owned the VW anyway.

The judge shook my hand and said, "You are not a bad man for an American, I think. No feeling hard, *si*?" I had to laugh.

"Sure judge, it was great, let's do it again sometime." I knew that he didn't get the joke, but I was in a good mood.

I walked with Duane down a cobblestone and brick street that looked like something from medieval times. Nick backed the truck up to a warehouse loading dock made from some poorly mixed concrete that was simply crumbling to powder. I drove the minibus out of the truck and handed the keys to its new owner. "I'm really sorry about killing your cow, you know?"

He took the keys and walked away without a word.

I climbed into the truck. "Tommy, you sure are in a good mood," Duane said, "all things considered."

"I really am," I agreed, "but being the guest of honor at a

firing squad helps put things in perspective."

"I'm willing to take your word on that, Tommy," Nick said while grinding the gears. "Let's not use first gear on this thing, okay? With the load off, it just isn't needed."

"I've seen enough of first gear for a while," I agreed.

We drove westward on the Pan American Highway. Crossing into Guatemala was accomplished with no more than the usual extortion. We entered Mexico in the late afternoon. We had been mostly lost to our own thoughts and I had even nodded off enough to feel rested. Duane, as usual, had been the least communicative.

I had been elected to drive the rest of the way to Tampico. I was headed north, the sun was setting off to our left, and I wondered what lay in store for me next. I was reflecting on the lack of direction in my life, and how I was oddly comfortable with the feeling, when Duane leaned forward and looked at me from the far side of the cab.

"Tommy," he said softly, "I think I have had enough of Central America for a while."

"I've seen enough to last me a lifetime," I responded. "And while I'm thinking of that lifetime, I just want to get serious for a minute. I never thought that I would tell another guy that I loved him, but I love you two. I'm never going to know any other people who would risk their lives to save mine. You guys had nothing to gain and everything to lose." I was rambling in my embarrassment. I felt myself choking a little and there may have been some dust stirred up in the cab, because I could see that the two of them were gulping just a little.

"Geez, Tommy," Nick said, "I just didn't want them to get your Rolex, ya know?"

"Yeah…well," Duane was struggling a little too, "so I was thinking. Since you are on leave from Honduras for at least a couple of months, and you like airplanes, how would you like to see Southeast Asia?"

Printed in the United States
44157LVS00003B/16-66